Amon's Mission

Books by Arnold Ytreeide

Advent

Jotham's Journey

Bartholomew's Passage

Tabitha's Travels

Ishtar's Odyssey

Easter

Amon's Adventure

Early Church

Amon's Secret

Amon's Mission

Amon's Mission

A Family Story About
Spreading the **GOOD NEWS**
(Acts 8–12)

Arnold Ytreeide

Amon's Mission: A Family Story About Spreading the Good News (Acts 8–12)

Published by Kregel Publications, a division of Kregel Inc., 2450 Oak Industrial Dr. NE, Grand Rapids, MI 49505. www.kregel.com.

Italics in Scripture indicate author's added emphasis.

Cataloging-in-Publication Data is available from the Library of Congress.

ISBN 978-0-8254-4873-7, print
ISBN 978-0-8254-7423-1, epub
ISBN 978-0-8254-7426-2, Kindle

Printed in the United States of America
24 25 26 27 28 29 30 31 32 33 / 5 4 3 2 1

For Grandma & Grandpa Ytreeide—

Thank you for the heritage of faith you
brought with you from a tiny church
in Norway over a hundred years ago,
and for passing that faith down
to your children and grandchildren.
This story would never have been told
if not for your example.

Character Universe

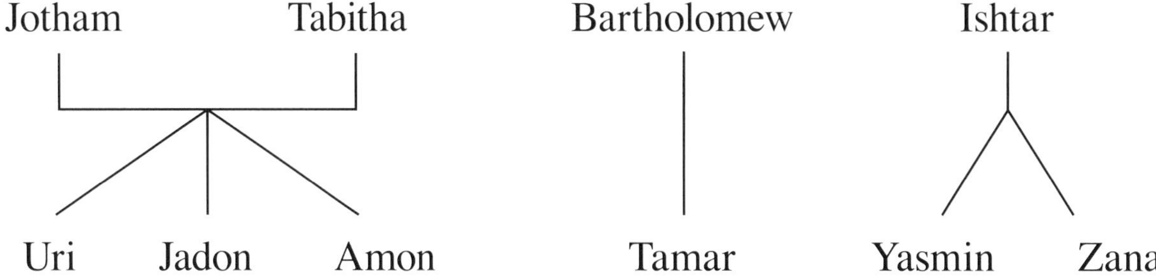

Before the Story

An Important Note to Parents and Teachers

No matter how you look at it, it's a tough story for kids. The early days of the Christian church were full of relentless persecution, barbaric punishment, and cruel death—all simply because some people believed that Jesus was their Savior and wanted to spread his message of forgiveness and salvation. For that, they were whipped, stoned, beheaded, and crucified.

It's just a tough story for kids.

But it's a true story, and a story full of truth, so it's a story kids need to understand. They need to understand—at appropriate levels for each age—that our faith must not be frivolous; it must be deep, dominant, determinate. They need to understand that each of us must be ready to defend our faith.

When I sat down to write this book, I at first struggled with how to present the next part of the story for a wide range of ages in a way that would inform but not traumatize children. My answer to that dilemma is the final product of *Amon's Mission*.

Stories are built on drama, and drama is based in conflict. Sometimes conflict is upsetting to children. While there is no graphic violence "on-screen" in this story, the plot does lead us through some scary territory. So if you have a child who is very young or particularly sensitive, I urge you to pre-read each chapter and leave out or soften any parts you feel would be too frightening.

Still, *Amon's Mission* is a story with meanings at many levels—more, probably, than even I am aware of. It is my prayer that your children—and you—will find a new and deeper appreciation for and understanding of this thing we call the church, and the faith each of us has that brings it to life.

Is This a True Story?

Amon's Mission is based on events described in the book of Acts, chapters 8 through 12. As with the other books in this series, I place those events within a fictional story, using a mixture of real and fictional characters. When a character is real, such as the apostle Peter, I try not to imbue them with any traits not shown in Scripture or inherent in all humans.

For instance, I might have Peter say, "I'm very tired today," because that's something probably all human beings say at some time. However, I would not have him say, "I'm sick and tired of all this talk of Jesus!" because that's a radical statement, and one not supported by Scripture. Likewise, I might have Peter compliment Amon on his cooking, invite him to go fishing, or give him scriptural spiritual advice, but I would never have him suggest they run off to Rome for a weekend of gambling.

As for the events of the story, I present them as written in Scripture but with details from dozens of commentaries, Bible dictionaries, atlases, ancient historians (Josephus, Tacitus, and Pliny in particular), and contemporary expert analysis.

Of course, the story of Amon, his family, and his friends is entirely fictional—but not entirely fiction. The way they live, the things they do, and the environment in which they live all stem from much research.

When I first started writing these stories, I was at a loss—how did a boy act two thousand years ago in an entirely different culture? But as I considered this question, it finally dawned on me that I'd seen the answer in my travels around the world: he would act exactly like any other ten-year-old boy in any other culture in any other time and place. "Boys will be boys, girls will be girls, and parents will be parents," became my guiding philosophy, and *Jotham's Journey* was born.

I've continued that philosophy throughout this series, including here in *Amon's Mission*. What did a sixteen-year-old boy in love act like two thousand years ago? Laws, rituals, and cultural expectations notwithstanding, he acted exactly as a boy in love acts today.

Time is the other necessary fiction in this story. The events of Acts 8–12 took many years to unfold—back then, one couldn't just say, "I'm going to run over to Rome for a minute," because it took months to travel to Rome. To reasonably fit these events into a story that children can follow, I condense them all into less than a year. If you read the Scriptures closely, it might also appear that some events are placed out of order. But, as I learned from many experts, the book of Acts is not presented moment-by-moment but theme-by-theme. For instance, the NIV version of Acts 9 begins with "Meanwhile," which is to say, "While all that other stuff I was talking about happened, this other stuff happened too."

So yes, the core of this story is true, to the extent it is detailed in the Bible, and to the extent that it impacts us spiritually. But where there's a gap between what we know from Scripture and what actually happened, I fill the gap with what I hope are reasonable conjectures, conclusions, probabilities, and possibilities, based on solid research.

How to Read This Book

Some of the previous books in this series were built around a particular time of year—Advent, Christmas, Lent, and Easter. Each chapter of those books was timed to coincide with the events of those celebrations. *Amon's Secret*, and now *Amon's Mission*, have no such seasonal connection.

So how should you read this book? I think the answer must be, "Any way that works for you and your family."

Like its earlier companions, *Amon's Mission* is broken into short chapters, each of which ends with a devotional thought. So, at whatever time of year works for you and your family, you could choose to read one chapter each morning or evening as a family or personal devotional for a month. My grandkids love this approach, and we read almost every night after dinner.

But since there are no external connections to think about, you could also just sit down and read this story, or give it to your children to read, at any time you'd like.

Pronunciation Guide

Biblical names can sometimes be difficult to pronounce. In reality, probably no one knows for sure what the proper pronunciations are. If you grew up in a Western culture, your mouth may not even be *capable* of pronouncing these names correctly! But for those who would like to conform to at least a pretense of a guide (admittedly inaccurate), here is how *we* have chosen to pronounce some of the names you'll encounter in *Amon's Mission*:

Aenaes = uh-NEE-uhs
Agrippa = uh-GRIP-uh
Amon = uh-MAHN
Caiaphas = KYE-uh-fuss
Cornelius = core-NEEL-yus
Gaius = GUY-us
Gamaliel = GAM-uh-leel
Herod = HAIR-uhd
Jadon = JAY-duhn
Jotham = JAW-thum
Raphu = rah-FOO
Tamar = TAY-mar
Uri = YER-ee

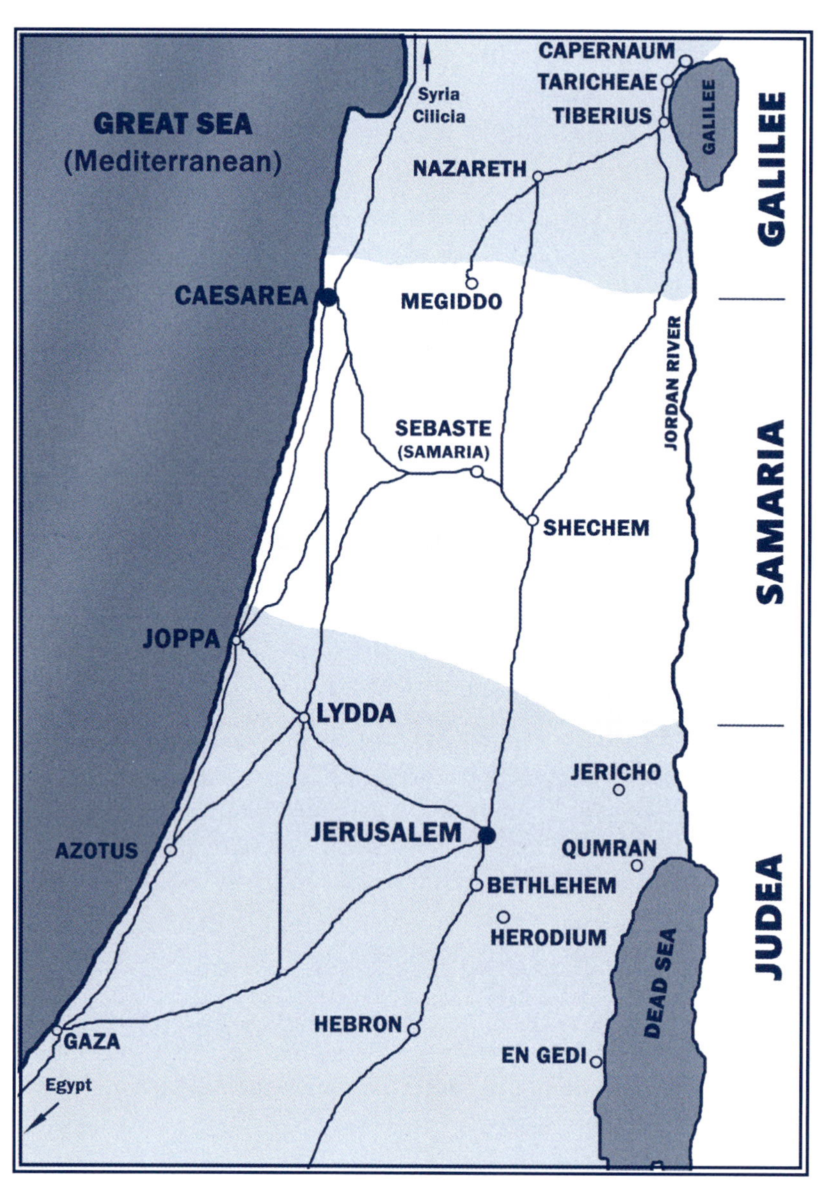
GREAT SEA
(Mediterranean)
Syria
Cilicia
CAPERNAUM
TARICHEAE
TIBERIUS
GALILEE
NAZARETH
GALILEE
CAESAREA
MEGIDDO
JORDAN RIVER
SEBASTE
(SAMARIA)
SHECHEM
SAMARIA
JOPPA
LYDDA
JERICHO
JERUSALEM
AZOTUS
QUMRAN
BETHLEHEM
HERODIUM
DEAD SEA
JUDEA
HEBRON
GAZA
EN GEDI
Egypt

Chapter One

Traditions

Hot sunshine pierced the stagnant air, roasting sixteen-year-old Amon like a sheep over a fire. Sweat streamed down his face and arms. He reached for another handhold, then pulled himself up the face of the rock. He had climbed this mountain a dozen times in his life, but that wouldn't keep his life inside his body if he made one wrong step and fell three hundred feet to the rocks below.

One more hurdle—the top ridge of the craggy boulder. Amon scraped his knee on the rough surface. Tiny drops of blood oozed from under his skin. His hands were already raw and his chest scraped up, even through his rough tunic. He pulled with his fingers, pushed with his toes. Finally he reached the top. He collapsed, his cheek in the dirt, breathing hard and staring out at the city below.

Jerusalem.

The white stone of the temple seemed to glow, though Amon didn't much care about that anymore. People swarmed around and through the city like ants scurrying to fill their nests with grains of food. Horses, camels, carts, and livestock filled in the rest of the spaces.

Even from here, Amon could see the strips of red and black cloth hanging on the inside of the city wall. This was the signal he had invented to tell followers of Jesus where and when to meet secretly each day. *The system has been working well for three years now*, he thought. *No need to change it*

He raised his eyes and saw the hills of Judea stretching ahead of him, and the Jordan Valley with its river on the other side of the hills. Nestled in those hills were several small towns, including one called Bethlehem.

Amon pulled himself to his feet, his breathing almost back to normal. He took a long drink from his water pouch, then began pacing the top of the hill as he always did when he came up here to think. He had a terribly difficult decision to make, and he'd learned long ago that terribly difficult decisions are best made in terribly difficult places to reach, where difficulty makes privacy possible. Below, both inside and outside the walls of the city, the people-ants were everywhere. Here, he could be alone.

"I thought I'd find you here."

Amon spun around, his back now toward Jerusalem, and searched for the source of the voice. He found it, leaning back in the shade of a rock, smiling.

"Benjamin! What are you doing here?"

"Waiting for you."

Amon wanted to say something really mean but held his tongue until he could tame the anger inside. "It is good to see you, but I came here to be alone."

"I know. That's why I came."

"You came here because you knew I wanted to be alone?"

Benjamin nodded. "Of course. You came here alone to think, and to make a most important decision. How could you do that without the help of your best of all friends?"

Amon stared for several moments, trying to follow his friend's logic. But then Benjamin held up a large bag of fruit. "I brought grapes."

Many thoughts collided inside Amon's head until there was nothing left to do but laugh. He walked over and sat in the shade next to his friend. "Okay, I give up." He tore several grapes off their stems and shoved them into his mouth. "Sho wha doo ooh ink uh shoo oo?"

Benjamin stared at him blankly. "What?"

Amon swallowed. "I said, What do you think I should do?"

"Oh. Well, you already know what I think you should do. The question is, What does God want you to do? Have you asked him?"

Amon looked sideways at his friend like that was the dumbest question ever. "Of course. And I know the Holy Spirit is inside me, guiding me. But sometimes it's difficult to hear him."

Benjamin nodded. "I know. It's like when I couldn't decide if I should play King's Ransom with Michael or Shepherd-Sheep-Wolf with David."

Amon looked sideways at him again. "Yes, this is exactly like that."

"You know what I mean. Sometimes there's no clear answer, so you just need to get up the courage to choose one. Which you already have. So do it. Peter says that Saul's going to be back any day now, you know. He's going to make a lot of fun of you if you haven't gotten this thing settled yet."

"Saul's been gone for three years. I don't think he gives me a second thought anymore."

"He's still our friend."

"Of course. But he has some important work to do, and he's not going to have time to tease some kid who used to hang out with him."

Benjamin looked at Amon in disbelief. "Dancin' camels, Amon, are you joking? I think you did a bit more than just 'hang out' with him."

Amon stood and started pacing again in the sunshine. "You see, this is why I wanted to be alone up here! I have an important decision to make and you're just getting me distracted with all kinds of other nonsense."

Benjamin pulled himself up and stood, arms crossed, next to where his friend paced. He was almost a full year younger than Amon, but they had been best friends since Amon's family moved to Jerusalem when Amon was five. "Amon, you and I both know what you're going to decide, and we both know what you're going to do. So why are you fighting it?"

"I'm not fight— I'm not sure I can—" He stopped pacing and faced Benjamin, a look of terror on his face. "What am I going to do?"

Benjamin calmly took him by the shoulders and looked him in the eye. "Amon, you're going to write up a ketubah, you're going to go see Bartholomew, and you're going to ask him for the hand of his daughter Tamar in marriage."

Amon searched the eyes of his friend. "But what if she doesn't *want* to marry me?"

"Don't be stupid, Amon!" Benjamin released his friend's shoulders. "She doesn't have a choice. You know our traditions better than I do—a girl marries whoever her father says she's going to marry. Period." Then he added under his breath, "Unless she *really* doesn't want to, I mean."

Amon pulled away and began pacing again. "But I don't *want* to get married that way. If I marry Tamar, I want it to be because she desires me as much as I desire her."

Benjamin sighed and sat back down in the shade. "Then go talk to her. Just ask her what she wants."

"Tradition does not allow such a thing. I must arrange the marriage with her father, not with her."

"Well, then, forget tradition." Benjamin waved his hand through the air as if shooing away a silly thought. "Those traditions are all way old. Hardly anyone keeps them anymore."

Amon frowned at Benjamin. "A moment ago you told me to force her to marry me even if she doesn't want to because it's tradition."

Benjamin shrugged. "Yeah, well, a lot has changed since then."

Amon smirked and turned away. Benjamin jumped up and followed him to the far side of the flat summit. "Okay, but some people *do* ignore tradition. And when they do, they don't die, they don't get sent to prison, their hair doesn't fall out—nothing happens."

"They disappoint their families," Amon said flatly. "They have to live their entire lives with the knowledge that they didn't follow the social rules their family expected them to follow."

Benjamin put his hands on his hips and shook his head. "Yeah, never let it be said that Amon broke even the dumbest rule." He sighed deeply, then his face lit up, and he followed Amon in his pacing.

"So why are we even talking about this? We both know Tamar loves you and wants to marry you. What's the problem?"

Amon stopped, his back still toward his friend. "You really think so?"

"Of course. You both follow Jesus, you both think alike—you even fight like an old married couple already. You're perfect for each other!"

Thinking, Amon looked back over his shoulder at Benjamin. Then he said, "C'mon," and headed down the hill toward Jerusalem.

~

Amon had started soaking the sheep hide in the stinky, fermented liquid of rotting acacia bark and leaves several days before. He had stirred it three or four times a day, preparing for exactly this occasion. After checking that it was ready, he pulled the hide out of the solution, using a wooden stick so he wouldn't get burned by the acid. Even as he continued thinking about what he would write, he rinsed it in water and saw that almost all the hair and fat had been dissolved away. He scraped away the few remaining strands, then rinsed and stretched the skin tightly over a frame, exposing both sides to the air. He ground some pumice into a fine power and rubbed it into the wet skin. This would create a smooth surface with a pleasing color.

All that night, Amon argued with himself over one particular point in the legal document—a point that would make his marriage to Tamar different from that of any other couple.

The following day, he removed the dried parchment from the rack and cut it into a rectangle. He burned some fish bones, pulverized them, then mixed them with honey to make ink. Using dyes made from insects and plants, he also created inks in several colors. *It's not how it's always been done*, one side of his brain would say about the legal debate. *Who cares? It's what I want done!* the other side would argue.

Finally, he found some sturdy reeds at the edge of the Pool of Serpents and cut their tips at an angle to make a set of pens. He sat down at a small table next to the sheep paddock to write in the traditional manner, as if the events he desired to have happen had already happened:

> On this, the seventeenth day in the month of Nisan, I, Amon, son of Jotham, in the city of Jerusalem, visited Bartholomew, an apostle of Jesus Christ, and asked him for the hand of his daughter, Tamar, as my wife, according to the practice of Moses and Israel. I have pledged that I will cherish, honor, support, and maintain her in

> accordance with the custom of Jewish husbands who cherish, honor, support, and maintain their wives faithfully. I pledged to provide her with food, clothing, and necessities, and to live with her as husband and wife according to universal custom.
>
> However, here I departed from the normal tradition of offering a sum of money to my wife, for the occasion, should it occur, of our divorce or of my death. I did not and do not offer such a sum, but instead offer all that I have, or will ever have; all that I own, or will ever own; all that I am, or will ever be. For I do not enter this marriage as a matter of law, or of contract, but as a matter of commitment, to Tamar and to our home. I therefore pledge that I will never divorce her, but if I do, or if I die, I will have nothing, and she will have all.
>
> We have followed the legal formality of symbolic delivery between Amon, the son of Jotham, the bridegroom, and Tamar, the daughter of Bartholomew, and we have followed all customs to strengthen that which is stated above, and everything is valid and confirmed by our signatures here written.

He then left space for himself, Tamar, and two witnesses to sign.

Amon laid down his black pen and used his colored pens to draw an intricate and beautiful design of flowers and vines around the whole border of the ketubah. When it was finished and dry, long after sunset, he rolled it up and went inside his father's house. His brothers, Jadon and Uri, had already gone up to bed, but his parents sat at the table—his mother, Tabitha, sewing, and his father, Jotham, dividing out coins to pay various debts.

"Father," Amon spoke with a husky voice. "Could you send word to Bartholomew that I would like to meet with him, and then could you and mother go up to bed?"

Jotham looked up at his son. "Why in all heaven would I want to invite Bartholomew over at this hour of the—" Jotham stopped when he saw the rolled-up parchment in Amon's hand. His eyes went wide; his mouth dropped open. Both he and Tabitha stared at their son for a long moment, then his father spoke in a hoarse whisper. "Oh! Yes! Yes, I could do that. Do you need— Would you like— I'll go get him myself."

Jotham jumped up and ran out the door. Tabitha quickly gathered up her sewing things, dropping needles and threads several times and stammering, "I'll just— I'm going to go up— Would you like some—"

By the time Jotham returned, panting, with a winded Bartholomew on his heels, Amon had cleared the table and laid out the ketubah.

"I'll just go up to bed," Jotham said, pointing up the stairs. "It is, uh, very late and I . . ." He ran up the steps faster than Amon had ever seen him move.

Suddenly filled with a feeling of calmness and certainty, Amon looked up at Bartholomew. "Thank you for coming. I have a legal matter I wish to discuss with you. Please, sit and be comfortable."

~

It had taken Amon hours to fall asleep on the flat roof of the house after that. Even though it was not yet summer and the air was still cold, the roof was a place he could be alone, and he had very much wanted to be alone with the thoughts buzzing through his head. He finally awoke in the daylight when a shadow crossed his face. He squinted and saw a familiar form hovering over him.

"Amon!" Benjamin barked, his hands once again on his hips. "Did you talk with Tamar yet?"

"Wha . . . what?"

"Tamar is very upset. I found her crying behind Samson's shop. Did you talk to her yet?"

Amon blinked and held up his hand to block the light. "Why is she upset?"

Benjamin made a sound of great exasperation. "Because she heard that you are betrothed."

Amon's eyes shot open wide, and he sat up. "How did she find out?"

"Your father has been telling everyone in town, including Josiah the cheese seller. Josiah told his family, including his daughter Keturah. Keturah told her friend Ruth, who told her friend Rebecca, who told Tamar." He turned aside and added as if talking to someone else, "And you'd better believe Rebecca loved every second of *that*."

Amon sucked in his breath. "And Tamar doesn't want to marry me?"

Benjamin turned back. "That's not it at all. She thinks you're betrothed to someone else."

"Why would she think that?"

"Amon, did you ever actually ask Tamar to be your wife?"

"Ask? Well . . . no. As I said, it's not tradition. But she knows how I feel."

"Amonnnnnn." Benjamin dragged out the name as if scolding a child. "You must go and ask her. Now." He threw his hands in the air as if to say, "I give up!" Aloud he sighed, "You must at least tell her sometime before the wedding day."

Amon jumped out of bed, threw on his outer tunic, and ran down the stairs. As he flew through the eating area of the house, his mother said, "Amon! I hear you may have . . ." but he was gone before she could finish.

Amon found Tamar still behind the shop that belonged to Samson the bread maker. She was turned toward the wall, crying. "Tamar?" he said softly.

Tamar snapped up straight and stiffened but kept her back to him.

"Tamar, why are you crying?"

She sniffled and wiped her eyes but still didn't face him. "I . . . I have just had a bad morning. It is nothing."

Amon slowly walked up behind her. "Tamar, have you not spoken to your father this morning? Or even last night?"

It took Tamar a moment to answer. "No. He left early to speak to the church group in Bethany. I do not know when he will return."

"Have you heard, then, that I am betrothed to be married?"

Tamar's body seemed to shudder, then she held still. Her back straightened again, and she forced herself to speak. "Congratulations. I am very happy for you."

Amon still wasn't sure if she was crying because she thought she was betrothed to him, or because she thought she was *not*. "Tamar, do you know to whom I am betrothed?"

Another long silence. "No, but I am sure you have made a logical choice, and a good business arrangement."

"Indeed I have," Amon said, now smiling. "Because, Tamar, I am betrothed to . . . *you*."

Tamar spun around, her face a flash of confusion and shock. "You . . . you . . ." was all she could say. She stared at him for a moment, finally comprehended what he had said, grabbed him around the neck, and kissed him.

If any priest or old woman happens by and sees us, Amon thought, *we're going to be in so much trouble*. A moment later he thought, *And I don't care one bit*.

Tamar pulled back and looked at him. "That is the last time I will be able to do that until our wedding night," she said with absolutely no concern about priests or old women. "Now go. Prepare our betrothal ceremony, so I may sooner call you my husband."

Amon grinned, nodded, then left the alley. His feet pointed toward his house, but his head was anywhere but at home—it was spinning wildly, with thoughts scrambled with other thoughts, and all scrambled with feelings he couldn't even identify. He trudged along, not even looking where he was going, until his feet became as lost as his head. A hand clapped him on the shoulder and a breathless cry clapped him on his ear. "Amon! I've been looking everywhere. Where are you going?"

It was Benjamin, and Amon didn't completely understand the question. "I-I am going home."

Benjamin shook his head in confusion. "Then why are you on the other side of the city, and why have you passed the Damascus Gate seven times?"

"I-I have not— How do you know how many times I've—"

Benjamin pointed to their friend Asa, a merchant of olive oil, at his stall just inside the gate. "Asa told me. I asked him if he'd seen you and he said, 'He's passed by here seven times in the last hour. Just wait a few moments, and I'm sure he'll be by again.' So I did, and then you were."

Amon looked around in a daze. "What am I doing *here*?"

Benjamin laughed. "That was my question, but I think I know the answer. You found Tamar, didn't you?"

Amon could feel himself blush, and he nodded his head slightly. "She kissed me."

Benjamin's mouth dropped open, and he gawked at his friend. He moved in close and lowered his voice. "You'd better hope a priest—or your mother—didn't see."

For the rest of the day, plans were made, food cooked, and guests invited. As the sun left the sky, torches lit up the night, and friends and family gathered at tables set up in the streets around his house. Large spits of meat roasted over a fire, vegetables filled bowls and trays, and so much bread was passed around that Bartholomew said it looked like the time Jesus had multiplied the loaves and fishes. All twelve apostles happened to be in town, so they came, along with Peter's wife, James the brother of Jesus, most of the "helpers" to the apostles, and most of Amon's extended family who lived close enough. *And this isn't even the wedding yet*, Amon thought.

Music filled the air, dancing filled the streets, and friends, neighbors, and complete strangers stopped by to congratulate the two young people. Halfway through the evening, Amon's father stood and called for quiet. "Friends, we are gathered tonight to witness the signing of the marriage contract my son has negotiated with the apostle Bartholomew, for the hand of his daughter Tamar. I will now read the contract." Jotham unrolled the ornate ketubah and read it loudly and slowly. He finished, then rolled the document out on the table. "I will now ask my son and Tamar to sign the contract in front of us."

Amon's hand was shaking so badly he was afraid the quill might fly from it, but he managed to scribble his name in the appropriate place. Tamar stepped up and swiftly and surely signed her name.

Jotham took the quill from his almost daughter-in-law. "And now, I would like to ask the apostle Peter and the apostle James of Zebedee to sign as witnesses."

Peter approached the table, saying, "This will be one of the great honors of my life." As James signed a moment later, his hand shook as badly as Amon's. "It is my great pleasure to bear witness to your happiness," he whispered to Amon and Tamar.

Jotham had asked the great teacher Gamaliel to pray the blessing. The old man stepped up behind Amon and Tamar, placed a hand on each of their heads, and prayed a prayer such as most in the crowd had never heard and never thought they would, since most in the crowd thought they would never in their lives be in the same place as the famous teacher.

Amon's mother and Tamar's father spoke words of blessing, then the celebration continued with a cheer. The men gathered on one side of the street, bringing Amon with them, while the women with Tamar gathered on the other. Benjamin put his arm around Amon's shoulders. "How does it feel to be betrothed, my friend?"

Amon sighed. "Lonely. Now I won't even get to talk to Tamar alone until the actual wedding."

"You'll live." Benjamin laughed. "You'll only have to wait two or three weeks."

A full moon traveled most of the way across the sky before a few people started drifting home. Amon finally had time to stand next to his father and thank him for the evening. "I am so proud of you, my son," Jotham said, his arm around Amon. "And so pleased that I will have my first grandchild in just a few years."

Amon grinned, a bit embarrassed. "Well, I do not believe it will be *that* long, father."

"Oh? You do know that it takes some time to grow a child, do you not?"

"Well, yes, but . . ."

"Good then. A year or so from now you will get married, and a year or so later I shall have my first grandchild!"

"A year! Why would we wait a year to get married? I was thinking more like next month."

Jotham held up his index finger. "Ahhhh, I forgot to mention something. Philip asked me today if you could accompany him on a journey he is planning, and I said that, of course, you'd be happy to."

Amon's knees went weak, and he collapsed onto a bench behind him. His mind raced with the words his father had just spoken and with the consequences of those words.

He looked across the yard to where Tamar was laughing and talking with the women. She saw him and waved.

Suddenly, Amon was the only person at the party who was no longer having any fun.

✦ ✦ ✦

Sometimes God makes it clear what he wants us to do, and it feels so right and clear to us.

Other times, not so much.

One morning long ago, while my wife was off teaching fourth grade, I suddenly got the idea, totally out of the blue, that I wanted to go back to college for an advanced degree. I searched the web, found the school and program I wanted, and emailed my wife for approval. Within minutes of her positive response, a different university called me up and asked me to teach a whole new program for them, in my area of expertise. "There's only one catch," they said. "You'd need to be working toward an advanced degree before we could hire you."

Coincidence? Possibly. But I took the job, got the degree, and spent two decades reaping countless rewards from that position. I'm pretty sure it was no coincidence.

Many other times, it hasn't been nearly so obvious or easy.

Amon is facing a new phase of his life and is starting a whole new mission. He is, and will be, trying his best to follow God's will. As he has discovered, though, it's not always easy to know what God's will is. Sometimes, instead of a phone call out of the blue, it's a matter of praying and then searching your heart for what you probably already know inside is the right answer. Personally, I take comfort in this: if it's really important, God will make it obvious.

Chapter Two

Philip, Not Philip

Oh Amon, stop whining," Benjamin scoffed when the betrothal party was over. "The patriarch Jacob had to wait seven years to get married. Surely you will survive if you must wait *one*."

Amon scowled at his best of all friends.

Benjamin cringed and went back to blowing out and collecting torches. "Or not."

All that night, Amon rolled around in his bed trying to sleep. But thoughts of his soon-to-be marriage and sooner-to-be journey fought a battle inside his head. Every so often the battle would pause for a terrifying second as Amon realized, *I am betrothed!*

The terror would pass, then the battle resume.

Legally he was now bound to Tamar for the rest of their lives. By his own hand and the ketubah he had written, if he called off the marriage now, Tamar would get everything he owned or ever would own. But they could not live together in marriage until the actual wedding day, sometime in the future. *Much further in the future, thanks to my father. He had no right to promise Philip I would accompany him. I hate Samaria. I don't want to go!*

In the light of early morning, as he and his father stacked chairs on the side of the house, Amon decided it was time to voice his frustration. "Father, I have something to say to you."

Jotham looked up. "Yes?"

"Father, is it not the responsibility of a man to choose his own path?"

Jotham nodded. "Yes, as much as Jehovah—and his wife—allow him." He snickered at his own joke, and Amon was sure he'd never heard his father make that sound before.

"Then why is it that you committed me to a long journey with Philip without even asking me?"

Jotham stopped stacking, crossed his arms, and looked down at the street. "Ah, I see your point. Perhaps it was not my place to make such a commitment." Amon smiled in triumph. "On the other hand"—Amon's smile collapsed—"you live under my roof, you eat food I provide, and you are, at the end of it all, my son." Jotham looked up with a grin. "So I feel no remorse in having accepted an invitation for you, an invitation I know full well you would have accepted yourself as soon as it was presented."

Amon huffed in frustration. "But a whole year! Half of my friends are already married, and I am only just now betrothed."

"That means the other half of your friends are neither married nor betrothed, so I would say you are doing quite well."

Amon turned away and paced, his hands behind his head. Jotham took him by the shoulder and guided him to the stacked chairs. They each sat atop a stack of three. "I was only teasing about the year," Jotham said. "It will probably only be one or two months. Three at the most. And then you can return and prepare for your wedding."

"You mean, prepare a place for us to live." Jotham nodded, and Amon looked down at the street. "I guess I have to ask . . . I should not assume . . ." He looked up into his father's eyes. "May I add our home onto yours?"

Jotham smiled. "Even if I said no, do you think your mother would listen to me? Of course you may add your home to ours. It is not only our custom, it is our delight. But you know, you must design and build that home yourself. Benjamin and I can help cut logs and lift heavy timbers, but our traditions say that a man must build a home for his bride by himself."

Amon sighed deeply. "I hope I am able."

Jotham laughed so loud it made Amon look around to see if it woke any neighbors. "I do not believe that the man who has every rich Jew and Roman in Jerusalem bidding for his inventions will have any problem designing an addition to a house. Amon, you have already created amazing things—including these chairs that stack. Why would you think you'll have trouble with *this* job?"

Amon looked down at the street again and spoke quietly. "Because this job is for Tamar."

Jotham sighed. "Ah, yes, that is true. We think that that which we do for the one we love must be . . . perfect. And remember, I am required to inspect this place you build, and must judge whether it is perfect enough for Tamar. Just in case you weren't worried enough." Jotham grinned a huge, fake grin.

Amon laughed, then took a deep breath. "I guess a month or two with Philip won't be a bad thing. It will give me time to plan. And besides, I like Philip. He has a keen mind for the Scriptures, and I can have many debates with him. I think he is one of my favorite apostles."

Jotham looked at his son with half a smile. "Amon, it was not Philip the apostle who requested your company, it was Philip the *helper*."

Amon jumped up and spun around to look his father in the eye. "The *waiter*?" he yelled. "How— You— Why would they send a waiter to do the job of an apostle?"

Jotham shrugged. "I do not know. Perhaps the apostles think he will be good at it. Perhaps he was called by Jehovah. Why do you call him the 'waiter'?"

Amon was pacing again. "Because . . . because of what Peter said. He said the apostles are too busy doing God's work to 'wait on tables,' meaning they're too busy to do the simple, menial tasks that anyone can do. So they chose seven—including Philip—to 'wait on tables' for them. In other words"—he stopped and looked his father in the eye again—"he's an organizer, a coin counter, a-a delivery person!"

"Jesus was a deliverer."

Jotham had said it so softly yet so sincerely that Amon's face turned red in anger. Jotham sighed. "All right, well, the end of it is that Philip the 'waiter' is going to Samaria to tell them of Jesus, he asked if you could go with him, I said yes, and that is that. Unless you want to refuse, which is your right as a man."

Amon felt trapped—more by his own conscience than anything. He knew what he *should* do, and what Jehovah would *want* him to do. But he didn't want to do it. He turned away from his father, crossed his arms, and resumed staring at the pavement.

"Very well," he said softly. "I will go."

~

It was Amon's turn to take the sheep to the afternoon market, where the best households in Jerusalem shopped for their evening meals. He had seven today, and he kept them moving through the busy streets with a click of his tongue and a tap of his long staff.

Benjamin was with him and every so often would run to the side to guide a stray sheep back to the herd. "You know, the Midianites have dogs to herd the sheep for them."

"Dogs are unclean. You are not. Well, not as much." Amon laughed at his own joke.

They turned onto the main street that ran across the top of Jerusalem. The street was blocked with people facing toward the other end of the city. They seemed to be waiting for something. Amon stood on his tiptoes and looked.

"What is it?" Benjamin asked. "What do you see?"

Amon leaned right and left, trying to get a better view. "A procession. Many horses and wagons coming from the palace, headed for the Damascus Gate." A moment later he added, "There's Pilate!

Riding a horse instead of in his chariot." He dropped back down to his feet and turned to his friend. "Nothing special about it. Just the usual." Everyone in the city was used to royalty and important leaders coming and going. After a few minutes, the traffic started moving again. Amon clucked his tongue and tapped the sheep, which then started up the street. Tens of thousands of people lived in Jerusalem, and that was all the more evident on a busy day like today. Many of them, Amon knew, were Jews who had returned from Babylon and other countries, where their ancestors had been forced to go hundreds of years before by King Nebuchadnezzar.

Benjamin sighed. "When do you leave on *your* trip?"

Amon's shoulders slumped. "Tomorrow."

"I will miss you." The lead sheep drifted to the right.

Amon stood up straight, smiling. "You could come along. I'm sure no one would mind."

Benjamin got the sheep in line, then moved back next to his friend. "No thank you. I think I will enjoy staying here and talking with Tamar."

"What? Why would you talk to Tamar?"

"We talk all the time."

"About what?"

Benjamin looked as if that was the dumbest question ever. "About *you*, of course."

Amon had a snappy reply on the tip of his tongue, but then he heard a familiar voice come from behind. "Amon! Wait!"

He grinned, then handed the staff to Benjamin. "Saul!" Amon reached for the hand of his friend, but Saul smothered him in a hug.

"I don't care if you *are* an old man now, I will greet you as my closest of friends." Then he leaned back and looked Amon in the eye. "Why aren't you married yet?"

Behind Amon, Benjamin laughed.

Amon frowned and ignored the question. "Did you just now arrive?"

Saul nodded. "Surely. And you are the first one I looked for, after I checked in with Peter and James."

They started walking, following Benjamin and the line of sheep. "Is it safe for you to be here? You've been gone three years, but Jerusalem has a very long memory."

Saul shook his head slowly, as if he was too sad to shake it any faster. "I do not know. I can surely understand why many people—especially the people of the Way—would hate me and not trust me." He stopped, turned, and held Amon by both shoulders. "But Jesus saved me. And you witnessed it. Even if the people don't believe *me*, surely they'll believe *you*."

Amon was quiet for a moment amid the morning street noise. "They probably will." Then he grinned. "They just need to see you *not* stoning people to death for a few weeks before they truly accept it."

Saul looked guilty and started to say something, but Amon added, "Tell me about the last three years. What have you been doing? What did you learn?"

Saul smiled and opened his mouth to answer, but a roar so loud it seemed to shake the ground erupted from the center of the city. Amon glanced over in surprise. Benjamin stopped and gathered the sheep in the middle of the street. Saul looked worried.

Amon identified the sound—people yelling. Yelling in victory, or yelling in anger? The roar seemed to have started near the temple, but now already reached the Valley of the Cheesemakers. In moments, he calculated, it would surround them.

They must have heard that Saul is back in town! The thought struck Amon like lightning. His next thought was of how to protect Saul. He scanned the area, looking for possibilities. Jubal's cistern was the closest, just a block away. If they could get there before—

The screaming reached the street they were on. Amon pulled Saul close, put him between himself and Benjamin. Perhaps he could make a plea, convince the crowd that Saul was not a—

But the people were not angry. They were cheering, celebrating. Amon listened closely to the words shouted from one to another up the street. "Caiaphas and Pilate have been fired!"

Amon's head spun. The chief priest, who had lied, stolen, and condemned Amon's father to death, was no longer chief priest? Pontius Pilate, who'd had Jesus killed, was no longer governor? Could this be possible?

Amon searched for a familiar face and finally found it in Josiah the cheese seller. "Josiah! Is it true?" he yelled.

Josiah had been dancing in circles and waving his arms over his head but now ran to Amon. "Yes! Yes, my friend. Governor Vitellieus sent word just now. Caiaphas and Pilate are recalled, and Pontius Pilate will go to Rome to stand trial for cruelty."

Amon cheered so loud he knew he'd have trouble talking the rest of the day. But he didn't care. He grabbed Benjamin and Saul by the hands and joined the dance that most of Jerusalem was dancing, forgetting all about the sheep.

As he danced, Amon noticed his friend, Raphu, captain of the temple guard, quickly walk by looking glum and worried.

In an instant, even as Jerusalem celebrated, Amon knew that something terrible was about to happen.

✦ ✦ ✦

Earthly kings (queens, presidents, governors, mayors, bosses, teachers) come and earthly kings go. Some are great leaders; some are walking disasters.

Why doesn't God send us only the good ones?

There are probably many answers to this, answers that have to do with us learning to grow and adapt, learning humility, learning to be subservient. But I'm guessing the real answer is this: God gave humans free will, and not everyone's will is the same as God's.

When the Israelites asked for kings to rule over them instead of God's prophets, God warned them what would happen—how much evil those kings would bring with them. The people didn't care. They rejected God and demanded their own way.

God let them have it.

And the Israelites suffered, as do we when we reject God's ways.

Free will. Amon is still learning about this idea and trying to learn to submit his own will to God. But he's also wrestling with the reality that free will allows bad people to do bad things.

That's just one reason Proverbs tells us to "trust in the LORD with all your heart and lean not on your own understanding" (3:5).

Chapter Three

Prying Eyes

As the news about Caiaphas and Pilate was heard, understood, and passed along, Jerusalem finally started to return to normal, though happy conversations and grinning faces filled the streets all day. Eventually Amon, Benjamin, and Saul got the sheep rounded up and to market, but they were there for only a few minutes. A long line waited for them at their stall, and Amon sold every single sheep in a matter of minutes. "Apparently there are going to be a lot of feasts of celebration in Jerusalem tonight," he said.

Benjamin sighed loudly as they walked home, Saul still by their side. "But wasn't Caiaphas just a puppet of the Roman government? Does it really matter that he's gone?"

Saul nodded. "They are all Roman puppets—all the high priests and other officials. Rome conquered the world—including Judea—a century ago, so Rome appoints the high priest. If the high priests don't cooperate, Rome will simply fire them and take over completely." Then he pulled his voice in close and added, "But Caiaphas was the worst of the worst. I should know."

Amon knew his friend was once again feeling the old guilt of his time working with Caiaphas and patted him on the back. "We need to find Raphu. I believe he has news we should hear."

Saul slowed his walking, looking Amon in the eye. "Is something wrong?"

"Perhaps. But we'll have to find Raphu to know for sure. I saw him after the announcement, and he didn't look very happy."

Benjamin grabbed Amon by the tunic and pulled him toward the Tyropoeon Valley. "I think I know where he'll be." He led them through the streets of the valley, past sellers of ointments, pottery, and woodworks, to an inn where they'd seen the captain of the temple guard eating his lunch many times. They found him there, sitting alone at a table, the only patron of the inn. They pushed past the people talking in the street and sat down at the table. Raphu looked up, nodded, then took a drink from his mug. "A day for celebration, is it not?"

Amon stared at him for a moment. "Then why are you not celebrating? What do you know that we don't?"

Raphu sighed deeply, then looked each of them in the eye in turn. "I read the orders," he said, looking down at the table. "The orders removing Pilate and Caiaphas from power. The people out there," he gestured toward the street, "they only know that much." He looked up at Amon. "But I read the entire document."

Raphu was silent, so Amon said, "And?"

Another deep breath. "And," Raphu continued, "the last line reads, 'Herod Agrippa is hereby appointed King over Judea.'"

Amon, Benjamin, and Saul slumped back in their chairs. "Another Herod?" Amon wheezed. "We just get rid of one enemy of Jesus, and another one shows up!"

"Amen," Benjamin said. "May the angel of darkness take him to the pit!" Then he sucked in his breath and looked up, terrified. "Oh no! Did I just commit a sin? Will the angel of darkness now take me to the pit for wishing that fate on a god?"

Saul shook his head. "Herod Agrippa is not a god. None of the Herods are, no matter what they think of themselves. Remember, it was his grandfather, Herod the Great, who murdered hundreds of babies in an attempt to kill Jesus when he was born."

"At least this Herod isn't as bad as that one," Amon said. "But he's bad enough, and I wish Rome would replace *him*."

Saul shook his head. "Rome will not easily replace Agrippa. He grew up with Emperor Claudius. They're like best friends. Herod would have to do something to embarrass Claudius terribly for that to happen."

They talked a bit more, then dispersed. Saul left them and headed to the upper city. Amon spent the rest of the day telling his clients he wouldn't be able to work on their houses for a time because of his trip. Then he packed and prepared, though his mind was really on Tamar, their wedding, the house he must build, and now their new king. After supper, he washed for his daily meeting with his bride.

Though traditions had changed over time and were even different from town to town and family to family, once they were betrothed, the bride and groom could only see each other once a day, and never alone. Tamar and her father were staying with a kind and generous woman named Mary, mother of John Mark, a good friend of the apostles. Mary was wealthy and often hosted church meetings in the courtyard behind her house. Because Tamar's mother had died when Tamar was young, Rhoda, the paid servant of Mary's house, would often fulfill the duties of a mother. Amon had first met Rhoda when he was eight. He had been running up the street and bumped into her, causing her to drop the urn of water from her shoulder. He still remembered the scolding he received, and still felt eight years old whenever she looked at him.

The time set for their daily meeting was sunset, and the place named was the communal well in the street in front of Mary's house. Benjamin, as best friend to the groom, would be his chaperone.

Amon had walked these streets thousands of times, had even walked them with Tamar hundreds of times. Still, as he approached the communal well now, he felt his stomach tumble end over end and then back again. When he saw Tamar, his entire body felt like a wet cloth that had been wrung out and hung up to dry. "Good evening, my bride," he finally squeaked out.

If she blushed, or smiled, or even noticed him, he'd never know. As was required, Tamar's face was covered in a veil whenever in public, and would be until their wedding day.

"Good evening, my husband." A breath later, she giggled. "That sounds so funny."

Amon laughed too. "Can you believe this? It happened so fast."

"It did. But now, I understand, it is to happen very slowly?"

Amon hung his head. "I fear so. My father made a commitment for me that I feel I must keep."

"Benjamin told me."

For a fraction of a breath Amon wondered when Benjamin and Tamar had talked that he didn't know about. "It should only be for a month or two."

Tamar was quiet for a long moment, and Amon wondered if she was giving him one of her looks of doubt from under the veil.

"Maybe a little more," he added.

"And then you still need to build our home."

Amon looked down and nodded. "But remember," he said without looking up, "the patriarch Jacob had to wait seven years for his bride."

She laughed. "You sound like Benjamin."

They talked for a few more minutes, interrupted several times by women or boys coming to the well for water. He told her how much he was not looking forward to traveling with old, boring, dull, and shy Philip, and she replied that she had thought exactly the same things about Amon at first.

Amon laughed. "I hope you have changed your opinion of me by now."

"Only a little," she said. Amon heard a tiny giggle behind the veil.

Rhoda cleared her throat, and Amon knew his time was up. He could not kiss Tamar good night, could not touch her hand, and could not even say he would see her the next evening. "I will be leaving early in the morning, so we will meet next upon my return."

"Be safe, Amon. I am so close to having you, I don't want to lose you now."

He stared at her until Benjamin grabbed him by the arm and dragged him away. "Come on, bridegroom. The sun has set for you."

When the sun was just about to rise again the next morning, Amon trudged up the dusty road out of Jerusalem, following the dusty footsteps of a dusty Philip the waiter. Amon looked back and was certain he could see Tamar on the roof of the house where she stayed, waving, and he waved back just in case. He couldn't see his own house, but he knew it was there. He ached to be working on the plans for the new addition so he and Tamar could finalize their marriage.

As the first of the sunlight lit up the top of the temple, they reached the top of the hill. Moments later, Jerusalem was lost to sight. Amon sighed and looked forward, at Philip's back, and thought about the horrible trip ahead.

I guess I'd better make the best of this, he thought. *At least he speaks Greek*. Philip was one of the many believers in Jerusalem who came from a Greek-speaking tradition known as Hellenistic Judaism. Amon grew up speaking the Aramaic of Jerusalem Jews but also knew Greek, Hebrew, Persian, and Latin. This trip would give him a chance to practice his Greek. "Are you not married?" Amon asked, since Philip was well past marrying age.

Philip shook his head. "No. I was, but she died before we had children."

Amon instantly felt ashamed for some of the thoughts he'd thought about the man. "My sorrow will be added to your own in God's ears."

Philip nodded. "It was long ago."

"Will you ever marry again?"

Now Philip nodded more vigorously. "It is certainly my plan, if it is God's."

Amon smiled to himself. "How will you know?"

"If God chooses a new wife for me, I will know it the moment I see her."

They walked in silence for a few minutes, then Amon asked, "Where in Samaria will we be going?"

Philip looked back over his shoulder and said in his soft, shy voice, "What do you mean, 'Where in Samaria'?"

Amon was confused as to why Philip was confused. "I mean, in which village or town will we be starting?" Amon was sure this was a silly question in any case. Philip wasn't an apostle or preacher; he was a storeroom manager and food distributor. If the apostles wanted to let him go try his hand at preaching for a few days, that was fine, but Amon knew it could only be in the smaller villages, close to Judea. Samaria could be a rough place, especially farther north and in the bigger cities.

"I believe you have misunderstood our mission," Philip said. He looked ahead at the road in front of them. "We are not going to the *region* of Samaria—we are going to the *city* of Samaria, which most people now call Sebaste."

Sebaste! He can't be serious. Amon's thoughts and feelings tumbled around inside him like a donkey gone mad. *We will surely die!*

Amon knew that, in the modern times in which he lived, what everyone called "Samaria" was a large region that stretched east to west from the Great Sea to the Jordan River, and from north to south was a day and a half's walking distance. The land north of Samaria was the Galilee region, where Jesus had lived, and south of it was Judea, where Amon lived. Centuries before, Amon knew, God had given the twelve tribes of the Jews the combined territory, dividing it among them. A few centuries later, those tribes got into a big fight about who should be king and split the territory into the northern region of Israel and the southern region of Judea, ruled by two different kings. During that time "Samaria" was just a city in the middle.

Over the years, though, and through many wars, Galilee shrank northward, leaving a gap between it and Judea. The gap in the middle was populated by people who were only part Jewish. Some had even married Gentiles from places like Macedonia. People from many other countries settled in the gap, as did Jews who had simply given up their dedication to Jehovah. This new land, the "gap," was called "Samaria," and the city with that name was renamed "Sebaste."

But Amon knew that some Jews still referred to the city by its old name, Samaria.

Amon stopped in the middle of the road. "You mean we're going to Sebaste?"

Philip stopped and turned, looking quite perplexed. "I, like many Jews, still call it by its proper ancient name, but yes. We are going to what you call 'Sebaste.'"

Amon had no idea what to say. The thought was simply insane. Most Samaritans rejected all but the first five books of the Scriptures, those written by Moses. Worse, the Samaritan Jews rejected temple worship as a means of meeting with Jehovah. But the people of Sebaste, he knew, were far worse than any of that. They were pagans, more Roman than Jewish. They worshipped idols and lived in unforgivable sin.

Jerusalem Jews thought the people of Samaria to be so stained with sin, in fact, that they wouldn't even allow a Samaritan to convert to Judaism if that person so desired.

Amon had walked this very road three years before, on the way to Damascus with Saul, and Saul had warned them to not even look at the little towns and villages they passed. So sinful were they, the old Saul had insisted, that good Jews would be contaminated even by the sight of them. Now Amon worried about his own spiritual health from just speaking the name Sebaste.

"And . . . and what is it we will do in . . . in that city?" Amon stared, still frozen in place.

Philip shrugged as he walked away. "We will preach the good news about Jesus, of course."

For a full minute, Amon stood in the middle of the road. He finally got his feet moving again, and eventually caught up with Philip.

"Do you not know how Samaria came to be?" Amon asked. "Have you not read the Scriptures? King Omri of Israel sinned greatly before the Lord, worse than anyone before him. But then he married off his son, Ahab, to a Phoenician devil worshipper named Jezebel. She brought all sorts of evil to Samaria, and when Ahab became king, he was even worse than his father. Jezebel killed all the Lord's prophets she could find. Even Elijah was so afraid of her that he ran as far away as he could get. After that, things just kept getting worse. And these are the people you want to go preach to?"

Philip looked back at Amon, nodded his head, and said, "Yes."

Amon shook his head in disbelief. For the rest of the afternoon he peppered Philip with questions about how they would preach good news in a city that knew only selfish evil, and for the rest of the afternoon, in a voice Amon often could barely hear, Philip simply kept repeating, "Jehovah will guide us."

Great! Amon thought. *I'm being taken to a place so sinful and dangerous even the apostles won't go there, and I'm being taken by a shy "waiter" who doesn't have a plan.*

The sky grew dark and dropped a torrent of rain on them. At almost that exact moment, Amon looked down to the side of the road and saw a stone etched with Hebrew letters that warned them that they should turn back, that there was danger ahead . . . that they were now entering the territory of Samaria.

✦ ✦ ✦

In the college classes I taught, I often used one of my favorite quotes from a man named Kenneth Burke, a literary theorist: "A way of seeing is a way of not seeing." In other words, if we become convinced that a thing has certain traits, and only see those traits, we'll miss out on everything else that "thing" might be.

When Amon "looks" at the Samaritans, he only sees one thing: evil. He's so convinced that they are beyond hope and beyond salvation that he doesn't see any other possibility.

Fortunately for us—for you and me—God doesn't just see one side of us. He knows us through and through, inside and out. When *he* looks at us, he sees everything we are, and everything we could be. He never prejudges.

Amon has already decided that the Samaritans can’t be saved.
Good thing he’s not in charge of the world.
And good thing we’re not, either.

Chapter Four

Sebaste

As soon as they passed the boundary marker, Amon started looking around nervously. In his mind he knew that the sins of this place could not fall on him like rain—that had been the belief of the *old* Saul. But he knew that people who willingly committed one kind of sin can easily commit another kind, such as robbery and murder.

Looking around, though, Amon began to notice that everything looked quite . . . normal. Wherever he looked, people worked in fields of wheat, or pressed olives in large, stone presses to milk them of oil, or tended grape vines. Women washed clothes, children played, and boys were learning lessons. *Strange*, Amon thought. *When I walked through here with Saul three years ago it seemed very different. Could it be that the old Saul painted in my mind a picture of Samaria that was not true?*

At sunset, Amon and Philip camped by the road, built a small cook fire, and talked. Amon tried several different ways to persuade this shy Jew that, perhaps, they should start their ministry somewhere smaller and build their way up to the big city of Sebaste. When that didn't work, Amon stated the obvious fact that the people of Sebaste were so sinful that they couldn't possibly be saved—that only the good Jews who lived holy lives were good enough for Jehovah.

After they finished eating, Philip leaned back against his travel bundle. "Amon," he said in his mousy voice, "you know Nebal, son of Timon, from our church group, do you not?"

"Yes, of course."

"He is fourteen, but he is somewhat, may I say, lazy? Though, like me, his father is one of the seven 'helpers' to the apostles, Nebal has not yet completed his lessons, has not yet become a man, and does not seem terribly anxious to do so. I believe he truly does want to know Jesus but isn't willing to do anything about that desire. Now, tell me, is Nebal son of Timon less important to God than, say, Peter? Or Saul? Or even James the brother of Jesus?"

Amon wiggled a bit, more uncomfortable with the question than with the hard ground. "No, I do not believe so."

"Then why do you believe that the citizens of Jerusalem are closer and more important to God than the citizens of Samaria? Sebaste?"

Amon took a deep breath to stall but finally had to answer. "I do not. But I do believe God is the last thing on the minds of the people in Sebaste and that they are unreachable."

"Ah, Amon, son of Jotham, has passed judgment on Sebaste, so we shouldn't even try to reach them."

Amon wiggled restlessly some more. "I-I am not passing judgment on them, simply recognizing the obvious. It's as futile as trying to preach about Jesus to Herod."

"I would love nothing more than an opportunity to speak to Herod about Jesus."

That seemed to end the matter for Philip, but Amon still wanted out of this hopeless mission. "That's fine, but why did you want to bring *me*? I am of no use to you, except as a companion."

Philip smiled and nodded. "And that is exactly why I requested you. I like you. You're smart, and I thought we could have some good debates together."

"But you didn't talk to me all day."

"Ah, yes, and for that I apologize. The climb up the hill out of Jerusalem tired me more than I imagined it would. But tomorrow is all flat or downhill, so we shall debate."

By the time they came to the outer wall of Sebaste the next afternoon, Amon's mind was as tired as his body. *He may seem shy and quiet*, Amon thought, *but he sure knows how to form an argument.*

It was midafternoon, and they stood in front of a thick rock wall as tall as a camel. Two round towers, each the diameter of a house, rose into the sky, blocking out the sun. Together the towers formed a gate that was guarded by four guards, through which merchants and travelers walked in both directions. The guards didn't seem to be stopping anyone, but Amon noticed that they looked carefully at every person.

On the other side of the gate, Amon could now see that the wall ran completely around a hill that was at least three times as tall as the temple in Jerusalem. A fine paved road that looked Roman led up the steep hill. Amon was huffing after only a dozen paces. "I thought you said there would be no hill climbing today."

Philip raised his eyebrows and shrugged.

At the top of the hill, the road flattened out, and Amon thought it must go on forever. It was long and straight and lined with tall marble columns that supported a narrow roof. Between each pair of columns was a shop offering goods for sale. Most shops simply consisted of a table with an awning hung over it. At many of these shops, women clothed in silk dresses called to Amon.

"I am betrothed," Amon whispered to Philip. "I do not believe I should talk to them."

"Very wise, young one." They stopped at a shop that had no dancing girls, and Philip treated himself and Amon to a pomegranate and some dates.

"Oh, this must be a sin," Amon mumbled, pomegranate juice running down his chin.

When it seemed like the street would reach to the edge of the earth, it turned slightly, and then Amon saw something he had never seen in his life—a city almost as big as Jerusalem, with huge buildings of white rock, streets paved in stone, an open theater, roofs made of red tile, and marble columns everywhere. Unlike the meandering streets of Jerusalem, these streets were laid out in squares. Amon instantly realized how helpful those would be in finding one's way around. In the center of the city was a huge rectangle of grass, surrounded by columns, that looked like some sort of playing field. At the end of the street, at the highest point on the hill, rose a temple to the Roman emperor Augustus, with at least twenty marble steps that were two house-lengths wide leading up to the entrance.

As amazing as the buildings were, Amon mostly gawked at the people. In Jerusalem, many kinds of people dressed many kinds of ways, but here it was different—everything was silks, colors, ribbons, and jewelry. But there was much less cloth per person here than in Jerusalem, and the silk didn't look like it would keep a person very warm.

At every street corner, it seemed, and on top of every staircase, and on every block of marble larger than a stool, women wearing thin, silky gowns in bright colors waved and called to all the men, including Amon.

"I am betrothed," Amon whispered again to Philip. "I do not believe I should even look at them!"

"I do not believe I should either!" Philip answered.

For lunch, Philip bought them two roasted chicken legs—a rare treat for Amon—then looked around at the bustling city. "There." He pointed to an unoccupied staircase. "We shall start there."

Amon looked back and forth between the stairs and Philip. "Start what?"

Philip looked at Amon as if he'd asked what they should breathe today. "Start our preaching, of course."

Amon had trouble hearing the smaller man amid the crowd, and he wondered what made him think he could preach effectively. "Should we not find a place to rest tonight before we get started?"

Philip brushed away Amon's concern. "No need. Jehovah will provide." He climbed to the top of the staircase and stood at the front of the top step. "My friends!" he yelled, and Amon was shocked.

Philip's voiced boomed out across the square and even echoed off the Temple of Augustus. "My friends!" he repeated. "Let me tell you the story of a man sent from God."

A passing Samaritan man, in a silky green cloak that failed to cover his large belly, scoffed as he walked by. "And why does a Jerusalem Jew call us friends? You who think us too dirty to even look at?"

"Because the man called Jesus the Christ has taught me to love all others just as he does, and to bring his message of salvation to everyone."

At this, the man stopped, along with several others nearby who had heard the exchange. "Go on then," he said in a much kinder voice. "Tell us your story of this man."

For the next hour Philip did just that. Using Scriptures with which the crowd would be familiar, as well as stories of the miracles of Jesus and the words he spoke, Philip preached a message such as Amon had never heard. He felt as if he were hearing the stories for the first time, and soon felt as if he were *living* the stories, not just hearing them. He could see that many others around him felt the same. In fact, he decided, it felt like some of the people were close to believing. But Amon knew that was ridiculous. It would take more than words from a waiter. Then a blind man in the crowd spoke up.

"I have heard many men preach salvation on these stones, but I have never seen any salvation delivered. If your Jesus be the Messiah, let him heal my blindness that I may gaze on his preacher."

Now Amon knew they were in trouble. This crowd would quickly turn on them and probably sacrifice them to Augustus when Philip couldn't heal the man. Yes, he'd seen miracles before, but those had been performed by Jesus or by his apostles, not by a store clerk. He looked around, deciding on an escape route, when Philip answered the man.

"If you are healed, will you believe?" he boomed.

The man took on a sarcastic tone. "Of course. If your Jesus can heal, I will believe."

"Very well then," Philip said as he jumped from the top step to the bottom. He grabbed the man by the collar of his tunic, stepped in close, and put his hand across the man's eyes. "In the name of Jesus the Christ," he roared, "be healed!"

Philip pulled his hand away. The man screamed and held up his arms to block the sun. He stumbled back, confused and disoriented. But then, as he blinked rapidly and as tears washed his eyes, he began to yell. "I can see! I can see!" He spun around this way and that, trying to see everything at once. "I can see! I can see!" He started to laugh and jump and leap and cheer. "I can see!"

It was clear to Amon that many in the crowd knew the man. They surrounded him, amazed, and then finally looked to Philip. "Tell us more of this Jesus," one woman yelled.

For the rest of the afternoon Philip did exactly that. Hundreds gathered, and all could hear as his voice boomed through the center of the city. He healed dozens of people who were crippled, blind, deaf, lame, or even paralyzed.

But then a young man came forward, looking ragged and dirty, covered in wounds and scars. The crowd pulled back. It was obvious to Amon that they knew this man and were afraid of him. "Sir!" the young man called. "Can you help me? I am possessed by an evil spirit that causes me to—to harm myself."

Philip didn't even hesitate. He strode over to the young man, put his hand on the man's forehead, and yelled, "Evil spirit come out!"

A shriek filled the plaza, so loud and piercing Amon thought that surely the sun had exploded. The young man went completely stiff. His back arched and his eyes rolled back in his head. Amon was sure he saw the man rise off the ground a few inches. But then he went completely limp and fell to the ground like a rag. Others helped him up. He stood, faced Philip, and then began to weep uncontrollably. "It's gone!" he cried. "It's finally gone."

Now many others came forward, reaching out and begging Philip to free them from the evil spirits that controlled them.

And Philip did.

As Amon looked on—and occasionally brought water to the "waiter"—Philip drove dozens of evil spirits from their victims.

After the last person had come forward for healing, Philip stood at the top of the steps again, hands on his hips, trying to catch his breath. A woman in the middle of the crowd yelled, "Tell us what we must do to be saved!"

Philip straightened and raised his right hand toward heaven. "Believe on the Lord Jesus Christ, only son of the only God, who sacrificed himself for you. Repent of your sins and be baptized, and you shall be saved!"

"I believe!" the first man in the silky green cloak yelled. "Baptize me in the name of this Jesus!"

Philip looked around and, seeing there was a pool behind him, yelled, "Come forward and be baptized, all you who would be saved."

Amon sucked in his breath in shock. How could Philip possibly baptize the hundreds of people in the square?

Philip turned to Amon. "You take the far end of the pool. I'll take the near end."

It took a moment before Amon realized Philip wanted *him* to help baptize. A thousand objections filled Amon's mind, not the least of which was that he had only done this a few times, three years before, and he wasn't sure he . . .

That was as long as he had to think about objections before the crowd pushed forward. With nowhere else to go, Amon stepped into the pool and invited the first person he saw—one of the young women in silky clothing—to step in and be baptized. He lowered her into the water, saying, "I baptize you in the name of Jesus . . ."

✦ ✦ ✦

Did you see what happened there?

First Amon decided the Samaritans couldn't be saved. Then he decided that Philip couldn't be the one to bring them the message of salvation.

God proved him wrong on both counts.

You'd think that with all the examples God gave us in his Word, we'd eventually get the idea that he knows more than we do and thinks differently than we do.

Nope. Just like Amon, we hold on to our human prejudices and think we know everything. We judge and condemn and hate others just because they don't conform to our idea of who God will and will not accept.

But the joke's on us: the only ones God will not accept are those who think they're safe simply because of who they are, what church they go to, what political party they belong to, what color their skin is, or a thousand other things. The only way to salvation is through belief in Jesus as the Christ and repentance from sins.

Remember this famous verse? "For God so loved the world that he gave his one and only Son, that whoever believes in him shall not perish but have eternal life" (John 3:16). We need to open our eyes and accept that the "whoever" in that verse includes even the people we don't like. It even includes you and me.

Chapter Five

James

As the sun disappeared behind the buildings, the last of those Philip and Amon baptized ran home to dry off. Philip had encouraged them to return the next day for teaching. He and Amon sat on the edge of the pool, their wet clothes in the cool air causing them to shiver. "Do you know how many?" Philip asked in his shy, quiet voice.

Amon had been through this a few times before and now realized he had been counting all afternoon out of habit. "Two hundred sixty-three on my side." He looked at his elder.

"Two hundred eighty-two," Philip said.

Feeling the cold all the way up to his earlobes now, Amon asked, "Where will we stay tonight?"

Before Philip could answer, a voice came out of the dusky evening. "You are welcome to stay with me."

Amon looked up and saw a young man, a little older than himself and wearing a red and gold tunic with several chains around his neck, walking toward them. "I would be most honored if you would allow me to host you this evening."

Philip sighed gratefully. "That would be a great weight off my mind, young man." They stood, picked up their bags, and then the man led them back across the square. For the first few steps, Amon was thinking that this young man—obviously rich and used to much wine and dance—couldn't possibly be reached with the message of Jesus. Then he captured those thoughts and invited them to leave his mind forever: with the first "silk lady" he had baptized, Amon finally understood that there was no one that God's Holy Spirit could not reach.

All the streets in the city ran either north-and-south or east-and-west and crossed each other at right angles. *This makes so much sense*, Amon thought again. The man took them down one of the wider streets and ushered them in through a large door.

Inside was a house of many rooms. He led them to a dining area with a large table. The house was adorned with fine cloth, rich pottery, and soft cushions. Amon sniffed the air. *Roast pheasant and bread!* After they had changed clothes, the young man gestured to the table. "Sit with me and eat." They sat, and Amon almost drooled at the sight of the huge roasted bird.

"I hire a woman who comes in and cooks for me each afternoon. My name is Gaius." Amon and Philip both looked up at him but said nothing. "I was afraid you would not come with me if I told you my name before. But I thought, 'Let them smell the pheasant first. Then they will surely stay.'"

Philip laughed and nodded, then blessed the food and broke the bread. "I will indeed enjoy this meal, but I would have sat with you even if you'd told us your name before. Out of curiosity only, why is it you have the name of a Roman?"

Gaius cut some meat off the bird. "My family is Jewish in most ways, but my father also enjoyed the luxury the Romans could provide us. In order to impress them, he gave me a name from their country."

Amon was well into a wing by now, grease covering his hands and face. "How old are you?"

"I-I am twenty."

"Are you not married?"

Gaius swallowed and looked down at his plate. "I am not married," he said so softly Amon could barely hear. "Many women have been my friends"—he looked up—"but none my wife."

Amon stared, understood, then began eating again.

Philip asked for water. When Gaius returned with it, Philip asked, "Why did you invite us to your home tonight?"

Gaius closed his eyes. "My sin is great." He sucked in a quick breath, and Amon thought he might start weeping. Instead, Gaius held his breath for a moment, then continued in a soft voice. "This very morning I cried out to God seeking deliverance and asked him to send me a sign if I could ever be forgiven." He looked up, straight into Philip's eyes. "Are you that sign?"

Philip looked sad, and slowly shook his head. "No, I am not." Gaius's shoulders fell and he stared down at his plate again. "But," Philip continued, "Jesus the Christ is! Come, confess your sins, repent, and be baptized, and you will not only be forgiven, you will be saved." Philip dropped his food and stood.

Gaius stared for a long moment, his mouth open, a bit of pheasant meat hanging out the corner. Finally he licked his lips, swallowed, and stood.

~

Soaking wet again, all three walked back from the pool a short time later, Gaius with a contented smile on his face. Philip put his arm around the young man's shoulders. "You will need much instruction in the coming days. I believe it would be best if you learned from Amon."

Amon looked up, shocked. This man was four years older than he. How embarrassing for him to be taught by one so much younger. But Gaius simply nodded. "It would be my honor to be taught by one so learned."

"Good then." Philip slapped Gaius on the back. "You can start tomorrow."

For many days, Philip and Amon preached, baptized, and taught as Gaius helped and learned. Every day many new converts came to know Christ. Every night Amon would sit at the table to work on his house designs but would fall asleep before he could draw more than two or three lines.

Amon grew to like Gaius a great deal. He asked the same kinds of questions Amon did, knew when it was time to be serious and when it was appropriate to joke, and always, at least since he was baptized, *always* wore a smile that seemed to say, "I'm Gaius, and I'm free from sin by the grace of God!"

After they'd gotten to know each other a little, Amon gathered up the courage to ask, "Where are your parents?"

Gaius's smile faded a bit for the first time since he'd been baptized. "They both died of the consumption. My mother three years ago, my father just last year."

Amon considered this. "So you inherited the big house, and probably some money, and spent it . . . doing whatever you felt like doing."

Gaius nodded. "Yes, it is so. Until I finally got so sick of myself that I cried out to God." He turned toward Amon, and his smile returned. "And that's when I met you and Philip."

Every day, more people seemed to show up to listen to Philip and be baptized than the day before. One evening as they sat, exhausted, eating their dinner, Philip said, "I am thinking the people of Sebaste need to see an actual apostle of Christ, not simply a helper. I would like you both to run back to Jerusalem to inform them of our progress and then invite them to come and take over. And I do mean run."

Amon's whole body felt the shock, and his mouth fell open but no words came out. The only word he could think was, *Tamar!*

~

It was easy running down the hill on which Sebaste sat. After that, Amon and Gaius started the slow uphill climb toward Shechem.

They had left long before sunrise. Philip had insisted that they make the trip in one day. "You cannot leave me here alone for very long," he'd said.

So they ran. For as long as they could, whenever the road was not too steep, they ran.

When they needed to catch their breath or sip some water, they'd slow, but rarely did they stop for even a few moments. Whenever they did slow to a walk, Gaius would pepper Amon with questions about his family, about Jerusalem, and about the old faith from which his family descended. At least three times Gaius asked, "Can I really be saved, though I do not know the Torah and have never been to temple?"

Each time Amon would assure him that, yes, it was Gaius's faith in Jesus and his repentance that saved him, not the laws of the Torah.

They arrived in Jerusalem just as the sun was setting. Amon's head twitched like a bird's a few times as he tried to figure out if he had gotten his days mixed up—the streets were empty. Was this the Sabbath? No, he was sure this was a Monday. So where was everyone?

With Gaius following, Amon cut across the upper city to his house. He opened his front door with a grin, expecting a surprised welcome. Instead, his house was filled with many people weeping in great sorrow.

Amon's mother looked up toward the door. Her face registered surprise, even through tears. "Amon! What are you doing back so soon?"

From the look on her face, Amon knew that someone had died.

And he was sure he knew who it was.

He scanned the crowd and asked the question he didn't really want answered. "Where's father?" He looked across the crowd of mourners. "Where's father?" he asked his mother again.

She started to fumble an answer, then Jotham's voice came softly down the stairs. People sitting there slid to one side, making a path for his feet. "Here am I."

Amon's heart was relieved for only a moment, as his mind quickly deduced the next question. "Where's Uri?" He saw his middle brother, Jadon, tending the small fire pit, but his younger brother was frail of both mind and body, and Amon could see him nowhere.

Jotham answered. "He's upstairs, playing."

Amon was most afraid to ask the next question, about Tamar, when his father said softly, "Amon, James was put to death today, on orders from Herod."

Amon's world had been spinning in a happy and miraculous way for days. Now it reversed and spiraled into a dark place of destruction and death. His legs wobbled, a woman in a nearby chair stood and guided his body to sit. After a moment he choked out the words, "Which James?"

"The Son of Zebedee."

Amon looked up in shock and jumped to his feet. "Herod killed one of the apostles?" All eyes were on him now as he lived through the same thoughts and emotions they had earlier in the day. "Herod cannot sentence anyone to death! Only a Roman governor can do that."

Jotham took the last two steps to the floor and stood next to his son, placing a hand on Amon's shoulder. "Herod grew up with Emperor Claudius. They are good friends. He can probably do whatever he wants."

Of the dozens of thoughts scattered across Amon's mind, one lit up brighter than the others. His eyes snapped up to his father's. "My marriage! James was one of the witnesses to our ketubah. Does this cancel—" he stopped suddenly as a much more important thought flew into his head. He gave a great gasp and yelled, "I have to see Tamar."

Jotham simply nodded, as if he knew this would be next: Tamar's father was an apostle. If Herod was killing apostles, Amon's father-in-law might be next. "I'll go with you," Jotham said. "Benjamin will be with his own family."

Amon quickly introduced Gaius and explained what was happening in Sebaste. Amon's mother sprang up to see to their guest as Amon's father grabbed his cloak.

As they walked quickly down the dark and deserted street, Jotham said, "You need not worry about your marriage. I already talked with Gamaliel about it. He assures me it is still legal, even with the death of one of the witnesses."

It was Amon's father who knocked on the door of Mary, John Mark's mother, a few minutes later. John Mark opened the door. Jotham didn't wait for greetings. "My son must see his bride immediately."

Rhoda pushed her employer's son aside. "It is not permitted. This is not the hour, and she is not prepared."

Jotham bowed to show his respect. "I understand, but those things are merely traditions, not laws. On a day such as this, the law of love and compassion must take precedence."

From some unseen corner farther back in the house, Amon heard the voice of Bartholomew say, "It is fine, Rhoda."

Rhoda clearly wasn't happy about it, Amon could see, but she said, "Wait by the well."

A few minutes later Tamar came from the house, a veil hastily thrown over her head. Bartholomew stepped out of the shadows and stood next to Jotham.

As soon as she sat next to him, Amon threw Tamar's veil back and saw the tears and terror in her eyes.

Rhoda started to step forward, but Amon's father put his hand on her arm and shook his head no.

Over by the well, Amon took Tamar's face in his hands and said, "He will be fine."

Tamar threw her arms around him. He could feel her trembling and wiped the tears from her cheek with the back of his hand.

"You don't know that," she said, her voice muffled by his tunic.

"Yes, I do. I don't know how I know it, but I do."

They continued to talk for a half hour. Before they parted, Tamar took Amon's hands and looked into his eyes. "Amon, you do realize, don't you, that if—if anything happens to my father, if Herod starts killing everyone we know who follows Jesus, or if we must flee and hide in the hills, I will not be able to marry you. At least not for a time. My father has no wife, and I must care for him in life, and mourn for him in death."

Such a thought had never presented itself to Amon's mind, and now that Tamar had placed the thought there, it sent a terror through his bones that he'd never before felt. On the outside he remained brave, saying, "Do not be afraid, Tamar. I will never allow that to happen." But on the inside, he was very much afraid of the things to come.

✦ ✦ ✦

James is dead.

He dedicated his life to Jesus and followed him around for three years. He listened, learned, believed.

Now he's dead, the first of the disciples to die a martyr's death, all because he believed in Jesus.

And yes, this really happened.

I hope you never have to face a test like this. I hope you live a long and happy life, with all the comforts and conveniences our modern world has to offer. But we must not allow those comforts and conveniences to become more important to us than Jesus. We can afford to lose the comforts. We can't afford to lose Jesus—even if someone demands that we do.

Amon is scared of what might be ahead. That's understandable, and very human. But in reality, neither he nor we need to be afraid—as long as we hold on to our relationship with Jesus and seek his peace.

Chapter Six

Requiem

When Amon and Jotham returned home, their house was empty except for their own family and Gaius. Uri was upstairs in bed, but Jadon was sitting with the adults. He was close to becoming a man but had not yet been called to the exams by his rabbi. Amon thought he looked terribly lost. "I'm glad you are home from Samaria, my brother," Jadon said quietly. "It seems like the world has split apart since you left. Nothing makes sense to me anymore." Amon put a firm hand on his brother's shoulder, then looked up at the other adults.

Now that he knew Tamar and her father were safe, his thoughts finally started thinking of others. "What about the rest of the apostles? What about Saul?"

Jotham lowered his body onto the bench. "Saul is fine. He left for Tarsus a few days ago. The other apostles are also safe, as far as I know."

Amon sat, exhausted, and accepted a plate of bread and cheese from his mother. "I believe Gaius and I would agree with Jadon. Nothing makes sense anymore." He looked at his new friend, who smiled and nodded. Amon swallowed a bite of cheese. "It seems to go in cycles. Jesus preached, and everyone cheered. Jesus was crucified, and everyone was scared. Jesus appears again, and everyone cheers. The Sanhedrin stones Stephen to death, and everyone is scared. Saul sees Jesus and becomes his follower, and everything calms down. I guess this is just the next stage of the cycle."

Tabitha broke off a piece of sweet bread and sighed. "I wish someone could stop the cycle."

Amon stared at his mother. "I'm already working on it, Mother."

~

In the morning, Gaius asked many questions of Amon's parents. When he found out that Jotham and Tabitha had both been present at the birth of Jesus, he had even more. Amon left them to go find Benjamin.

“What are you doing here?” were Benjamin’s first words. Amon explained, telling him about Gaius, that they must return to Sebaste immediately, and that he’d seen Tamar.

“You talked to her without me?”

As they sat by what they had started calling “Tamar’s Well,” Amon explained the danger that stalked Tamar’s father—something Benjamin hadn’t yet thought of. Then he asked his friend about all that had happened in the last few days.

“It was the morning you left,” Benjamin began. “It seemed like the whole Roman legion suddenly crammed its way into Jerusalem.”

Amon looked up in surprise. “Wait a minute. *Roman* soldiers? Not temple guards?”

Benjamin nodded, his lips pursed. “It seems our new problem is worse than both our old problems put together.”

Amon dipped his hand in the bucket of well water and took a drink, then wiped his mouth. “When I heard that Caiaphas and Pilate had both been fired, I thought our troubles were over.” He looked directly at Benjamin. “Now I guess we need to get rid of Herod too.”

Benjamin nodded again, absentmindedly agreeing, then his head snapped up. “Wait! What? Are you saying—”

Now Amon was the one to nod. “Yes, Benjamin. You and Tamar and I are going to figure out how to get rid of King Herod.”

~

There had been times when, walking through Jerusalem, Amon had feared for his life. Threats hid everywhere among the alleys and dark corners, and violence was always a possibility—from thieves, temple guards, or Roman soldiers. With Herod’s new lunacy, it now seemed to Amon that threats and violence were growing ever more real. As he and Benjamin, accompanied by Gaius, made their way to the house where some of the apostles stayed, Amon could feel the difference. The streets were almost completely deserted. Only a few shops and stalls were opened for business. *Just like after they stoned Stephen*, he thought.

Amon knocked, a suspicious eye peeked out, then the door opened. Peter strode forward, his hand outstretched. “Amon! It is good to see you, but what are you doing back here?”

“I have been asked that many times in the last few hours.” He explained about Sebaste and his mission as he, Benjamin, and Gaius sat and accepted dried apricots from the owner of the house.

“Baptized? He *baptized* people? In *Sebaste*? Is repentance even possible in Samaria?”

Amon put his arm around Gaius's shoulders. "Yes. And here is the proof, sent to you by Philip."

The apostles quizzed Gaius and Amon until the noon meal. Between bites of bread, James the brother of Jesus spoke for the first time. "I am shocked, but I should not be. My brother himself sat and had a salvation conversation with a Samaritan, and a woman at that. And he told a parable about a Samaritan man who helped an injured Jew after a priest and Levite passed him by. Then he told us to go out and do the same." James looked across the rest of those present. "We should not be surprised to hear that someone we thought lower than ourselves because of where they were born has been called and saved by the Christ Lord Jesus."

Peter slumped back against the wall from his place on a stool. With half a smile he said, "When Philip the helper said he wanted to go preach in Samaria, we thought he was crazy. We didn't think he could ever be a preacher, as shy as he is, and we didn't think there was anyone to preach to in Samaria." He looked up at the others, now with a grin on his face. "Perhaps we were wrong."

"And perhaps," Andrew added, "we should stop calling him Philip the helper and start calling him Philip the evangelist!"

Hasty plans were made, and it was decided that Peter and Andrew would return to Sebaste with Amon.

Gaius requested to stay with the apostles and learn from them so he could return to Sebaste later and teach the new converts there. The apostles agreed. They also decided that they'd hold a special meeting of the congregations late that evening, to mourn and remember James the son of Zebedee.

"I would like your advice on one other matter," Amon said to the apostles. They gave him their full attention. "I have been called, I believe, to develop a plan to get Herod replaced as king. I would like your thoughts on how to accomplish this."

"Called by whom?" Matthias asked.

Amon shrugged. "By God, I guess."

"Well," Peter said, stretching after sitting so long, "if God has asked you to accomplish this task, who am I to deny it? After all, I was one of those who thought Philip would never be able to preach. I will try to think of some things that will help you. But don't you also have another important task to complete?"

Amon sighed and leaned back in his chair. "Yes, and I am trying to work on it." He looked around at his friends. "But building a house for my bride seems to keep getting interrupted!"

~

Amon's father was standing outside their house, staring into the sky, as Amon, Benjamin, and Gaius returned. "Oh no," Amon wailed in mock distress, "my father has once again gone mad and lost his thoughts in the clouds."

Jotham turned and raised his eyebrows at his son. "My thoughts are only as high as the roof of my house. I'm trying to see where we might add on rooms for you and your bride." He returned to studying the structure. "Has my son given even a moment of consideration to this problem?"

Amon shook his head. "I have tried, but there have been many other matters to occupy my mind."

"No loss," Jotham said, his back still turned to them. "It will not bother me in the least if your wedding is delayed until you're thirty or forty years old. I could use the help around here." Amon laughed, then told his father of the last-minute meeting to happen that night.

"We have much to do," Jotham said, now facing the three and stroking his chin. "I will put the chain in motion and alert the ostiaries."

Three years before, Amon had designed a system to pass a message from one believer to another all across Jerusalem. They'd only had to use the system a few times, but Jotham would now put it to work once again. The ostiaries, or "doorkeepers," would help everyone get into the secret meeting place safely.

"And can you do one other thing for me?" Amon asked. "Could you come with me to convince Rhoda that we need Tamar to help in assembling the people?"

Jotham frowned. "You do understand, do you not, that I am terrified of that woman?"

Amon grinned. "Which is why Jehovah will richly reward you for helping me in this matter."

An hour later, as the sun began to slide from the sky, Amon, his father, and Benjamin approached the door of Mary's house, and Jotham knocked. Rhoda opened it.

"Blessings on you and on this house, Rhoda," Jotham began. "I wanted to be sure that you've received the message about the meeting tonight."

Rhoda looked at Amon's father like he had gone mad. "Of course. We heard through the message chain. As we always do."

"Ah, yes, good," Jotham mumbled. "Well then, allow me to discuss another matter with you." He explained how Tamar played a vital role in the safe assembling of the people, argued again that the rules about betrothal were only traditions, and emphasized that Tamar and Amon would always be in public.

"Besides," Benjamin added, "I'll be there to chaperone."

Rhoda pursed her lips and narrowed her eyes. Then she looked down her nose at them and said, "As will I."

"At least she agreed," Amon whispered to Benjamin as they walked down the street toward the north end of the city, toward the city wall. Amon was on one side of Benjamin, Tamar on the other, Jotham in front. Right behind Amon, with a donkey-swatting stick in her hand, walked Rhoda.

Three years earlier, Amon, Tamar, and Benjamin would sit atop the city wall next to the Damascus Gate whenever the believers in Jerusalem were to meet. They would hold sticks in certain ways to let the ostiaries below know when it was safe to send believers into the secret meeting cave called "Uri's Place." They had decided, after a couple years, that it looked odd for three older teens to be playing with sticks. So they changed the signal to cups of pomegranate juice. When the three of them would take a sip or pour a new cup in a certain combination, the ushers below would know that no Roman or temple guards were around, so it was safe to send people to the cave.

Rhoda seemed perfectly at home sitting on top of the wall next to Amon. She talked and laughed with the teens as if they all were the best of friends and did this every day. Jotham, however, was full of nerves. He kept looking over the edge at the forty-foot drop to the rocks below. Amon tried to act natural, laughing as if he were telling a hilarious joke, as he said, "Father, relax. You look very suspicious."

"I cannot relax," Jotham hissed. "Death is calling to me from those rocks down there, and I don't care to answer!"

For over an hour, people strolled into the meeting place as directed by the ostiaries, then the five watchmen went down to join them.

James the brother of Jesus led the congregation in a somber song of worship, then began to speak. Seated on the stone floor of the secret cave, Amon looked around and calculated that only about one-third as many people as usual were present.

James spoke about the life and death of James the son of Zebedee and led prayers for James's family and close friends. He closed with words of encouragement. "Consider it pure joy, my brothers and sisters, whenever you face trials of many kinds, because you know that the testing of your faith produces perseverance. Let perseverance finish its work so that you may be mature and complete, not lacking anything."

John then stepped up onto the "preaching rock." He was one of the three disciples who were closest with Jesus. He was also the brother of James, the apostle who had been murdered. Together, Jesus had called the two of them the "sons of thunder" because they were so loud and rowdy. John stepped forward but didn't raise his head. This time he was anything but rowdy.

The cave went completely silent.

"My brother died because he believed in Jesus as the Messiah," John began.

Amon glanced over to see what effect this had on Gaius. He could not tell.

John finally looked up at those gathered. "My brother died because he believed in Jesus and would not change that belief even in the shadow of a sword!" He went on to encourage and comfort the congregation, ending a few minutes later with, "My brother died because he believed in Jesus, and I am ready and willing to do the same."

Shouts of praise and "Hallelujah!" filled the chamber as John stepped down. Peter came to the front. He explained that, even as tragic events unfolded in Jerusalem, miraculous events were unfolding in Samaria.

This caused shouts of a different kind.

"Samaria?" one man shouted. "Samaria? And especially Sebaste? It—it is full of sinners, sinners who cannot be redeemed!"

"So thought I," Peter said. "I thought it a barren wasteland, filled with the spiritually dead." He waved for Gaius to stand. "But our friend Philip—not the *apostle* Philip, but the helper Philip—felt called by God to go there and preach. And this is the fruit of that mission." He gestured at Gaius. "Many Samaritans have already come to follow Jesus."

Gasps and exclamations swept across the crowd.

"I know, I know. I didn't believe at first either. But my friend Gaius here is but one example. Amon has told me that he and Philip baptized thousands. It would seem, my friends, that God is making changes in our church, and we had better prepare to accept and welcome many more whom *we* thought were unworthy. Obviously God does not find them so."

Slowly, cautiously, the believers accepted Gaius, and some even invited him for a meal or a conversation. Eventually the meeting ended, though reluctantly, with prayers and praises.

Amon was exhausted when they returned home. Uri and Jadon were immediately sent to bed, and Gaius dragged himself up the stairs, but as Amon said good night to his parents, his father called for him to wait a moment. "I know you are tired, my son, and have many important things on your mind, but I must add one more. I will not require it, and I will not even ask it, since it is such a heavy burden. But I believe there is someone you might want to invite to join you on your journey back to Sebaste. Someone who needs you and the example you set."

When Jotham spoke the name of the one to whom he was referring, Amon's head flopped back, his eyes rolled in his head, and he whispered an exhausted, "Oh, no."

✦ ✦ ✦

"God is making changes in the church."

That could be the theme song for much of the book of Acts.

It's easy to understand why the Jews of the first century were so suspicious of Jesus and his message: for centuries, they had been told to believe, behave, and worship in very specific ways or else face spiritual death.

If that was hanging over *our* heads, I'm pretty sure we'd be suspicious of changes too. One wrong move and you're dead, even if it wasn't on purpose.

Then this guy Jesus comes along and says everything has changed. It's not surprising that many Jews refused to listen.

But God had carefully prepared his people to hear such a message. He sent them prophets who told them, in a poetic sort of way, exactly what was going to happen. He then sent them his Son, who fulfilled those prophecies perfectly and performed miracles as proof. So why didn't they listen? Maybe by then they'd become so used to maintaining the organization that they forgot to listen to the organizer.

And therein lies the lesson for us: we need to keep our eyes on the Jesus of the church, not the church of Jesus. That's what Peter did, and Saul and James and the rest—they kept their eyes on Jesus even as they were building the church. In fact, I think it's why the apostles handed off the day-to-day operation of the church to helpers. Those activities were important, but the apostles were concentrating on sharing the life-changing message Jesus had commissioned them with.

Keep your eyes on Jesus. (I believe I've heard that a few times in my life!) I think I'll challenge both you and myself to apply it to every situation and every conversation, every day.

Chapter Seven

See for Yourselves

Amon's father had said he wouldn't require him to do the difficult thing he was asking, that it was Amon's choice. Deep inside his chest, Amon knew that wasn't true. Yes, he could deny his father's request, but on what grounds? There was no logical, practical, or spiritual reason for such action. He could only deny on the grounds that it would inconvenience and irritate him, and those would be selfish motives.

And besides, Amon's conscience kept whispering in his ear, *hasn't Father sacrificed much, for years, to help me grow into who I am?*

Amon stood up straight with a sigh. "Yes, of course, Father. I will do this thing for you."

Jotham smiled, then climbed the stairs. A few minutes later Amon heard a cry of "Father, no!" from Jadon.

All this required Amon to completely rearrange his thinking. Now he had to consider not only his own needs but those of his brother. Food, clothing, the route to take, what places to avoid, where they would sleep in Sebaste—many new questions and problems occupied Amon's mind such that he was able to sleep only a little that night. *And you can quiz him on his Torah lessons*, he remembered his father saying. Yet another duty to occupy his mind.

In the morning, with their parents, Uri, Benjamin, and a once-again veiled Tamar waving and shouting blessings, Amon and a pouting Jadon joined Peter and Andrew, passed through the Damascus Gate, and started up the road to the north, out of Jerusalem.

They had not even reached the top of the first hill before Jadon said his first "How much farther?"

~

The first day of the journey was slow—Peter seemed older than he had been just a week before. His bones didn't want to move quickly, and his spirit seemed to carry many more burdens than a person his age should expect. *And he's not that much older than me.* Then Amon realized: *He's troubled by the murder of James and carries the weight of the entire church.*

As they walked, Amon began to quiz Jadon on his knowledge of the Scriptures. Soon Peter and Andrew joined in and made a game of it, and Amon wished *he'd* had such help when learning his own lessons. Toward the end of the day, Jadon asked a perplexing question of his own. "Peter, if Jesus has fulfilled the law and the prophets, and if righteousness now comes from accepting him as Savior and repenting of sins, why then must I still learn these lessons and be tested by the rabbis on the *old* law? Isn't believing in Jesus enough?"

Amon thought it was a pretty good question, but Peter turned a bit grumpy. "I will have to think on these things," he mumbled.

As they passed small villages and fields of wheat, Amon remembered how fast he and Gaius had covered this ground in the opposite direction. He ached to move more quickly, but he had "old" men and a "young" boy to consider.

They reached the city of Shechem late the next morning, after a night at an inn. "Here is where God appeared to Abram," Peter told Jadon, "and said he would give this land to Abram's descendants." He turned to the boy and added, "That's us, in case you didn't pick up on that."

Jadon laughed.

"Here is where Jacob purchased land and buried the bones of Joseph after God rescued them out of Egypt. Here is where our people have much history." He pointed down the hill, to the north. "And right down there is Tirathana, where not too long ago Pilate's army wiped out many Samaritans." He looked again at Jadon. "Which is why Pilate has been recalled to Rome and why we no longer need to worry about him." He shifted the load on his back and said, "But we don't have time to stop and see the sights. We must keep going."

Instead of continuing on the main road around Mount Ebal, they turned left onto another road. Amon had taken this route in the valley between Mount Gerizim and Mount Ebal twice before. That afternoon they arrived at Sebaste. They passed through the two enormous towers and started up the long road to the center of the city. Amon stopped dead in his tracks. "We're in the wrong place," he announced. "We must have taken a wrong turn in Shechem."

The other three looked at him, trying to understand.

Amon continued to stare up the road. Only a few food vendors filled the spaces between the columns, and there was no music, no dancing, no women in silk clothing. He started walking; the others followed. When they reached the city itself, instead of prancing women and games of chance, there were only groups of people—five, fifteen, thirty in number—sitting or standing around the gymnastics field. "Now I *know* we're in the wrong place," Amon said.

As they passed between the groups, Amon could hear them discussing Jesus and the good news of his sacrifice for everyone. Peter leaned over and whispered, "Amon! You have brought us here as a joke. Everyone here already knows about Jesus."

Amon's face went pale, and he stumbled on his words. "No, Peter, no! I promise you it was not like this five days ago."

Peter grinned, and only then did Amon realize his friend was teasing. He looked around, trying to find Philip, but did not see him. "I guess we'll have to search the city," he said.

Peter looked at Amon, then looked around at the groups of people. Instead of answering Amon or looking for Philip, Peter walked up to a group of eleven people—seven adults, one teenager, and three children—and started talking to them. "Excuse me, friends. May I ask, have you received the Holy Spirit?"

The people looked at each other with shrugs. One of the men said, "We have not heard that there is such a spirit."

Peter explained that, after Jesus ascended into heaven, God's Holy Spirit had come to the believers in Jerusalem. Then he held his hands over them and prayed that they might all receive the Spirit. Andrew came over and joined Peter. Just as Amon had experienced at Pentecost, the Spirit came upon the people, giving them the ability to speak languages they did not know and filling them with even greater zeal for God. Others started to gather now, and asked that they too might receive this thing of which Peter spoke.

"You're here!" Amon heard the voice but had to search the crowd behind him to find the source.

"Philip! What happened? Sebaste is not the same as I left it."

Philip shrugged modestly. "I simply told the story of Jesus to all I met, and the people believed."

Peter and Andrew came over and greeted Philip, looking at him in awe. "Perhaps we misjudged you, my friend," Peter said. "I see God had more in mind for you than simply distributing bread to widows and orphans."

For the rest of the day, the five disciples of Christ continued ministering in Sebaste. The first time that Jadon told someone about Jesus and that person believed and was baptized, Jadon went behind the Temple of Augustus and hid. Amon followed him there and found his brother on his knees, weeping. Amon knelt next to him. "Brother, what is it? What sorrow do you carry?"

Jadon sniffed and wiped his face but didn't look up. "I-I led someone to believe in Jesus and accept him as their Messiah."

Amon was confused. "That seems like a happy thing, not a sad thing."

Jadon finally looked up in anguish. "You don't understand. I am not *worthy* to tell others of Jesus! I am full of sin and selfishness."

He turned away, weeping again, so Amon pulled him close. "Jadon, have you truly accepted Jesus as the Messiah and repented of your sins?" Jadon nodded. "Then you are as worthy as me or Peter or Andrew or anyone else. There are no degrees of salvation—either you are saved or you are not. There is nothing more you need to do—or *can* do—to be worthy. We all keep learning and growing—as are Peter and Andrew, even now—but none of us is any better or any more worthy than any other."

Jadon looked up again and wiped his face with his sleeve. "Truly?"

"Truly. So catch your breath, then come back out there and help us minister. There are still hundreds of people to talk to." Amon stood, started back out to the plaza, then stopped and looked back. "And Jadon," he called. Jadon looked up. "It is a testimony to the sincerity of your faith that you felt yourself unworthy. I feel that way myself every day."

Jadon nodded, and a few minutes later was back talking to strangers about a strange new faith.

At the end of the day, they met at the house of Gaius, where Philip was still staying. Amon explained to the others, "Gaius told me before we left Jerusalem to make ourselves comfortable and eat all his food. He told his cook to prepare meals for anyone who stayed here. He doesn't know how soon he'll be back."

For many more days they ministered, until it seemed there was no one left in Sebaste who had not heard about Jesus. Most of those who heard had believed and were baptized.

"Even a sorcerer was converted today," Andrew reported at one evening meal. "He was a little confused at first, but Peter gave the man his usual pep talk, and that brought him around."

Amon grinned. "I believe I have heard that 'pep talk' a few times. Did it involve fire and damnation?"

Andrew nodded, and they laughed.

At breakfast a few days later, Amon was still tired and sore from walking around the plaza, talking to so many, and baptizing so many, for so many days. The others seemed to feel the same. But a large clay pot on the table held a soup that tasted of barley, wine, and roasted chicken, and soon no one was talking about aches or pains.

The door to the outside opened, and Philip entered. Amon thought he looked a bit strange. Philip sat at the end of the table, and Peter patted his hand. "You almost missed breakfast. Is your body complaining about the work your mind has brought you to?"

Philip shook his head. "No, quite the opposite." He looked at them across the table. "An angel of the Lord visited me in the night."

Everyone stopped eating, and Jadon stared as if Philip had suddenly turned into a ghost, or a god.

✦ ✦ ✦

Jadon didn't feel worthy of leading someone to Jesus. Even though he was a believer, he thought his own soul so corrupt that he couldn't rightfully help another find God.

I feel that way every day—every time I sit down to write, every time I pray for my family and friends, every time I receive a note of thanks from a reader. I feel so unworthy to even live in the shadow of Jesus myself, let alone do anything like lead another to him.

But even though it was a conversation between fictional characters, what Amon told Jadon is true for every one of us who has accepted Christ: There are no degrees of salvation. Either you are saved or you are not. If you truly have accepted Christ as the Lord of your life and repented of your sins, then you are as saved—and as worthy—as anyone else who has.

Jadon went on to lead many more people to Jesus. I'm sort of feeling a challenge here to do the same. Would you like to join me?

Chapter Eight

Official Business

Everyone stared at Philip, anxious to hear his story.

"An angel of the Lord visited me and said I am to travel south, on the desert road to Gaza."

Amon waited for more, but Philip was silent. Finally he asked, "To do what?"

Philip shrugged. "He didn't say."

Peter leaned back and crossed his arms. "Then I guess you'd better go. And perhaps take Amon and Jadon with you."

Amon's head snapped up, and he shouted, "No!"

The others looked at him, surprised.

"I mean, um, I do not think that to be a good idea."

Peter was curious. "Oh? Why is that?"

Amon's mind spun in twelve directions as he tried to come up with a reasonable reason he shouldn't go. "Uh, Jadon is not yet used to long travels, and, uh, our mother expects him home. We should leave for Jerusalem today."

Peter stared at Amon, who studied the ground to avoid making eye contact. Peter smiled, and said gently, "I know you did not choose to come on this mission, but often God calls us to do things we would not choose. So you must decide which is more important—to build a home for your new bride, or to do that which God has asked you to do."

Amon sighed, then nodded, but he still desperately wanted to go home. Peter leaned forward, his arms resting on the table. Amon knew he was about to tell a story of Jesus. Usually Amon loved to hear Peter's stories, but he suspected this one was going to be about doing what you didn't want to do.

"After Jesus rose from death but before he ascended to heaven," Peter began, "I was out fishing on the lake one night. James and John were with me, along with a few other disciples. We caught nothing. But early in the morning, I saw a man on the shore, and the man shouted to us to put our net out the right side of the boat. We did, and our net was so full of fish we couldn't even haul it in."

Jadon sat up straight suddenly, his eyes wide. "It was the Lord, wasn't it?"

Peter smiled and nodded. "That's exactly what John said. Until then, none of us had recognized him."

"So what happened?" Amon asked.

Peter looked Amon in the eye. "I was so excited I jumped out of the boat and swam to shore. The others followed, pulling the net. Jesus had a fire going and had cooked a breakfast of bread and fish. After we ate, Jesus asked me to walk with him. He asked me not once, but three times in three different ways, if I loved him enough that I would take care of his people no matter what. Naturally, I answered that of course I loved him that much."

Jadon started to ask another question, but Amon knew that Peter wasn't finished, so he raised his hand slightly to stop his brother. Peter looked down at the table, remembering, and continued in a voice so quiet that Amon had to lean closer to hear.

"As we walked along the beach, he told me, out of the hearing of the others, that my death will not be of natural causes. He told me . . . he told me that my death will be like his, at the hands of others, in anger and hatred." Peter took a deep breath, sat up straighter, and looked again at Amon. "And then he asked me to follow him, even though I knew what it would cost. So you see, Amon, being a follower of Christ must mean that he is more important than anything *you* want, that you will do whatever is necessary to further his kingdom, that you have given up your own agenda in order to follow his."

Outside the windows, Amon could hear the city coming to life. Around the table, there was silence. Finally he nodded and said in almost a whisper, "Jadon and I will go with Philip."

Peter smiled. "It is a difficult decision, I know. But I'm beginning to think that the difficult decisions in life end up being the most important decisions we make." He sat up straight. "Andrew and I will finish here before we return to Jerusalem."

"So be it, then." Philip stood. "We will pack and leave immediately."

Jadon looked at his brother, eyes wide open, as if silently pleading to be excused from this journey.

"We'll be fine," Amon whispered. "Philip's bringing along an angel to protect us."

~

Philip set a fast pace out of Sebaste and down the hill to the plain between the mountains and the Great Sea. They passed through a small town named Lydda, but Philip didn't even stop. By dark they had arrived on the road from Jerusalem to Gaza. As they camped next to a pond, Amon knew that his home, and Tamar, waited just on top of the ridge to their left.

Jadon seemed terribly nervous, and Amon finally realized this was his brother's first time sleeping somewhere without walls and beds. He remembered his own first night on the road to Damascus with Saul and had great sympathy for his brother. "Don't be afraid," he said to Jadon. "There is nothing here that will hurt you, and you can sleep between Philip and me."

Jadon didn't look convinced but forced a smile and a nod.

In the morning, they continued on the road toward Gaza. Amon kept wondering why they were going where they were going. The farther south they traveled, the drier and more arid the land became. There were no other travelers on the road, which wasn't surprising to Amon since its nickname was "deserted road."

"Where are we going?" Jadon whispered to Amon. "I'm getting thirsty."

"I don't know." But they had full stomachs and full water skins, so he wasn't concerned.

The sun was just starting to move from comfortably warm to uncomfortably hot when the three travelers heard something approaching from behind. All three turned to look. Amon was shocked. Two white horses, with red blankets trimmed in gold and red and ornate headdresses studded with jewels, pulled a large two-wheeled chariot of white and gold. It was driven by a charioteer in front. In back, a green canopy fringed in gold and held up by four poles shaded a dark-skinned man on a seat. Behind the chariot, a squad of twenty soldiers on horseback followed at a distance.

Philip stepped to the side of the road and pulled Amon and Jadon with him. Suddenly, Philip pulled off his carrying bags and outer cloak and piled them on Jadon. "The Spirit is telling me to run alongside this chariot."

As the horses trotted by, Amon could smell their sweat. The chariot itself passed, and he saw that the man on the seat was reading aloud from a scroll. A second later he was surprised to hear words he knew: "He was led like a lamb to the slaughter, and as a sheep before its shearers is silent . . ."

The chariot passed them going a little faster than a fast walk. Philip started running next to it. Instantly, Amon heard and then saw the front two horses of the column behind them galloping forward. Amon jumped back from the road and pulled Jadon with him. As they watched, the man in the chariot waved the guards back, then motioned for Philip to climb into the chariot with him.

"Come!" Amon said to his brother, and they began running to keep up with the chariot. Amon took most of Jadon's load onto his own back and was sweating hard within moments. As they ran, Amon asked his brother, "Did you hear the man reading?"

"Yes," was the only word Jadon could get out between gasps.

"And what was it he read?"

A few moments and several gasps later Jadon answered, "Isaiah."

Amon smiled. "Very good, brother. You may be ready for your exams after all."

The chariot continued for some time. Amon and Jadon would run a while, catch up, and then slow to a fast walk. The chariot would pull away again, and they'd run some more. Whenever he got close, Amon could hear Philip talking with the dark-skinned man, though he couldn't tell what was being said.

Finally the chariot stopped at another small pond. Amon and Jadon collapsed onto the sand. The two men climbed out of the chariot and walked into the water, where Philip baptized the other man. Back on the road, the two men embraced. The other man climbed into the chariot and rode away.

Philip walked back to Amon and Jadon, grinning like he'd just gotten married. "Well now, that was interesting." Amon waited for the story, but instead the evangelist said, "We have fulfilled our purpose here, and the Spirit is leading me to Azotus. You may come with me, but if you reverse direction and follow this road, you'll be in Jerusalem by sunset. It is your decision."

Amon stared at the man, his mouth hanging open until he said, "Philip! What happened?"

"What?" He looked back at the chariot and its dust cloud, now far up the road. "Oh, he was an Ethiopian official who adopted Jewish Scriptures and ways long ago. He had gone to the temple in Jerusalem to pray and was on his way home. He was reading from Isaiah and didn't understand the words, so I explained them to him. That's all."

Still Amon stared, dumbfounded. "That's *all*? You baptized him. Did he accept the message of Jesus?"

"Oh yes, oh yes," Philip answered in his quiet voice.

"What kind of 'official'?"

"What's that?"

"You said he was an Ethiopian official. What *kind* of official?"

"Oh, he was, uh, he is in charge of the treasury for the queen of the Ethiopians."

Amon's head felt like it was full of buzzing bees. They had just been in the presence of a powerful man from another nation. *And I'm just a sheepherder!*

Through the buzz, Amon managed to make a decision: he and Jadon would return home. They thanked the evangelist for the education and experiences he'd given them, then turned to face Jerusalem and started walking. They reached the bottom of the hill, and as they started up, Amon asked Jadon, "Do you remember the last instructions Jesus gave us as he ascended to heaven?"

"Of course. Though I do not believe it will be on my exams."

Amon laughed. "No, indeed not. But tell me what he said."

"He told us to go into the world and make disciples of all nations."

"What about that is different from the teachings of your rabbi?"

Jadon thought for a long time. "Oh! Jesus was saying the news about him was not just for the Jews but for all people."

Amon nodded. "Very good. Now tell me what just happened this morning."

Again Jadon thought, then suddenly stopped walking and fixed his eyes on his older brother. "We just witnessed the news of Jesus being given to a man of a different culture, a different country, and a different race. And that news is now on its way to a part of the world far, far from Judea."

Amon smiled. "That won't be on your exams either, but I believe you are ready to be a disciple of Christ."

They arrived home late in the afternoon. Their parents were surprised but happy to see them. Gaius was out meeting with one of the apostles. "I thought you'd be gone much longer," their father said as he and their mother worked in the sheep pens beside the house.

Amon and Jadon stood outside the pens and watched their parents separate blemished lambs from unblemished. "It was even more amazing than my *first* trip to Sebaste," Amon said. "The Holy Spirit swept across the entire city. Well, almost the entire city. Peter and Andrew couldn't believe it either. But then an *angel* visited Philip and sent us on a whole different mission."

Amon let Jadon tell that part of the story as he watched his mother care for the lambs. It had rained that morning, so the pens were muddy, and the lambs were cute with their muddy faces. But the glare on Tabitha's face was hardly cute.

"You took Jadon to the plains alone?" The tone of Tabitha's voice took Amon back to his days as a child.

"I . . . I . . ."

Jotham held up his hand between the two. "Tabitha, Amon is a man three years now, and has proven his strength and wisdom many times. If he took Jadon to the plains, I have no doubt it was a wise thing to do."

Tabitha relaxed a bit. "Yes, of course."

"Besides," Jotham continued, "Jadon will soon be a man himself." He looked at his second son. "Your rabbi talked to me. He said it is time for your exams."

Jadon sucked in his breath, and a terrified look crossed his face. Then he turned and ran into the house.

"Where's he going?" Tabitha asked.

Amon answered, having been in Jadon's position so recently. "To study."

His parents continued working. Amon moved closer to his father and quieted his voice. "I believe it was wise of you, father, to send Jadon with me to Sebaste. He learned much and grew taller in his spirit."

Jotham smiled at his eldest son. "Amon," he said softly and gently. "I did not send Jadon with you for *his* education, I sent him for *yours*."

Amon looked up, shocked. Jotham set down the lamb he was checking and leaned in close to his son. "All your life you have only had to care for yourself, and occasionally Benjamin. You could come and go, commit yourself to a course of action, and never worry about where your next meal would come from. But soon you will be married, and never again will you have such luxury. You will need to send *your* desires to the back of the line and think first of the needs of your wife and your children. That is the lesson I was hoping you'd learn by taking Jadon with you."

Amon was in awe of his father. "You—you are the wisest of men." He thought about his father's words, analyzed what he'd learned on the trip without even knowing it, then nodded. "Yes. Yes. I did learn much on this trip. And for that I thank you."

Jotham stood straight and leaned his head back so he faced the heavens. "Ahhh, how long I have waited to hear those words." Then he looked at Amon and laughed. "Now my life is complete, and I may die."

Amon laughed at the joke, then turned serious, leaned forward, and touched his forehead to his father's.

No other words needed to be spoken.

✦ ✦ ✦

Before we go on, I'd like you to jump in your car (if you're young, your parents must drive), head out from where you live to some isolated road, and keep driving until God tells you to stop and do something.

I don't see you moving.

What? You don't want to go?

I wouldn't either, unless an actual angel appeared and told me to do so.

But not many people see angels these days—at least not any we recognize as such—so how do we tell the difference between something God wants us to do and something we're just making up out of our own desires?

I have two answers. First, it's those little "coincidences." For me, it's usually a string of events, conversations, or messages that are so completely improbable and out of the blue that the chances of them being a coincidence are statistically impossible (as long as I did nothing to prompt or encourage them, of course!).

Second is prayer. Many years ago, I was given a quote by a pastor that finally helped this make sense to me: "Waiting in prayer is a disciplined refusal to act before God acts." A refusal to act—just as David twice refused to act against King Saul (1 Samuel)—even if all your friends and advisors are urging you to act. If it's really God asking you to do "the thing," he'll let you know. Maybe with an angel, maybe with a miracle, maybe with an email. In the meantime, until it's clearly from God and not yourself, you wait.

That doesn't mean you should wait for a miracle before you tell your friends about Jesus or invite them to a Bible study. But before you start a new building campaign, change what church you attend, feel God's call to go live among the natives of Nepal, or decide that God is telling you to become a movie star, you might want to wait and pray, pray and wait.

Even Philip had a visit from an angel before he took off down the road.

Once you *do* get the clear word from the Lord, don't hesitate for a second—jump right in and get busy!

Chapter Nine

Plans

Amon had lain awake much of the night and was awake again now, just before sunrise. He was on his bed mat, on the roof of the house, surrounded by his two brothers, his parents, and Gaius, all asleep. But there were too many questions spinning inside Amon's head to leave any room for sleep.

How would he get Herod removed as king and save the lives of Jesus followers?

How would he design the new addition to the house?

What did it mean that Samaritans—those Jewish Gentiles—had received the Holy Spirit and apparently been accepted by God?

What did it mean that the veil in the temple was torn in two from top to bottom when Jesus died? Did it mean that the temple was no longer the place to meet God? That thought had been circling Amon's mind, but now that he'd seen Samaritans and an Ethiopian find God without the temple, the thought roosted in the attic of his mind.

And the final question was the most difficult: How would he survive, emotionally, the many months until he could marry Tamar and once again hold her in his arms?

Amon's thoughts had always been organized and catalogued. Now he flitted from one to another. *Maybe we should build onto the back of the house, into the hill. Caiaphas was a thief and murderer. I wonder if the new high priest will be too. Do we even need a high priest anymore? Maybe I could see more of Tamar if she was helping me with the Herod plan. An addition could work well on the left side of the house. How do you trick a king into resigning? Should the rooms connect on the inside, or should I keep our rooms separate? The new high priest should be named any day now. I wonder where Herod sleeps? I hope Gaius will be here long enough to help us build—he's a good friend.*

"Amon, stop!" It was the voice of his father, whispered out of the darkness.

"Stop what?"

"Stop thinking so many thoughts. You're exhausting me."

"But . . . what . . . You can't hear my thoughts!"

"No, but I know you're thinking them, so I'm thinking them too. We must sleep now."

Amon laughed to himself. "Yes, Father. But it will be daylight in just a few minutes."

He heard his father sigh. "Yes it will. Perhaps we should surprise your mother with a breakfast she doesn't have to cook. She's been very tired these last few days."

"Maybe. But do you remember the last time we did that? She woke up coughing from the smoke."

Jotham chuckled. "You were much younger then. We'll do better now."

By the time Uri came downstairs, Amon and his father had fresh-baked bread on the table, along with olive oil, olives, dried figs, and thin slices of fried lamb. When Uri saw the feast on the table he yelled, "Is it my birth celebration?"

Jotham laughed. "No, Uri. It is just a good day to celebrate, because our family is once again together."

The others came down a short time later, Tabitha being the last. "What a wonderful surprise," she said between yawns. "I guess I've been working too hard on the clothing for the poor. I'm tired all the way down to my bones."

Amon's mother had been working for three years gathering and organizing donations of clothing for the needy ones among the Way, and sewing many clothes when there weren't enough donations.

Breakfast was loud and fun. In the middle of it, Benjamin walked in. Many years before he'd been told he was such a part of their family that he never needed to knock before entering. "I smelled the lamb the moment I stepped out of my house," he greeted. It was decided that, though the flat fried bread wasn't quite flat enough or fried enough and the lamb was a bit tough, Jotham and Amon could cook breakfast for the rest of them anytime they wanted.

After breakfast, Amon and Benjamin left to make an irregular call on Tamar. Outside, Amon walked backward up the street for a time, studying where they had just come from.

"Planning your new house?" Benjamin asked.

Amon nodded. "I can't find a plan I really like. But I can't get married until I do, so I think I'll just throw something on the side of the house and call it good."

"How about building *up*?"

"I thought about that, but the walls of the lower floors won't support that much weight."

They were still in sight of the house when Jadon ran out and caught up with them. "Can I go with you?"

Amon's mind thought up a mean response, but he caught it before it found his mouth. He really didn't *want* his little brother tagging along—he had always enjoyed his times with Benjamin away from family. But then he thought about how well Jadon had done on their travels. "Okay, you may. But when I'm talking with Tamar, you'll have to stay with Benjamin."

Jadon didn't realize that staying with Benjamin meant also staying with Rhoda. The older woman made Jadon sit on the bench straight-backed and still between her and Benjamin.

On the bench around the well, Amon and Tamar sat in private discussion. Tamar looked into Amon's eyes as if she could see his soul. "Could we not just kill him and be done with it?" she whispered.

Amon smiled as if Tamar were the only woman in the world. "I'd love to, but I'm pretty sure Jehovah is against murder."

Tamar laughed loudly, and Rhoda squinted to see if there was something inappropriate going on. She had no idea.

When they first sat down, Amon had filled Tamar in on their travels, the miraculous events, and his plans—or lack of plans—for both their house and for removing Herod from office. They continued their game of trying to look as if they were talking about their deep love for each other while talking about very different subjects.

Tamar's laugh trailed off. "So what should our plan be, if not murder?"

Amon sighed and tried to look as if they talked of future children and home life. "I have a vague thought that maybe we could embarrass Herod. Rome does not like their puppet kings to look foolish. Maybe we could find a way to humiliate Rome through Herod."

"Oh, my lovey dovey, that sounds so wonderful. I'm sure you'll come up with something."

"I can't do this alone, donkey-poo. I need your help. And Benjamin's, and everyone's."

Behind her veil, Tamar was trying to hold in a laughing fit. "Donkey-poo? Is that supposed to be a romantic term of affection?"

Amon bit his lip, trying not to laugh. "Sorry," he squeaked. "I'm not very good at terms of affection."

"No, you're not." The laugh Tamar was holding in seemed to bounce back and forth off her ribs as her whole body shook. Then she saw Rhoda stand and clear her throat. "I believe we're being told our time is up."

"All right, I'll see you tonight."

Tamar's voice showed her surprise. "Twice in one day?"

Amon nodded. "My father arranged it, since we spent so many days apart."

Tamar sighed a satisfied sigh. "I love your father."

Amon, Benjamin, and Jadon walked down the streets of Jerusalem headed nowhere. "Just because I haven't been here in so long," Amon said.

"You were only gone a few weeks," Benjamin reminded him.

"Yeah, but it felt like forever."

"Amen," Jadon said softly.

Benjamin gave Amon a little shove with his shoulder. "So what were you and Tamar talking about that was so funny? Or was it all mushy married stuff that I don't want to hear about? Yet."

"It wasn't mushy. We were talking about murdering Herod." Amon sucked in his breath and his eyes flashed over to Jadon.

"What?" Jadon said. "I'm not going to tell anyone."

"I was, uh, just kidding, Jadon. I didn't really mean—"

"I *know* that, Amon. I'm not six anymore. I'm almost a man. But if you *do* murder Herod, I want in on it."

"I'm not—I was just joking, Jadon."

"So was I. You see, I'm old enough to joke about serious things. Of *course* I don't want to murder him. Or hurt him. Or anyone. And if you *were* serious about it, I'd tie you up and not let you loose until you came to your senses." Jadon smiled. "Or at least tell Rhoda, and *she'd* tie you up."

Amon relaxed. "No thanks. And I'm sorry—after all we went through on our journey, I should have realized that you're more mature now."

"Yes, you should have. So how are you going to do it?"

"Do what?"

"Get rid of Herod without murdering him."

"Who said . . . I'm not . . . Okay, I give up." Amon turned to his friend. "Benjamin, meet my brother, Jadon. He's all grown-up."

"Nice to meet you, Jadon. And welcome to our world."

Amon sighed. "The answer is, I don't know. And I don't have much time to think about it because I have so many other things to think about."

"Amon!"

The call from somewhere behind them startled Amon. He spun around and saw Gaius running after them. He slid to a stop, breathing hard, and held a parchment out to Amon. "A mess—a message from Sebaste."

Amon took it, read it, then looked up at the sky and thought for a moment. "Thank you, Gaius. Benjamin, could you please go to the houses where the apostles are staying and tell them we need to meet immediately?"

"Surely. Where should I tell them we're meeting?"

Amon raised an eyebrow and stared at his friend.

"Oh. Right. Of course," Benjamin said. "Right away."

Benjamin turned to run, but Amon grabbed his arm. "Bring Barnabas too."

"Who?"

"Barnabas—Joseph the Levite."

"Oh, yeah. Why do you call him Barnabas?"

Amon gave a look as if he were a teacher and Benjamin his student who had asked an obvious question. "What does 'Barnabas' mean?"

Benjamin thought. "Uh, 'son of encouragement.'" He saw Amon staring at him, eyebrows raised, and finally got it. "Oh!"

"Yes, 'oh,'" Amon said. "Who do you know who's more encouraging, patient, and kind than Joseph the Levite?"

Benjamin didn't answer but instead said, "So it's a nickname."

"Yes, it's a nickname. One his family gave him, because . . . ?"

"Because he's so encouraging, patient, and kind."

Amon nodded. "Exactly. And besides, if it weren't for Barnabas, the apostles probably would never have accepted Saul when he came back from Arabia. Now go!"

Benjamin ran up the street, pushing past elders and jumping around carts. Amon turned to the other two.

"Jadon, could you take Gaius back to our house, please?"

Jadon started to protest, then saw the look in his brother's eyes. "Yes, Amon."

As he and Gaius turned and started up the hill, Amon called after him. "Jadon, I trust you. But I am not allowed to take you where I must go. It is not my decision."

Jadon looked back, nodded, then turned again and climbed the hill.

Amon turned the other direction and ran toward the temple. He skidded around several corners and ended up at a heavy wooden door. He watched overhead, above the roofs, where thousands of workers still chiseled and sanded and carved stones to finish the temple. He knew that one of them, known only as "Simon the Temple Builder," was already a member of the Way, and another, "Alexander Who Made the Gates of the Temple," was beginning to believe. Of the other ten thousand builders he did not know, so he made sure none of them were watching. When he was sure, he unlocked the door and slipped inside. He opened a door to a closet, then a secret gate inside that, and descended a long stone stairway. After he'd lit lamps around a large room, he straightened up parchments and rolled maps out on the table. Sheets of papyrus hung on the walls, each with a name on it: Peter, John, James the brother of Jesus, Andrew, Saul, and so forth. Under each name was a list of dates and places that the apostle or elder was visiting. The bottom entry on the list was their current location. For most of them that entry said, "Jerusalem." The last entry on Saul's sheet indicated he had left for Tarsus. The sheets for Peter and Andrew listed "Sebaste." Next to those, someone had scribbled a note saying, "Really?!"

Amon made a new sheet and nailed it up. It read: "Philip (evangelist): Sebaste, Gaza, Azotus." A short time later, the apostles began to arrive.

Matthew was first. Amon liked all the apostles, but Matthew was one of his favorites. And Mark. And John. Then he decided there really wasn't an apostle who wasn't his favorite. As Bartholomew entered, Amon thought, *I guess he'd better be my favorite now.*

"Greetings, almost son-in-law."

Amon bowed his head. "Greetings, my already father-in-law." Neither of them was ever sure what to call the other before the actual wedding.

Bartholomew leaned over and whispered in Amon's ear, "Tamar misses you terribly."

"And I her."

The underground chamber filled up, with Benjamin trailing the last of the apostles, along with a few leaders, such as Barnabas.

When they had greeted each other and sat down, James the brother of Jesus called them to order. "Well, Amon, what is so urgent that I must leave a very fine nap to come to our headquarters?"

Amon held up the parchment. "A note. From Peter and Andrew." James reached for the note, but Amon pulled it back. "It's in Greek," he said, knowing that most of the apostles knew little if any of that language.

James sat back. "It must be serious." They all knew that Aramaic and Hebrew, not Greek, were the languages spoken by most people in Judea. If Peter wrote in Greek, he must have wanted the contents to be private. James nodded at Amon, who began to read aloud to the group.

✦ ✦ ✦

Benjamin (a fictional character for this story) was confused about who Amon (another fictional character) meant when he said the name Barnabas (a real person in the Bible).

He's not the only one, and Barnabas is not the only character there's confusion about.

The twenty-seven books of what we call the New Testament were not written by one person as one long history book. They were written by several different people at different times and compiled later. And each author wrote about many people with many names, assuming their readers would know who they meant. If I'm writing a letter to my family about "Andy," they know I mean my friend. But if someone else reads that a thousand years from now, they may wonder which of millions of Andys I meant.

To make it even more confusing, many people in the Bible are called by more than one name, such as if I also called Andy by the name James, his middle name.

Historians think that "Barnabas" is the same person as "Joseph the Levite," and that the disciple "Bartholomew" in the first three Gospels (a real person, and father of the fictional character Tamar for this story) is the same person as the disciple "Nathanael" in the Gospel of John. But we're not a hundred percent positive.

Confused yet? So was Benjamin in our story. So am I in real life. Often.

But in the end, it doesn't really matter if we get those names exactly right. What we need to get right are the *ideas* Jesus taught, and those are crystal clear in the New Testament: love the Lord your God with all your heart, soul, and mind, and love your neighbor as yourself.

There's simply no confusion about that.

Chapter Ten

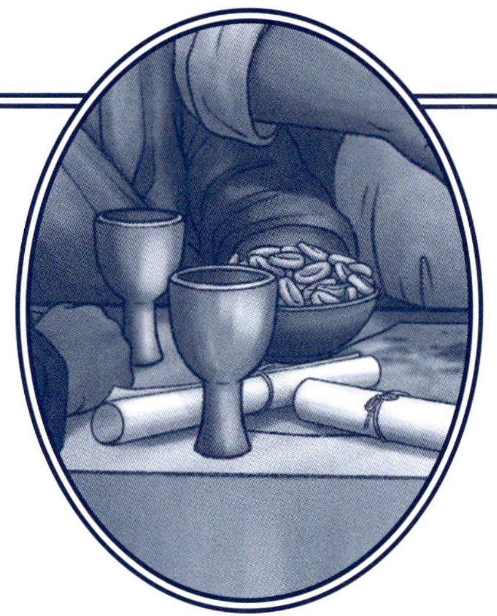

The First Letter

Amon read the note from Peter aloud, translating from Greek to Aramaic in his head:

> "My friends and fellow workers in Christ. Our surprising work here in Sebaste continues, though Philip has been called by Christ to minister elsewhere. Amon can fill you in on that. Andrew and I would like to return to Jerusalem and further spread the word along the way, but we don't want to leave the flock here unattended. Please select two of our brothers to relieve us and continue the work.
>
> "The more urgent concern is the work in Antioch. The persecutions there seem to be waning, but they continue all the same. I feel we should check on the church, and perhaps assist Saul in his ministry. You might discuss sending a representative there as well. Andrew and I will return to Jerusalem as soon as the Spirit allows. Greetings to you all in the name of our Lord Jesus Christ."

Amon refolded the letter as John Mark asked, "So why did that need to be in Greek?"

It was quiet for a moment until Bartholomew answered. "Because it deals with the comings and goings of the apostles." He looked at each of the others around the table. "With the death of James of Zebedee, we now know that none of us are safe. We must be terribly cautious, both here in Jerusalem and as we travel."

A long discussion followed, which Amon and Benjamin simply watched. It was finally decided that Jude and Thomas would be sent to Sebaste, as they were the most available at the moment. Gaius would return with them.

"Of course, if you're too busy to go," Matthew joked with Thomas, "you can always send your twin brother. Who would know the difference?"

The apostles laughed, including Thomas. "My mother, and anyone who has ever met me!" he answered. "My brother and I are alike in appearance only."

Amon thought it was good to hear them laughing. Since the death of James of Zebedee, and with Herod on the hunt for people of the Way, there hadn't been much humor in the group. *Perhaps I should tell them that soon Herod will no longer be a threat*, he thought. But then he reconsidered. *I should at least have a plan before I bring it up again.*

A second discussion led to a decision to send Barnabas, "a good and faithful evangelist," to Antioch. Barnabas was to report on the conditions in Antioch and help out Saul where he could.

Amon recorded these decisions on the schedule sheets and maps and charts on the wall of the chamber. He had started keeping track of the apostles and other important evangelists three years before, after Stephen's death had sent them traveling in different directions. "So we know who is where, and what they're doing," he had explained then. Now he moved Barnabas, Thomas, and Matthew to their respective destinations on the charts.

Since they were together, the apostles discussed many other things. Benjamin kept notes of it all. When everything was said that needed saying, Matthew asked Amon in front of the whole group, "How is the new bridegroom coming with the wedding plans?"

All the apostles turned their attention to Amon, grinning and anxious to hear the report. Amon felt his face flush. "Well, so far I've been too busy to do much. But soon I will turn my attention to building our home."

The group then ate and drank and joked. *More like the old days*, Amon thought. A moment later he decided he was wrong. *Not like the old days. Back then the joking came from joy at the resurrection of Jesus. Now it is covering up tension and concern about Herod.*

The meeting broke up, and Amon gathered his parchments and quills. He was surprised when James the brother of Jesus took him aside. "Amon, I have a great favor to ask of you."

"I will do anything to help you," Amon replied.

James hesitated, and Amon thought he seemed a bit embarrassed. "I would like to write a letter." He stopped, as if waiting for an objection. When Amon gave none, he continued. "A letter to all the Jews spread around the world, to teach them how to be followers of Jesus, and guide them in their daily lives."

Amon smiled and nodded. "Yes, I think that's a very good idea. Especially coming from you."

"Yes, well . . ." James looked down, stroking his beard, hesitant.

"Is there a problem?"

"Well, yes, in a way." He looked back up at Amon. "I'd like to write it in Greek."

Amon shrugged, thinking this an excellent plan since so many Jews now lived in Greek-speaking countries, and many had been born and raised there. A moment later, Amon understood the problem. "You don't speak or write Greek."

"Not as well as I'd like," James confessed. "And not enough to write clearly, with passion and authority."

Amon suddenly realized what James was saying. "You want me to help you."

James smiled. "I would be most grateful if you could. It would not take long—maybe a few weeks—and I would pay you what I can."

In his heart, Amon wanted to laugh and say, "No!" He already had a king to depose—to remove from the throne—and a wedding home to build. He didn't have time for something more.

But in his head, Amon thought, *This is the brother of Jesus. How can I say no?*

Amon tried to make sure it was the thoughts of his mind and not the feelings of his heart that showed on his face. "Of course I can help you. But you need not pay me—my wages will be the great gift of trust you place in me. When would you like to start?"

James shrugged. "Tomorrow?"

Amon's heart again wanted to protest, but he made his mind speak the word. "Perfect."

~

"Oh, wait! I have three more back here." Tabitha dragged out three bags of clothing from behind the stairway by her cooking place. A man named Uzziah lifted the bags as if they were pillows and took them out to the handcart.

Amon swallowed his bite of parched wheat. "Sit and eat, Mother. You cannot walk to Joppa on only a few dates and a sip of pomegranate juice."

Tabitha waved away his concern, then thought better of it. She sat on one stool and put her feet up on another. "I'm tired already, and we're not even out of Jerusalem."

Amon laughed. "I do not believe I've ever seen you with your feet up."

"Well, I'll be on my feet all day, so I think they deserve a small rest right now."

Jadon came in from outside. "We're almost loaded, Mother."

"Then come and eat more. You'll need your energy."

Jadon's eyes lit up. He came and sat at the table and seemed to pour a bowl of parched wheat right down his throat.

It was still dark out, early in the morning, a week after the apostles' meeting and several days after

Barnabas left for Antioch. Tabitha and nine other people representing the Jerusalem church were taking as much clothing and food as they could gather and transport over to the coast to Joppa, a distance of two days' walking. She was taking Jadon with her, for "protection," she said, but Amon suspected she really just wanted some time with her second son before he became a man. Amon and his father would stay and watch over Uri.

Jadon was excited about the trip, no longer afraid of far places and dangerous roads. Jotham entered and reported that everything was loaded and that the travelers should leave immediately if they wanted to make it to Lydda, which was a little over half the distance to Joppa, before sunset.

It was strange, Amon thought, for his mother and little brother to go on a trip and leave him and his father at home. But Tabitha was always working to help the poor, the widows, and the orphans, and these days that meant distributing food and clothing far beyond the walls of Jerusalem.

With shouts and waves, those staying home sent off those traveling, and Amon watched until they were through the Essene Gate and out of sight. Then he, Uri, and their father went back to bed.

After a second breakfast, Amon left the house with his quills and papers in a flat bag. James would be meeting him at the house of Jesse for another day of writing. *And rewriting*, Amon thought. *He wants everything to be so perfect, like this letter is going to be around for all time or something.*

Jesse was a wealthy believer living in the upper city. An old, empty cistern on his property was one of the meeting places for the congregations. Several such cisterns existed around Jerusalem, and members of the Way could meet with their local congregations in them twice a week for prayer, praise, and lesson gatherings. Each week, Amon created the schedule of which congregations would meet at which cistern and at what time to prevent onlookers from noticing a pattern. He had simply not scheduled any group in this one until James was done with his letter.

Amon crossed the top of the city, surprised at how few people were about. *Did I forget a holiday?*

Sunlight tickled the tops of the towers at the praetorium as Amon passed. This was where the Roman governor of Judea, whoever that might be, lived and ruled—the place Pilate had just vacated. Amon had been inside the palace many times, trading his inventions and labor for the life of his father. At one end of the mighty complex, three towers punctured the sky. Amon always wondered if they were more for show than any practical defensive purpose.

Around the corner, to the right of the Garden Gate, was the palace of the Jewish king—another ornate witness to the self-centered greed and cruelty of most of the Herod family. *In fact*, Amon thought, *I'm not sure there's a Herod who—*

"Halt!"

Amon snapped upright, swung around to his left, and froze. Two temple guards stood not ten feet away, swords drawn. *How did I not see them?* Amon wondered.

"Your name and your business, boy."

Fear tried to cripple Amon, but he quickly shooed it away and relaxed. "I am Amon, son of Jotham, and by right and tradition I am a man. What business do you have with *my* business?"

Amon had no idea where the words had come from but instantly knew he'd just made an enemy.

The soldier on the left stared at him, eyes wide, flames shooting out his nose and smoke blasting from his ears. Amon knew that the man had no legal cause to challenge him, but he also knew it really made no difference: the soldier held a sword, Amon held a quill, and in all practical ways the quill was not mightier than the sword.

The soldier took a step forward, his eyes locked on Amon's. A second step, a third, and the soldier was so close Amon could feel the man's hot breath on his face. It smelled of rotting meat and sour eggs.

Amon didn't blink. He breathed slowly and calmly. If this soldier wanted to kill him, then it would be so. Amon would not offer him the pleasure of seeing his prey cower.

The soldier stared for many long seconds, then glanced down to see what Amon was carrying. He locked eyes with Amon again. "What is the punishment for lying to the king whom God has appointed to rule over us, or for lying to his servants?"

Amon knew this was an old trick used by the Sanhedrin—the legal court of the Jews. Gamaliel had warned him about it many years before: ask the accused to name their own punishment and it sounds like a confession of guilt. Amon would not play that game. "*Rome*, not God, appointed Herod as king."

The eyes of the soldier narrowed, and in the next moment Amon thought, *Uh oh, this time I may have gone too far.*

✦ ✦ ✦

James the brother of Jesus has decided to write a letter to the "Diaspora"—the Jews who were taken from Galilee and Judea centuries before and forced to live in other countries as slaves. Of course, those particular Jews *died* centuries before, so James is writing to their descendants, the "twelve tribes scattered among the nations." These Jews don't live in Judea or Galilee but rather are scattered around the world.

But here's a funny thing: just like we don't always know who the specific *people* mentioned in the Bible are, we also don't always know the exact *author* of a book in the Bible. The book we call "James" starts out, "James, a servant of God and of the Lord Jesus Christ." But that could mean any of several different people named James, or theoretically, even a James not mentioned anywhere else in the Bible.

I would say that most of us who study such things agree that the book of James was written by the brother of Jesus. But we could be wrong. So the question again is, Does it really matter? The book of James—a letter written to help people live a Christian life—is included in our Bible by design of God's Holy Spirit. It therefore has the same authority as any other book.

And here's another point: the books of the New Testament were not written centuries later but close to the time these things happened, by the people who were there, who lived through—and were living through—these events. These books were written by people who either knew Jesus personally or were intimately involved in the birth of the church. They were eyewitnesses.

It makes me feel almost like I was there.

It should make us *all* feel that we can trust the Bible as the inspired Word of God.

Chapter Eleven

You, Boy!

The soldier's eyes were barely more than slits, and his mouth was pinched tightly closed. He slowly brought the tip of his sword up directly in front of Amon's throat, without taking his eyes off Amon's. He stared for several moments, then his lips parted just enough to hiss, "Your rightfully appointed king is asking you a question, *boy*. Who is the Clever One?"

Amon's blood froze as solid as the ice of a winter storm in Jerusalem. For three years he and every follower of Jesus had tried to hide his secret identity from the Romans. And now, apparently, the Roman-appointed king and his army were hunting him again. How long would it be before they tortured Amon's name out of some unfortunate Christ follower?

Amon held on tightly to the shivers of fear that shook his chest and desperately wanted to shake his whole body. He hoped the battle didn't show in his eyes as he answered carefully. "I know many clever people, but I know of no friend, acquaintance, or enemy, whether Jew or Roman or anything else, who is called by that name."

He knew he was being clever in his answer, of course. He knew of no friend, acquaintance, or enemy called the Clever One because that was the name by which the followers of Jesus called *him*.

The soldier kept glaring and took several angry breaths. He glanced again at the writing materials Amon carried. "Who's your rabbi, boy?"

Amon didn't hesitate. "I told you, I am a man, and it is an insult for any Jew to call someone a boy who is a man. It is loathsome in the eyes of Jehovah. But *my* rabbi is Gamaliel. Who is *yours*?"

The soldier's eyes shot wide open in fear. Amon almost laughed as he saw the soldier calculate the odds of his own survival if he dared harm a student of the most honored and beloved rabbi in Jerusalem.

The soldier didn't answer Amon's question and said simply, "Then you'd better get to your lessons."

~

"They were testing to see if you are a Jesus follower," James said a few minutes later, after Amon had escaped the soldier's interrogation. James shook his head. "Someone has told Herod of your nickname. It was bad enough that Caiaphas and Pilate knew about the Clever One. I was hoping that knowledge had left Jerusalem with them."

They were once again in the brightly lit and empty cistern of Jesse.

"Do you think I lied by naming Gamaliel as my rabbi instead of Jesus?" Amon asked.

James stood and paced across the small space. "I do not know, Amon, but I do not think so. He asked you a question, and you answered it truthfully. Gamaliel is, and always will be, your rabbi. Nothing can change that. He taught you the foundations of faith, and even compassion. In many ways, you are who you are because of him. That you now follow a new rabbi as well does not change any of that and is not what the soldier asked you."

Amon nodded. "Actually, there was something else about the whole incident that bothered me even more."

"Oh? More than being threatened with death for following Jesus? What is that?"

Amon looked a bit shy as he asked, "Do I really look like a twelve-year-old boy?"

James was surprised, then laughed loudly. "Why do you ask such a thing?"

Amon shrugged. "The soldier called me a boy. Twice. But he's a Jewish soldier. How could he not tell I am well over the age of becoming a man?"

"Ah, I see. It's your feelings he hurt instead of your body. Well, I would say that yes, you do look a bit younger than your age. But not twelve. Perhaps"—James started to pace again and stroked his beard—"perhaps an angel of the Lord made him see the papers in your hand as lessons, and your face as that of a boy, to keep you from becoming our next martyr."

Amon grinned. "Oh, I like that explanation."

"Good, then let's get to work. Where did we leave off?"

Amon sorted through the parchments on the table and found the last one. "'Speak and act as those who are going to be judged by the law that gives freedom, because judgment without mercy will be shown to anyone who has not been merciful. Mercy triumphs over judgment.'"

"Ah, yes." James paced again, his eyes searching the empty cistern for his next words. "Write this: What good is it, my brothers and sisters, if someone claims to have faith but has no deeds? Can such faith save them? Suppose a brother or a sister is without clothes and daily food. If one of you says to them, 'Go in peace; keep warm and well fed,' but does nothing about their physical needs, what good is it? In the same way, faith by itself, if it is not accompanied by action, is dead."

Amon stopped writing and held up his hand. "Wait, wait, wait." He looked up at his elder with a face that said he meant no disrespect. "Are you saying that there are things we must do to prove our faith before God will accept us for salvation?"

"No, no, not at all. I'm saying that if you truly have faith, you won't be able to hide it like a lamp under a basket. Instead, it will show in the things you do, for all to see, like a city on a hill."

Amon frowned and shook his head. "I don't understand the difference."

James thought for another moment. "Would you, Amon, *could* you, Amon, if you saw someone by the side of the road, injured, walk by them without helping?"

Amon's answer was instant. "No. Of course not. I could never pass by someone in need."

"Yet, in one of the parables Jesus told us, that's exactly what both a priest and a rabbi did to an injured traveler—they ignored his pleas and passed him by. But a Samaritan—someone that even I thought could never find God until a few weeks ago—stopped and helped the man, even to the point of parting with his own cloak. So who had a true faith in God? The priest who spoke good words? The rabbi who taught good lessons? Or the Samaritan, who gave up all that he had to help someone in need?"

Amon nodded, understanding that James didn't really expect him to answer.

"So I'm saying, Amon, that there is nothing a person need do to secure salvation beyond acceptance of Christ and repentance. But if that person truly has accepted Christ and repented, their faith will show in their treatment of others. At least eventually."

Amon considered the words for several moments. "Jesus told that parable?"

"Yes. It was one of many."

Amon leaned back in his chair and sighed. "I wish I could have followed him around and listened in."

"You couldn't," James said, quite abruptly. "You were too much of a little know-it-all kid to listen to anything you didn't already believe."

Amon looked up, shocked, until James started laughing loudly again. Then Amon laughed too, and James added, "Of course, so was I, and I was his brother."

As they stood hours later and put out the oil lamps, Amon, still thinking about their conversation, asked, "Do you think that James of Zebedee was murdered by Herod's guards because he would not tell them that I am the Clever One?"

James stopped and stared at Amon in the dim light of the last lamp. Amon thought he seemed surprised, as if he'd never considered this possibility. "I think," James said finally, "that James of Zebedee was murdered because he was a follower of Jesus, and because Herod is a man who is sick in his head, full of the demons of pride and lust for power and glory."

Amon thought for a minute, then nodded. "I think that as well." *But still*, he said to himself, *it would be just like James to sacrifice himself to save someone else.*

~

Amon spent a few hours working for his clients—some of the wealthier Jews—installing "rocks you can see through" in their windows and wind machines in their bedrooms. He rushed home late in the afternoon to prepare dinner for his father and Uri, watching carefully for temple guards and Roman soldiers in every shadow. After dinner he rushed down to the well to see Tamar. When Rhoda eventually shooed him away, Amon rushed back home to put Uri to bed so his father wouldn't have to.

As he tucked a cloth-and-straw camel toy in next to Uri's cheek, Uri asked, "Amon, is mother dead?"

Amon flinched. "What? Why would you ask such a thing?"

"Well, once when father went away, you said they might make him dead. Now mother is gone. Will she be dead?"

Amon gave his most compassionate smile. "No, Uri. Mother is just on a trip. To help other people. No one is going to . . . make her dead. She'll be home in a couple of weeks."

Uri smiled, nodded, then closed his eyes.

As he came down the stairs after that, Amon saw his father sitting at the table, working on his ledgers for the family sheep business. He sat across the table and laid his head on his arms. "I'm so exhausted. I need to work on my house design, but I don't think I can keep my eyes open."

"How is the writing coming with James?"

Amon shrugged underneath his head. "Fine, I guess. I'm not really sure what his goal is, so I can't tell if we're making progress toward it."

Jotham kept writing in his ledgers. "Why don't you go up to bed? House designing can wait."

Amon thought for three or four blinks. "Yes, I think I will." He stood and started up the stairs but stopped on the fourth step and sat. "Father, I have a . . . delicate question for you."

Jotham stopped writing and looked up.

"I want—I have decided that, for the good of the Way, I must find a plan that will force King Herod to be removed from office."

Jotham laid down his quill and gave full attention to his son. "I'm listening."

"I just think—well, Herod thinks anyone who believes in Jesus should die."

"There are many in Jerusalem who think that."

"Yes, but Herod has the power to make it happen. Now that Caiaphas is gone and Pilate is gone, he's the last threat to the Way." Amon saw the look on his father's face. "Okay, maybe not the last there will ever be, but the last in Jerusalem. For the moment."

"So what is your plan?"

"That's my point, and my question. I have been so busy that I haven't had time to think. But also, I cannot think well about such things without the help of Benjamin . . . and Tamar."

Jotham's eyebrows shot up, and Amon felt like his father was about to laugh.

"So, you would like me to arrange for you to meet with Tamar more often? For a longer duration? Or in private?"

"Yes."

"Yes to which one?"

"All three."

Jotham chuckled and rolled his eyes, and Amon thought that was a very funny thing for someone his age to do. "Go to bed."

Amon nodded. "Yes, Father."

Then he crawled up the stairs and into his bed next to Uri.

✦ ✦ ✦

Just like many people today, Amon is confused by what James is writing. At this point in history, the brand-new church is struggling with the change from the "Old Testament" rule of law to the "New Testament" rule of love.

The rule of law says, "You must *do* this and this and this to be holy and acceptable to God."

The rule of love says, "There's nothing you *can* do to be acceptable to God, except believe in the Lord Jesus Christ and repent of your sins."

In the beginning, we humans walked with God in the garden. Then we sinned and were evicted into a cold, cruel world of laws. Accepting the sacrifice of Jesus allows us back into that original garden relationship.

But then James comes along and says that if you truly have accepted Jesus, it will show in the things you *do*.

Say what?

As Amon's response demonstrated, these words caused a lot of confusion for the new believers, and still do for some believers today. But James wasn't saying we must *do* certain things to be *saved*. I believe he's saying, as Jesus himself said in the parable of the Good Samaritan, that if we are filled with the Spirit of God, how could we possibly treat people poorly?

Treating others with kindness and respect, helping them when we are able, and being generous with what God has given us may not come easily or naturally. But let's work at it day by day, person by person, just as Jesus commanded when he said, "Whatever you did for one of the least of these brothers and sisters of mine, you did for me" (Matthew 25:40).

Chapter Twelve

Herod

He laughed?" Benjamin asked.

"Yes. Without even thinking about it. Then he told me to go to bed."

Amon and Benjamin wandered the streets at the far end of the Tyropoeon Valley, near the Pool of Siloam, about as far away as you could get from Herod's palace. They had walked up and down the crowded alleyways and visited many of their vendor friends—who were weaving and dying cloth, making sandals of leather, and extracting precious oils from plants—simply to talk and think.

"Well, you don't have to do what your father says, you know. You're a man now."

Amon sighed. "Yes, legally that is true. But I respect my father too much to throw legalities in his face."

Benjamin gave him a strange look, halfway between a grin and a grimace. "You did not always respect him so."

"That is true. But I won't make that mistake again. I've learned that he is wise and I'm a fool."

They passed the Pool of Siloam, where more than three thousand Jews had been baptized into the Way on the day of Pentecost.

"Is it strange not having your mother home?"

Amon shrugged. "Yes. It is the first time in my life she has not been there. I'm glad it is temporary. But I'm also glad she has found a way to serve others."

Amon's stomach told him it was lunchtime, so they headed back to his house. "I need to get lunch for Uri in any case." As they approached, they were surprised to hear laughter from his house. Amon opened the door and found Peter and Andrew at the table with Uri and Jotham, already finished with their lunch.

They greeted one another, then Amon asked, "When did you get back?"

Peter answered, "This very morning. We came straight here to let you know that the work you and

Philip started in Sebaste has spread across the whole of the city. And it is not a temporary hysteria or emotional demonstration either. The Holy Spirit has come to them, and lives have been changed."

"Gaius is also doing well," Andrew said. "He learned much in his few weeks here and is teaching large crowds day and night."

Peter shook his head in amazement. "I still cannot believe that half Jews and lapsed Jews can be saved and receive the Holy Spirit."

Amon asked, "What of the other places you visited in Samaria?"

"It was much the same in most," Andrew said. "Once people heard that those in Sebaste had believed and been baptized, it was much easier for those in the smaller villages to accept our message."

After Peter and Andrew had left and Amon and Benjamin had eaten some lunch, they headed upstairs to start planning. When the two young men were halfway up the stairs, Jotham, still clearing the table, called to them, "Where are you going?"

"Upstairs to start planning," Amon answered.

Amon was almost to the top when his father said, "Aren't you going to include Tamar?"

Amon stopped, then rushed back down. "You arranged it?"

Jotham flashed an overly large smile.

"Father! Thank you!" Amon jumped down the last two steps and hugged him. "What are the terms?"

Jotham cleared his throat. "You must meet at a table in the courtyard behind Mary's house. Benjamin must be there and must sit between you and Tamar, or you must sit across the table from her. Rhoda will be there as well, but she will sit back by the house where she won't be able to hear, if you whisper. Tamar must be veiled, and you two may not touch. You may meet for one hour, twice a day."

Amon looked at his father like he was an angel. "You are the most holy man in all Judea. How did you get Rhoda to agree?"

Jotham looked some combination of embarrassed and guilty. "Uh, well . . . I bribed her."

Amon's mouth dropped open. He stared for a moment. "With *what*?"

Jotham shrugged. "A new roof on Mary's house, so they can sleep there when it's hot."

"That's a good price," Amon said, nodding. "That shouldn't take you too long."

"It will take me no time at all. I told her that you and Benjamin will do it, after you and Tamar are married."

Amon laughed. "A fair trade."

As fast as they could gather their parchments, tablets, and quills and run down the street, Amon and Benjamin were at Mary's door. Rhoda opened to their knock. "Wait over there," she snapped, pointing to a gate at the side of the house.

The wooden gate was attached to a waist-high stone wall. A few minutes later, Rhoda came from the other side and opened the gate without a word. Amon led the way to the back, pushing through a dozen goats hoping to be fed.

Tamar sat at a small table, a veil across her face. The courtyard was large and had both an opening to a small water cistern and an opening to a large oven, in addition to vines of grapes along the stone wall and several fruit trees.

As agreed, Benjamin sat next to Tamar and Amon sat across from her. Rhoda took up her station on a bench outside the back door of the house, where she kept busy feeding goat kids that apparently had no mother.

Amon tried to see behind Tamar's veil, but Rhoda had chosen one difficult to see through in the daylight. After exchanging greetings, Amon explained their mission. "We must find a way to get Herod transferred or replaced. He is a threat to every member of the Way and will not stop until he has hunted and killed every one of us."

"Is he worse than Caiaphas was?" Tamar asked.

"Much," Amon answered. "Caiaphas had to answer to Pilate and could only do what the Romans allowed. Herod answers only to Emperor Claudius in Rome, three weeks' journey by ship."

Benjamin prepared to write, pulling out a tablet and stylus. "What are our options?"

Amon counted on his fingers as he answered. "Well, one option is to murder him, but we already know we're not going to do that. Second, we could humiliate him before Claudius so he'd be recalled to Rome. Third, we could reveal him as a thief who steals from the taxes he's supposed to send to Rome. That's as far as I've gotten."

Tamar held up four fingers. "Fourth, we could convince him he *wants* to leave Judea, from either fear or desire."

Amon scrunched up his face. "Desire for *what*?"

"For Rome. He grew up among hills rich and green with everything you could want to eat, in a city built of gold and marble, that is cool and comfortable all year, near a sea where fatal storms are rare, among Romans who think and talk as he does. None of that describes Jerusalem. If we could convince him he misses Rome, maybe he'd go back there."

Amon nodded, impressed once again with Tamar's wisdom.

Benjamin held up five fingers.

"What?" Amon asked. "What's the fifth possibility?"

Benjamin spoke even more quietly. "Fifth, we could convince him that Jesus is the Messiah, and that he should pray for salvation and forgiveness."

Amon was embarrassed that he hadn't thought of that first. "You are exactly right. Though I suspect praying for Herod would be a lost cause."

Tamar sighed. "Isn't that exactly what you and everyone else except Philip thought about Samaria?"

Amon was embarrassed for the second time in five breaths. "Yes, you are correct."

"So, which option do we start with?" Benjamin asked.

Amon thought for a long time. "Number five," he said at last. "I think we start by trying to convince Herod that Jesus is the Messiah."

"I know it was my idea," Benjamin said, "but how do we do it?"

All three thought for some time. "Maybe we could write down our personal testimonies of Jesus," Benjamin suggested, "and send them to Herod."

Amon swallowed a drink of water. "Would we sign them?"

"Of course." A moment later, Benjamin realized this would mean instant death. "Or not."

"That would be the problem," Tamar said. "If we sign them, we die; if we don't, they have no power to persuade Herod."

Amon tapped his fingers on his chin. "Perhaps if we compiled the prophecies about Jesus and sent them to Herod anonymously, the Spirit may open his eyes."

Tamar sighed. "We tried that with Saul, before Jesus called him, but he had already made up his mind."

"Herod is a Jew!" Benjamin spat. "Surely he must care at least *a little* about Jehovah."

"Saul is also a Jew," Amon answered. "But look how hard it was to convince him about Jesus."

At that moment, the sun reached a point in the sky where it lit up Tamar's veil such that Amon could see her eyes. He sucked in his breath and started to make a comment when he suddenly found himself butted off his stool by a large male goat. He flew several feet and landed in the dirt.

Tamar laughed until she cried. "I believe Rhoda is telling you it's time to leave."

Amon looked at her, shocked, then looked toward Rhoda. She was rewarding the goat with a treat. "What! She—she *trained* a goat to butt me off the stool?"

"It would seem so."

"Why? Doesn't she like me?"

"Once we're married, she'll probably love you. But right now you are the lowest, sneakiest, foulest form of life—a bridegroom."

Amon stood, brushed himself off, and gave a nod and fake smile to Rhoda. "Come on, Ben. Let's go." To Tamar he added, "I'll see you tonight."

As they let themselves out through the gate, Benjamin said, "That's the first time you ever called me 'Ben.' I think I like it."

Amon's intent was to turn right and head up the hill toward his home, but a sound to his left, toward the north end of the city, caught his attention. "What is that?"

Benjamin listened. "Sounds like fighting."

Amon grabbed the front of Benjamin's tunic. "Come on." They ran up the street to the north, past the praetorium, to the Garden Gate, and climbed to the top. The north end of the city lay before them, with the Fortress of Antonia to their right. Below them was another market, this one with dealers of wool and timber, metal workers, and makers of clothing. On the other side of the far wall, beyond the Damascus Gate, large crews of men seemed to be digging a trench. Amon couldn't see on the other side of the small hill of Bezetha, but it looked like the trench started at the left corner of the wall, went entirely around the hill, and came back to the right corner.

"Dancin' camels!" Benjamin whispered in awe. "What are they doing?"

Amon leaned on the stone barrier next to where they stood. "I don't know. Drainage, maybe? Some sort of defensive system?"

"You boys!" The gruff yell startled Amon. Coming toward them from their right was a Roman soldier carrying a spear. "What is your business here?" When the soldier stopped, he towered over Amon, creating shade from the sun.

"Uh, we heard some commotion and just wondered if Jerusalem was being attacked or something."

The soldier seemed to relax. "It is the opposite. Your 'king' Herod has ordered that the city wall be extended around the northern settlements to protect them. They started building the foundation at sunrise."

Benjamin made a startled sound. "That means the Damascus Gate will be—"

"Thank you, officer," Amon interrupted. "We'll leave now."

The soldier grunted. "I'm no officer, and I don't wanna be. But you'd best not seem too curious about Herod's affairs. The man is a—" He stopped abruptly, got a strange look on his face, turned, and walked back along the top of the wall.

"Sorry," Benjamin whispered. "I just realized they might find Uri's Place."

Amon studied the scene in front of them. With Jerusalem crammed full of both people and buildings, many new arrivals had started making their home to the north, outside the city walls, around the area of the garden tomb where the body of Jesus had made a short visit.

And around the entrance to the secret caves they called "Uri's Place."

To his right, the wall they stood on continued over to the temple, past the palace of—

Amon jumped back into the shadow of the gate and pulled Benjamin with him. Above them and to the right, King Herod was strolling on the roof of his palace tower, watching the construction of the wall. The king's eyes wandered across the city and came to rest on the Garden Gate. Then he looked directly into the eyes of Amon.

✦ ✦ ✦

Sometimes it's easy to see the stories in the Bible as just that—stories. They don't seem a lot different than other fiction, fantasy, and adventure stories we read. They're set in places that aren't real to us, things that we know are actually impossible in our world happen, and like any good story, the characters are bigger than life.

But the Bible isn't just a storybook; it's history. And we know from other books and sources outside the Bible that Caiaphas really was replaced, Pilate really was relieved of duty, Herod really was appointed king of Judea, and on and on. Those things are historical facts—just like the things the apostles said and did and the things that happened in the church.

Amon gives us an example of how we can respond to the wonders of God's workings. Keep reading or listening and he'll lead you to the true Jesus.

Because it's not just a story.

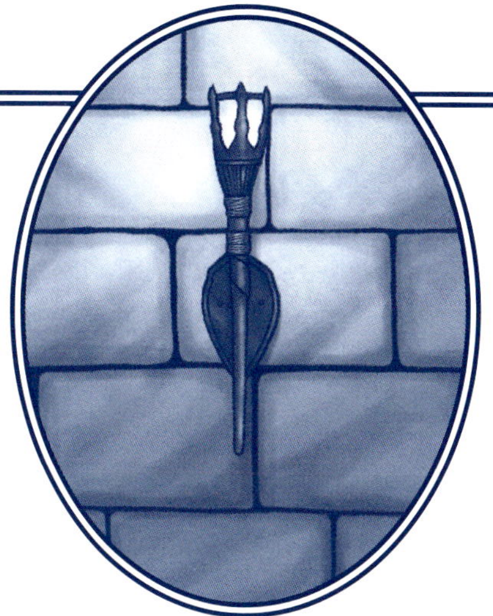

Chapter Thirteen

Squirrels

"No!" John slapped the table hard to cement his objection in the minds of everyone in the room. "We must not allow this."

Matthias leaned forward and folded his hands on the table. "And just how do you propose we stop it?"

John's mouth moved as if a hundred angry words were fighting each other to get out, but he had no answer.

"John is right." Matthew sighed. "This puts the entire Jerusalem church at risk. If they finish that wall, Uri's Place won't be outside the city anymore—it will be right in the middle. Someone is sure to find it."

Amon and Benjamin sat back and listened as the apostles debated what, if any, action to take against the building of the wall. They were once again in the secret underground chamber near the temple. All the disciples were there, except Jude and Thomas, who were still in Sebaste.

Amon thought back to his earlier encounter. Herod had stared at him for many long moments—so many that Amon wondered if the king knew who he was. *Does he suspect me of being the Clever One, or is he just trying to figure out who I am?* he had wondered. Either way, Amon's own pride made him keep staring, and the king was the first to look away.

"I think we need more information," John said. "Amon?" Amon snapped back to the present, realizing he hadn't been paying attention. "You and Benjamin used to spy on Pilate using those tunnels there." He pointed to the tunnel entrance at the corner of the chamber. "Could you, perhaps, do that again to find out what's going on?"

Amon shook his head. "It is not possible. There were many places in those tunnels that we could barely squeeze through. We always came back scraped up. That was three years ago, and both of us have grown much bigger now."

Bartholomew, Amon's future father-in-law, spoke for the first time since the meeting started. "I'm wondering if we should be spending our time worrying about what might or might not happen regarding some earthly king. I believe our focus must continue to be on the heavenly king."

"I agree," Peter said. "Besides, they're building the wall around the outside of the north end, far from Uri's Place. There's no reason they'd be anywhere near our caves."

Philip the Apostle sat back and crossed his arms. "Unless they decide to do inspections and repair work on the wall *around* Uri's Place while they're at it."

This started a whole new line of debate. Eventually, Peter asked Amon, "What did Herod look like? How was he acting?"

Amon hadn't thought about that yet, but now quickly gave a name to what he'd seen. "Smug. Defiant."

More debate followed, but the only decision made was to delay a decision and pray that Jehovah would take care of the problem for them.

"As long as we're gathered," Peter continued, "I should tell you that God has called me to take another missionary journey, to Lydda." Matthew was most of the way to a nap, but now his eyes popped open and he sat up straight. The rest of the apostles were also surprised.

Andrew spoke in a soft tone, as if trying to calm a rabid dog. "And you are . . . sure . . . that this call is from God?"

Peter looked at Andrew as if his younger brother were still a child. "Of course. Why would I say it if it were not true?"

The apostles looked at each other around the table. They all seemed to hope someone else would say something. *They're afraid he's going to ask them to go with him*, Amon realized. Benjamin kept looking up at Amon, a question on his face, but he also kept silent.

Finally John sat up a little straighter. "If God has called you, you must go. May I ask—that is, I think what we're all wondering is—did God tell you to take one of us with you?"

Peter scowled as if a great battle were going on inside his head. "Not yet. We're still working on that."

An uneasy silence followed. Amon figured the men thought that if one of them spoke, Peter might see it as a sign to take that person with him. After several embarrassing moments, Amon spoke up. "Say, has anyone heard anything of Philip? The waiter—I mean—the evangelist?"

"Yes," came a slow, deep reply. Amon tracked it to Bartholomew. "I heard he is still in Azotus."

Amon looked at Peter and shrugged. "Perhaps you could travel with *him*. He makes a very good companion."

Peter's face twisted, and Amon wasn't sure if it was a scowl, a frown, or a bit of indigestion.

~

Benjamin pulled on Amon's tunic to get him to slow down. "My mind had a question for you in there, but I did not think it proper for me to speak." They were walking home after the meeting to take over watching Uri so Amon's father could do his work. "Why were the apostles so afraid of Peter and of going with him on his journey?"

Amon took a moment to organize his thoughts. "Most of the apostles were only teenagers when Jesus first called them. They were of marrying age, but not yet betrothed."

Benjamin elbowed Amon in the ribs. "Like you, huh? Dragging out the decision until you're almost too old?"

Amon scowled at his friend. "I am *not* too old. Many of our older friends are not even betrothed yet."

"What about Hezeria? He's already married, and he's only fourteen."

Amon nodded and sighed. "Yes, that is not unusual either. But I was just pointing out that most of the apostles were still young when Jesus called them. Peter was one of the exceptions. He was not only married, but several years older than the others. I think that's why he's sort of been their leader."

"What about James the brother of Jesus?"

"Well, yes, he is *now* sort of the leader of the apostles, and older, but back in the day, while Peter faithfully followed Jesus, James thought his brother was a lunatic."

"Okay, so Peter was the leader. So what? Why is everyone afraid to travel with him?"

"I think they see Peter as kind of the father of their group, even though Bartholomew is technically the oldest. And what teenager wants to travel with their father?"

"Ohhh, I get it. It's like when Jadon was playing King's Ransom with his friends last year and you wanted to join them. Remember the look he gave you that said, *Go away*?"

Amon frowned. "Yes. And thank you for that painful memory."

Benjamin opened his mouth to reply, but instead they both heard "Halt!" *Not again*, Amon thought. But then he turned and looked.

A Roman soldier was walking toward them quickly, a spear in his hand. The man was as big as an ox, Amon thought, and could easily skewer both him and Benjamin at the same time. Behind the soldier, a higher officer stood with two other soldiers, waiting and watching. From the corner of his eye, Amon saw Benjamin twitch as if getting ready to run, so he put a hand on Benjamin's arm to hold him still.

"King Herod has ordered more men to be brought in to work on the new wall. You are now both employed by the Roman legion."

"We're being conscripted?" Amon asked in disbelief.

The soldier lowered his voice and, with his back still to his commander, said, "Only for the day, if you are wise." The soldier's eyes looked down toward the ground several times. Amon finally got the message and looked down as well. Fire flashed through his nerves when he saw the arc of half a fish drawing, made with the point of the soldier's spear.

Amon swallowed, fighting down his fear. If he drew the other half of the fish, it would identify him as a follower of Jesus. If the soldier wasn't really a believer—if this was a trap—then he and Benjamin would be dead before the sun set. But if the soldier was a member of the Way, Amon wanted to hear what he had to say. Finally, Amon acted. As if he were simply shifting his weight, he reached out his toe and completed the fish.

The soldier smiled. For a moment, Amon wondered if it was a smile of friendship or the smile of a successful hunt. The soldier pulled out a parchment and quill, making it a bigger task than it needed to be so he had time to whisper. "You must get out of Jerusalem, Clever One. Herod searches for you. Work hard today, and keep your mouths shut. Tonight, leave the city. Now, when I ask, give me false names."

Amon's head was spinning. He felt like it had been most of an hour since the soldier stopped them, but it had only been seconds.

In his loud and gruff voice, the Roman said, "Give me your names."

Amon's thoughts swirled around on themselves for a moment, then he said, "Eliazer, son of Ishtar." *Why did I give the name of my father's Persian friend?* he thought. *This man's commander might know that no Jerusalem Jew would have such a name.*

Benjamin, having had a few more seconds to think, said quickly, "Simon, son of Moab."

"Very well. Report to Lucius Ranius Optatus on the east trench. You'll know him by the purple feather in his helmet."

Amon was too stunned to speak and too stunned to move until the soldier shouted, "Now!" The soldier winked. Amon and Benjamin stumbled up the street, followed at a distance by the Romans. When they were out of hearing range, Amon increased his pace and said, "I can't believe we've been conscripted."

Benjamin almost had to run to keep up with Amon. "I can't believe we were just conscripted by a Roman member of the Way!"

"Yes, I wonder if that was just a trick. I wonder if the Romans have figured out our codes and secrets."

They turned right, onto the street to the Damascus Gate. There were soldiers everywhere, so Benjamin lowered his voice. "I don't think he would have warned you to leave the city if it was just a trick."

They slowed to a walk, went through the Damascus Gate, and turned right, walking past Uri's Place without looking. They found Lucius Ranius Optatus at the bottom of the hill, shouting orders from atop a horse, purple feather and all. *That looks ridiculous,* Amon thought.

Optatus looked down at Amon and Benjamin. "Conscripts?"

"Yes, sir."

"Where are your tools?"

Amon looked around quickly, trying to understand. "What tools?"

The Roman frowned, then spat on the ground. "You are required to provide and maintain your own tools."

"Sorry, sir. We were just conscripted moments ago."

Optatus turned away and said something into the wind. He turned back, his eyes warning them of future death. "Tomorrow you will bring tools. Today you will be squirrels!"

✦ ✦ ✦

How old were the disciples when they followed Jesus around Galilee?

The paintings we have of them were all made hundreds of years later and were completely made up by the artists. For most of those centuries, people assumed the disciples were mature, grown-up, even old.

But that's probably not true. While there's still a lot of debate, it seems probable that they were much younger than they're usually shown in paintings. Some scholars believe that John may have been as young as thirteen or fourteen, which seems likely since Jesus was crucified in about AD 33 but John didn't die until about AD 100. (Remember that in the Jewish tradition, a boy can be considered a man when he's thirteen.) Because people in general lived much, much shorter lives than we do today, young people would get married and have children as early as thirteen. Since none of the disciples except Peter were married yet, there seems to be a pretty good case that most of them were under the age of twenty—not the thirty or forty years old we usually see in the art.

What difference does it make? None, really, except for this: just because you happen to be twenty, or seventeen, or thirteen, or even younger, it doesn't mean Jesus isn't calling you to follow him, or even to be a leader in your church group and share Jesus with others. There are no age restrictions on following Jesus, and no age limit on making a decision to care more about others than yourself, just as he did.

Chapter Fourteen

Gone Again

Amon looked at Benjamin to see if he understood what it meant to be a squirrel, which Benjamin did not. To Optatus he said, "Squirrels?"

This set off a whole string of yelling at and by various soldiers until Amon and Benjamin found themselves inside a giant wheel just wide enough that they could stand side by side. The curved outside wall of the wheel was made of wooden slats about a hand-width apart right in front of their faces, but was open to the air on their left and right. It hung on a large axle above and behind their heads. "Lift!" the construction foreman yelled. Amon and Benjamin stared at him, completely lost. The foreman glared, then made a motion like walking. Finally, Amon got it. The two young men started walking up the curved wall of the cage. As they did so, the entire cage rotated under their feet so that they actually walked in place.

As the cage turned, ropes wound around the wheel and lifted the load attached to the other end—a heavy stone cut into a rectangular shape. When the stone was two feet off the ground, the entire mechanism—a crane, Amon heard them call it—was rotated sideways by other men, dangling the stone over the prepared trench. Amon and Benjamin then walked up the opposite side of the wheel to slowly and precisely lower the stone while men in the trench guided it into place.

Halfway through their first stone, Amon started feeling queasy in his stomach. The slats of the spinning cage, right in front of his face, were making him disoriented. From Benjamin he heard, "I think I'm gonna be sick."

A worker on the outside of the crane said, "Don't look straight ahead. Look to a fixed point outside the cage."

Amon choose the top of one of the towers on the Jerusalem wall and felt much better after that.

As he got used to the work, Amon looked around the construction site. Almost all the workers were Jews and other conscripts, while the designers and foremen were Romans. The ditch they dug was an average of four foot-lengths deep and six wide.

Other workers used a *libella* to perfectly level each stone. Amon watched as a worker set one side of the triangular tool on the stone with its peak pointed up. A string with a weight was attached to that peak and hung straight down. When the weight pointed to a mark in the center of the bottom side of the triangle, the worker knew the stone was level. This would give the wall a level base around the hill. The stones Amon and Benjamin lifted would be the foundation of the wall.

Water and bread were brought around to the "squirrels" in all the treadmill cranes several times an hour. Amon suddenly realized they were the "engine" of the crane, and engines, like horses, mules, or fires, need fuel.

When the bottom of the setting sun touched the top of the mountains to the west, a bell was rung and work stopped. Amon and Benjamin collapsed on the bottom of the cage for several minutes, catching their breaths. "Be back here before sunrise," purple-feather-man yelled. Then they trudged home, hardly able to put one foot in front of the other. At first both of them had trouble walking because they would lift their feet too high for the next step, as if still inside the treadmill.

Benjamin looked at his friend as they stumbled up the street. "You know," he said with a raspy voice, "all in all, I think I'd rather have spent the day playing Shepherd-Sheep-Wolf. Even if you got to be the wolf."

Amon nodded, his head moving only about an inch. "Yeah, those were the days." He looked at Benjamin. "I guess we're not children anymore."

"I hope not," Benjamin answered. "You're getting married pretty soon."

As they passed Mary's house, Amon shook his head slowly and said, "It doesn't seem like it." They kept trudging up the street as he added, "I'll come back to see her after we clean up."

Finally they fell through the door and onto the floor of Amon's house. Jotham rushed over to them. "Where have you been? Are you hurt? How can I help?"

Amon panted, lying as flat as he could on the dirt floor. "We were conscripted today." Both then took turns telling the story. Jotham sent Uri to fetch Benjamin's parents, who lived close enough that it was a safe thing for Uri to do. Uri was thrilled to be able to help and to do something on his own. Bartholomew also arrived, heard the story, then sent a neighbor boy for Peter. Over a dinner of undercooked bread and burnt meat—Amon's father insisted on cooking for his friends—the group decided that Amon would leave Jerusalem before sunrise and accompany Peter on his journey. Benjamin would come and live at Amon's house to help with Uri and the sheep. And no one would ever utter the names Eliazer son of Ishtar or Simon son of Moab again.

Though he had agreed, Amon was once again reluctant to leave with Peter. "I have no idea what I'm doing. God did not call me to this journey. I am only using it to run away from the Romans. Will he still protect me? Guide me? What possible good can I do when I have no gifts or wisdom to offer?"

Peter patted Amon's hand. "Amon, it is obvious that God *has* called you. He has called you through circumstance and the wisdom of those you trust. And if God has called you, you can know without doubt that he will supply whatever courage, wisdom, and knowledge you require."

Amon nodded at Peter's words, but he didn't really believe them.

Benjamin led Amon down the street to talk to Tamar. She was sad that Amon was leaving on another trip. "It feels like all the angels and demons are trying to keep us apart."

Amon leaned against the side of the well, his body still throbbing from the unusual work of the day. "Angels, demons, apostles, tyrants—it seems like *everyone* is trying to keep us apart."

Back at the house, Amon sat and pondered his fate in front of the fire. After a time, he asked Bartholomew, "Weren't you once a slave of the Romans? It seems like father told me such a story back when—back when I did not believe his stories."

Bartholomew nodded slowly. "Yes, it is so. The Romans came and burned our town—Tarichae—when I was ten. They took most of us as slaves. I was sold to a Roman official in Caesarea and worked a few months for him."

Benjamin sat up, curious. "What happened?" Bartholomew looked as if he were in great pain. Benjamin said, "Never mind. I should not have asked."

Bartholomew took a deep breath. "No, it is fine. I will tell the story." He looked up and told them of hard work, long days, beatings, and a complete lack of freedom. "But then," he continued, "one morning I wasn't paying attention and did something that made the master terribly angry. He ordered the household staff to—to do a horrible thing to me."

It was silent for a moment, until Amon said, "What? What did he order?"

Bartholomew shook his head. "That I cannot speak, even today. But before they could harm me, I jumped out a window and escaped. Roman soldiers chased me through Caesarea until an old monk named Nathan saved me. Well, I suppose he wasn't that old, but I was only ten, so he seemed old to me. Then a most miraculous thing happened." Bartholomew stopped and looked at Amon and Benjamin, and they could see the wonder in his eyes. "By a miracle of God, a young Roman soldier by the name of Cornelius, who had sympathy for Nathan and the God of the Jews, helped me escape the city."

Amon sat up straight. "Cornelius was there? The same Cornelius who helped me free father?"

"The same."

"Wow! I had no idea he'd been around that long."

"He was a very young man back then. Barely older than you are now." Bartholomew talked about his escape for a few more minutes, then excused himself to go back to Mary's house to sleep.

Amon and Benjamin were asleep before they could even say good night to each other. They were shaken awake what seemed like a few moments later. "Amon! Benjamin! Arise," Amon's father said as he shook them. "It is an hour until sunrise, and Peter is here, ready to depart."

Amon said goodbye to his father, brother, and friend, and lifted his pack onto his back. He and Peter slipped out the Gate of the Essenes. As they climbed the hill behind Jerusalem, Amon kept looking forward, then back, and forward, then back. He knew he was leaving great danger behind in Jerusalem, but he also knew there was great danger ahead.

Even though he was wearing an outer cloak and climbing a hill, the air felt chilled to Amon, and he wished for the sun to rise. When they were out of sight of the city, he finally spoke. "Tell me again why we're going to Lydda."

"Because Jehovah has ordered it so."

"But, why? There is nothing *in* Lydda."

Peter stopped walking and turned to look at Amon. "There are *people* in Lydda. Are people *nothing*?"

"No, of course not. I just meant, it is a small town, with nothing but houses and—"

"You have been there?"

Amon felt as if God himself was questioning him. He shrugged slightly. "No, not really. I just walked through it once."

"Then perhaps we should finish our mission before you pass judgment on an entire city." Peter stared at him for a moment, then laughed and started walking again. "I'm just teasing you."

Amon pouted for a few steps. "You know, I'm supposed to be building a home for my bride right now."

Peter stopped again and stared at Amon without saying a word. Finally Amon got the message. "Oh yes, you have a wife you are leaving behind as well."

"Yes, I do. And I have left her behind far too often since Jesus entered our lives. But she and I both know that his mission is more important than our desires."

Amon wilted under Peter's continued stare. "Yes, of course. Forgive my selfishness."

Peter laughed again and started walking. "You are not being selfish," he called over his shoulder. "You are being human. And when we're done with our journey and arrive home once again, I will personally help you build your home, as much as I'm allowed."

The sun peeked over the horizon behind them, causing a bit of warmth to touch Amon's body and long shadows to stretch out in front of his feet. The road was still deserted, other than themselves, which made Amon nervous. There was safety in a busy road.

The path leveled out and joined the major road coming out of Jerusalem. They passed a Roman check station. It was manned by a single soldier in a small building made of stone, but Amon knew that if he made any trouble, they would instantly be surrounded by another dozen soldiers. Apparently this soldier didn't think them to be thieves, runaway slaves, or merchants transporting goods, because he simply nodded as they passed.

As they walked, Amon realized he really *didn't* know anything about where they were going. "Can you tell me about Lydda?"

Peter used a walking stick to steady himself. "You are correct that Lydda is small, but it lies at an intersection of this very road that runs from Jerusalem to Joppa, and one of the north-south highways that connect all the world. Perhaps God thinks that the word of salvation planted there will touch many travelers and spread throughout creation."

Amon processed this thought as he walked. "It seems that, perhaps, God is doing that in many ways, through many people. The word has already spread to Jewish communities across the world, and to the Jews who weren't very Jewish in Sebaste. Now it even travels to Ethiopia with a high government official. Do you think God intends us to take his message to the Gentiles as well?"

Peter seemed to shudder just a bit as they started around a curve in the road. "This I do not know. It is difficult for me to think such a thing, but Saul seems to think so. I . . . I just do not yet know."

From behind an olive tree at the side of the road, a booming voice said, "And what is it you do not know, my friend?"

Peter and Amon skidded to a stop as two large, dirty men stepped into the middle of the road in front of them, both holding tree limbs as thick as Amon's wrist. The men grinned at them with black and crooked teeth, their stringy hair hanging down almost to their waists. Amon instantly began to assess his chances of outrunning the thieves when he sensed movement behind him. He turned his head slightly.

Two more men with large sticks had stepped out onto the road.

✦ ✦ ✦

Amon always asks such tough questions. This time it's whether or not God plans to send his Spirit to the non-Jews—called the Gentiles—in addition to the Jews. This was a question that worried the apostles of Jesus for many years as the church grew.

Obviously, you and I believe God *did* send the Holy Spirit to the Gentiles, because most of us are Gentiles and have accepted Jesus as Messiah. But back in the days of the early church, it was a perplexing question. The Jews had always been taught that they were God's special people, set apart for his special purpose.

And they were right.

Before Jesus, only Jews or Jewish converts were God's chosen ones.

Jesus changed that and made it possible for all of us to come into his presence and be part of his kingdom (remember the "whoever" of John 3:16). But it took the apostles and other Jews several years to fully accept that.

For me, the knowledge that everyone is welcomed as a Christian is what makes the gift of Jesus in my life even more special.

Chapter Fifteen

Signs

I ask you again," the thief who seemed to be in charge said, pacing slowly and looking at Peter, "what is it you do not know?"

Peter stood up straight. "I do not know if God will invite someone such as you, a Gentile, to join him in his kingdom, or if that right is reserved only for the Jews."

"Ahhh! A preacher." The four thieves laughed at this. "And what is it you would preach to me, preacher? Will you preach that those coins in your bag are not for me, but for God only?"

Amon felt a warmth fill his body, as if God's Spirit was giving him strength. He took a step toward the thief, who snapped his stick up between them. Amon stopped, never taking his eyes off the man. "Of silver and gold we have very little," he said softly, "but the riches we have we give to you freely. Repent of your sins, turn from your wicked ways, and God might have mercy on you. I do not know this to be true, but it seems God may be working in those outside our faith. If he is, he is your only hope for salvation."

This time, the thief's laugh was nervous and full of uncertainty. "I'll let you keep your God, and I'll have whatever silver and gold is in that bag of yours." He pulled back his stick, ready to swing it at Amon's head. "And I'll take it *now*!"

Amon stared at the thief. Oddly, he had absolutely no fear. *How strange*, he thought. He stared into the eyes of the man, which seemed to make the man more nervous—nervous enough to speak another threat. "You understand, don't you, that this will end only one of two ways? Either I will have your money and you will go on your way, or I will have your money and leave you broken and bleeding on the side of the road. It is your choice. Either way, I *will* have your money."

Amon kept staring but said nothing. Next to him, he sensed Peter starting to say something. But before any words could come out of Peter's mouth, a look of absolute evil crossed the face of the thief.

A growl started in his throat as he pulled the stick further back over his shoulder, ready to let it loose onto Amon's head. The man's arm twitched, and Amon knew if he ducked it would be Peter receiving the blow instead of himself.

The thief started his swing toward Amon's head.

"Halt!"

The thief checked his swing and jumped back, startled. From behind trees and around the corner they'd just passed, eight Roman soldiers ran out onto the road. The four thieves tried to scatter in four directions, but the soldiers anticipated this and easily had all four trapped in seconds. They were quickly bound with chains and taken away, screaming and fighting.

The soldier who had yelled walked up to Peter and Amon. It was the same one who had been at the check station two miles back. Amon sucked in his breath, wondering if the alarm had yet been raised about two young squirrels who didn't show up for work in Jerusalem.

The soldier looked them up and down. "It is not wise for an old man and a boy to walk these roads alone. Best to travel in groups."

"Thank you, officer," Peter said with a bow. "We will remember that."

The Roman stared at them for another moment, then suddenly flipped a gold coin to Amon, who caught it in midair. "We've been trying to catch these four for weeks. When I saw you pass this morning, I knew you'd make excellent bait. Remember that the Roman legion rewards those who help keep the peace." He gave them one more unfriendly stare, then turned and followed his seven soldiers and four screaming prisoners back up the road.

Peter took a deep breath. "Well now, that was certainly an exciting interlude to our journey. Wherever did you find the courage to stand up to the thief like that?"

Amon suddenly realized he was trembling. "I do not know," he whispered. "The words just seemed to sprout from my mouth."

Peter put his arm around Amon's shoulders, and they started up the road again. "Ah, yes, that is often how it is when the Holy Spirit speaks through you."

As they continued their journey, Amon's only thought was, *The Holy Spirit spoke through me?*

The road to Lydda climbed again, peaking at Beth Horon pass. As the sun was straight overhead, Amon and Peter stopped for lunch at the town at the top of the pass, which overlooked the coastal Plain of Sharon. From here Amon could see the Great Sea, and the road was all downhill. They made good time, arriving at Lydda long before dinner.

The town was small and fairly flat, with a stream running through it. Stands of trees and swampy pools surrounded Lydda, but it was an otherwise typical Jewish settlement. As they entered the town,

Amon realized he had no idea where they were going. "Do you know someone here? Are we staying at a friend's house?"

Peter shook his head. "No, no one. Jehovah will provide."

Amon's eyebrows raised in concern as Peter kept walking, but then he remembered the first night in Sebaste with Philip and relaxed.

Since it was at the crossroads of two major routes, the people of Lydda were used to strangers walking through. No one seemed to notice the apostle and his apprentice until they neared the intersection of the two roads, where many sellers at booths had goods for sale—food, clothing, knives, lamps, urns of oil, and strange things Amon couldn't even name.

"Young man," a vendor called from a stall. "Some cheese for your journey?"

Amon was hungry, so he went over to the covered stall. Along the wooden countertop sat three kinds of cheese in various sizes from blocks to bites. Amon eyed a white cheese that looked and smelled good. "A taste?" the vendor offered.

"Yes, please."

As the man cut off a small sliver, he said, "Goat cheese, cured with fig sap. This is exactly the cheese David took to his brothers' commander before he slew Goliath."

Amon gave the man a look like a father catching his son in a lie. "You can't know that. The Scriptures do not say what kind of cheese it was, and there is no other way to know."

The man handed the sliver to Amon with the tip of his knife. "Try it."

Amon did, and his face melted into a look a pure joy. "Okay, I'm a believer. This must be the cheese of David. I'll take two pieces." He paid for the cheese, then caught up with Peter, handing him a piece.

Peter's face also lit up when he tasted it. "Oh, this must be the cheese David took to his brothers' commander—"

"Before he slew Goliath," Amon interrupted. "Yes, I agree. So, now what do we do?"

Peter looked around at the booths along the road, and the houses and buildings behind them. "God's Spirit will lead us."

The market was busy because the roads were busy. Amon looked up the big road—north toward Syria and Cilicia, south toward Egypt—and wondered where and why the people were traveling. Some pulled handcarts, some rode horses, a few led camels, but most just walked, like him and Peter.

They crossed the road, headed toward the sea, and gazed at the people and places of the town. Amon was about to suggest they find a place to sleep when he saw something on the side of a stone inn. He walked closer, followed by Peter, then pointed and whispered. "Look! The sign of the fish." He felt a strange feeling flash through his body as he studied the symbol of the Way he had invented—the outline of a fish with Greek letters inside—on a building far from Jerusalem.

They entered the inn, where sunlight streamed through openings in the ceiling. Several people sat at tables eating. A woman balancing three plates of food on each arm set the plates down at a table, then came toward Amon and Peter. "Something to eat? A place to sleep?"

"Both, perhaps," Peter said.

The woman looked at him like she didn't have time to play games. "And when will you decide, that I may plan the rest of my day?"

As the two of them continued to talk, Amon drew in the dirt with the toe of his sandal.

"Well, that is the price of lodging," the woman was saying to Peter, "and if you don't—"

She stopped, staring at the ground. She swallowed, then looked up and continued talking as she moved her own sandal through the dirt. "If you don't like it, then I may just have to allow you to sleep here for free."

Amon looked down and saw that she had completed the fish he had started.

"That would be most agreeable. I am Peter, from Jerusalem, and this is my companion, Amon."

"Peter!" she gasped. "You—you're—" She looked at the young man before her. "And you're Amon? *The* Amon, who stood up to Pilate?"

Peter smiled and looked at Amon. "I believe we have found a place to stay tonight."

"Yes," the woman said. "Yes of course. I am Naamah, and you are welcome here." She went to two of the other tables and whispered to the people there. They came over and shook the hands of Peter and Amon. All asked questions and told stories so that everyone was talking at once.

After a while they pulled three tables together and sat to eat. Peter asked how many believers lived in Lydda. Naamah was busy tending to guests who kept arriving at the inn, so a man named Joseph answered. "About twenty. But we must be careful. The rabbi in charge of our synagogue does not believe in Jesus and is very much against us spreading his message."

As the conversations continued, dishes on the tables emptied, and the sun set, Peter leaned back and patted his belly. "A fine meal, Naamah. I will stay at your inn any time I pass this way. Are you here alone?"

All the others at the table lowered their eyes, and Amon was sure Naamah was going to say that her husband had died. Instead, she said, "No, I live here with my husband."

Amon thought Peter looked confused. "Well, we must meet him then!"

Naamah looked concerned, but she nodded to four men who got up and followed her down a hallway. They returned a few minutes later, carrying a man lying on his bed mat. The men set the mat down next to the wall.

"This is my husband, Aenaes," Naamah said. "He was paralyzed eight years ago and has been bedridden ever since."

Peter immediately stood and went over to the man. With a tone that said, "Well this is ridiculous!" Peter spoke loudly. "Aeneas, Jesus Christ heals you. Get up and roll up your mat."

Aeneas sucked in his breath as if he'd just seen a snake. He looked around, confused, then stood to his feet.

Gasps and cries went up across the inn as everyone witnessed the miracle. Then it was stone quiet for a moment as Aenaes walked across the floor between the tables. From the others in the room came whispers of, "It's really him," and "This is a miracle!"

Those at Peter's table were shocked for several moments, then began praising Jesus.

Peter sat down and drank the rest of his wine as if nothing unusual had happened.

Which it didn't, Amon thought. *If we believe in Jesus, we should just believe that miracles will happen*.

Once the shock passed, the inn filled with noise as everyone started talking. Most of those at the other tables had never heard the name of Jesus and were anxious to learn of him. Someone ran and got the local rabbi, who stormed into the inn looking for a fight. Peter greeted him warmly. "Rabbi, allow me to tell you how the prophesies of Scripture have been fulfilled." The rabbi was so distracted seeing Aeneas flitting between tables that he didn't object.

Peter stood and told the story of Jesus to those at the inn, making sure to emphasize how Jesus fulfilled all the signs of the Messiah recorded in the Scriptures.

When he was done, almost everyone, including the rabbi, asked to be baptized in the name of Jesus. Aenaes led them to a pool in the center of town, where Peter and Amon baptized everyone who wished.

For the next ten days, Peter and Amon, and others as they gained courage, preached salvation through Jesus and taught his followers. Amon found himself saying words he hadn't thought of as he preached in the streets, in the squares, and in homes as he was invited.

Aenaes ran up and down the roads all day long, telling every traveler about his miracle. Most pushed him away, many listened politely but didn't believe, but every day a few would believe and be baptized.

At the end of the tenth day, Peter found Amon at the signposts of the crossroads. Because so many people passed by this intersection, someone long before had put up posts on opposite corners where everyone could see. Here, travelers could leave messages for family and friends they knew would be

passing this way. Amon was standing on a rock nailing up such a message as Peter approached. Peter saw the sign and read aloud. "Tabitha—Amon is here. Find me at the Inn of Naamah." Peter laughed.

Amon looked at his elder. "Well, the prophet Jeremiah tells us to 'set up signposts,' so here is mine. I suddenly realized today that my mother will be traveling home soon and will pass right through Lydda without knowing I'm here."

"She can't possibly miss that," Peter said. "But you know, Joppa is only half a day's walk. You could go there and visit her if you'd like."

Amon jumped down. "Perhaps. When we near the end of our ministry here. But there is still much to be done."

Many more days passed, and many more people made the decision to believe in Jesus. At the inn one morning, Amon and Peter sat eating a breakfast of bread and olive oil with Aenaes and Naamah. Peter was just saying, "I believe our work here is about complete," when the door to the inn slammed open.

Two young men, bent over at the waist and gasping for breath like horses at the end of a chariot race, searched the room frantically. "Peter!" one of them yelled between gasps. "We need the apostle Peter!"

Peter jumped to his feet and quickly went to them, Amon at his side. "I am Peter. What is it you need?"

"We have been sent—sent by the believers—in Joppa." He sucked in three more deep breaths before saying, "They ask that you come immediately."

Peter shook his head in confusion. "Come to Joppa? But why? How did you know I was here?"

"Travelers spread the news of your work here. But you must come at once."

Peter gave him a look that said there is nothing Peter must do except follow God. "Why must I come at once?"

The messenger lowered his gaze and said through his panting, "One of the disciples has died."

Everyone in the room cried out in anguish.

"Who?" Peter demanded. "Who has died?"

The young man took three more breaths, still doubled over at the waist. He looked up into Peter's eyes and said, "Tabitha. Tabitha from Jerusalem has died!"

✦ ✦ ✦

Peter healed Aenaes.

I believe that. For me, it is a fact.

Of course, he and the other apostles healed many others as well.

Then why don't we see such miracles of healing today?

I believe we do. I have seen such miracles many times in my life. Maybe not ones as dramatic as the blind being able to see, withered limbs being restored, or the lame being able to walk, but still miraculous healings for which there was no earthly explanation.

So why don't we see that every time we pray?

I think that's a question we won't have any answer to until we get to heaven, other than to say that his ways are not our ways. God heals. You should ask. You should have faith that healing is possible. You should believe God can and will heal if it fits his purposes. And before you pray, you should confess and repent from your own sins.

What God will do with the situation after that, only he knows. But now you've done your part to work *with* God. And remember—Saul, Peter, and the other early believers also faced many cases of sickness, injury, and hunger that God didn't miraculously heal or eliminate, so you're in good company.

But you'll also be in good company if, as I've seen so many times, God *does* choose to heal those you pray for!

Chapter Sixteen

Tabitha

Amon's scream cut through the quiet morning air of Lydda for blocks in every direction.

Inside the inn, Amon fell to his knees, pushing away the words as if they were attacking vultures. "Noooooo!" he screamed, over and over and over.

Peter dropped to Amon's side, put his arm around the grieving young man. As the messengers looked on, one of them said, "We have been sent to ask you to please come at once."

Peter looked up at Naamah and Aenaes. "Does anyone in town have a chariot or wagon with horses?"

Naamah nodded. "I'll be right back." Light from the door opening splashed across Amon, making him glow like an angel, but an angel in agony. The door closed again, and the shadows returned.

"Amon, we will get you to Joppa as fast as we can," Peter said. "I will come with you. You must trust in Jesus. Your mother is with *him* now."

Amon's screams turned to wails, and the wails turned to sobs. He fell onto his side on the bricks, tucked his legs and arms in, hugging himself as he sobbed. Peter knelt next to him, holding him tightly.

The door slammed open, and Naamah ran in. "Lamech is coming with his horses and wagon. I'll fetch your things."

A few minutes later the wagon arrived. It was big enough to hold Amon, Peter, the two messengers, and Lamech the driver, but little else. Two sleek white horses pulled the wagon. Lamech flicked his whip over the heads of the horses, and they headed for the main road going west.

As soon as they passed the edge of Lydda, Lamech drove the horses to full speed. The wagon bounced down the road, Lamech cracking a long whip just over the heads of the horses. Only a few travelers were out yet, and they dove to the side when they saw the animals charging toward them.

The ride in the wagon was rough. With one hand, Peter held on to an iron railing along the top of one side of the wagon, with the other he held on to Amon. It was a half a day's walk from Lydda to Joppa, but Lamech got them there in less than an hour. They were stopped at the gate to the city by a squad of Roman soldiers.

A legionnaire held up his hand. "Where are you coming from?"

Peter answered, then the soldier inspected the wagon. When he saw Amon lying in the bottom, he jumped back. "What's wrong with the boy? Is he sick? Does he have the fevers?"

"No, no, legionary. He is in mourning. His mother has died."

The soldier raised an eyebrow. "How did she die?"

"I do not know. We only received the news an hour ago."

The soldier studied them for a minute. "Very well. Make sure the body is properly disposed of, according to instructions from the legion *dissignatores*."

Peter nodded. "Yes, yes, I will."

The soldier waved them on, and they entered the city.

The poorer area of Joppa rose slowly to a sharp ridge, which overlooked the water of the Great Sea and the side of the city where the wealthy lived. The other side of the ridge dropped quickly to the sea, creating steep streets and odd-shaped buildings. A short distance offshore, a series of small, rocky islands jutted up from the sea, creating a natural breakwater and harbor. The wagon stopped just inside the wall on the poorer side of the hill. Peter helped Amon out of the wagon, then followed the messengers up narrow, crooked streets.

Amon could hear the wailing of the mourners before they could even see the house. They turned a corner and stopped. The street was packed with grieving women crying and tearing their clothes. Amon wondered for a moment who had paid for all these mourners, then realized they weren't being paid—the people were actually mourning. Peter pushed through the crowd, saying, "Pardon us—the eldest son is coming through."

They entered the tiny, dark home. When people realized Tabitha's son had arrived, several stepped outside to give them room. The crowd parted, and Amon saw Jadon lying on a couch. Jadon saw Amon and jumped up. They grabbed and held each other tightly and wailed in grief. After several minutes, Amon leaned back so he could see his brother's face and asked, "What happened?"

Jadon had trouble getting words out. "She—she took ill—three days ago." He wiped his eyes with his sleeve, but the tears kept coming. "We thought she was getting better, but then this morning they—they found her—" He buried his face in Amon's chest again and wailed out his grief.

A few minutes later, a woman who seemed to be in charge approached Amon. "We have washed the body of your mother, but we left her eyes open so you may do your duty as eldest son."

Amon nodded even though this was a duty he did not want to perform. She led him up the narrow stairs. Amon had to push past a line of mourning women as they climbed. He pulled Jadon behind him, never letting go of his brother's hand. Peter followed them.

At the top of the stairs was an open door to a single small room. Stacks of neatly folded clothing lined the walls, and women with their faces veiled stood in front of them, weeping. Shafts of light stabbed in through the windows, which were open for fresh air. As they entered the room, the woman leading them, still in tears, waved her hand across the stacks. "You see all this clothing? Dorcas made these, for the widows, and the orphans." Some of the mourners held up robes and tunics to show them.

Jadon was clinging to Amon. "Who—who is Dorcas?"

Amon leaned over and whispered in his ear. "Dorcas is Mother's name in the Greek language." Jadon nodded.

The mourners parted. Tabitha's body lay on a bed against the far wall, all but her face covered in a sheet. "My husband is out preparing a tomb," the leader of the women whispered. "She died in the night, so we must anoint and bury the body as soon as we can."

Amon didn't acknowledge the woman, but stepped slowly forward, followed by Jadon. Fresh grief swept through him as he saw his mother's face, eyes looking straight up into nothing. He knelt, reached out, and pulled his hand across her face, closing her eyes. Then he and Jadon grabbed each other again and cried.

After several minutes, Amon felt Peter's hand on his shoulder. "If I may," Peter spoke to those in the room, "I would like to ask you all to leave the room for a few minutes."

Amon was surprised and looked up at his friend and elder. "Please," Peter said directly to Amon, "just for a few minutes."

Amon couldn't understand what was going on, but he swallowed, stood, and turned toward the mourners. The women stared at him, confused. He said nothing but gently shooed them toward the door with his hands. They went back out, herding the mourners down the stairs as they went. Amon, the last one out, closed the door behind him. Jadon turned to him. "What's going on?"

Amon shook his head slowly. "I do not know. There is no ritual that requires a priest or elder to be alone with the body."

It was instantly hot and stuffy in the narrow space of the stairway. Amon was about to ask the women on the steps below him to move down to the bottom floor so they could breathe when the door suddenly opened. Peter stood there smiling. "Amon, Jadon, bring the widows and come."

Amon climbed back up the last two steps and entered the room.

Standing in the middle of the floor, very much alive, was his mother.

She blinked.

And then she said, "Come here, boys," and held out her arms.

Amon screamed the not-quite-deep scream of a young man. Jadon screamed the voice-just-now-changing scream of a thirteen-year-old. They both ran to her, both buried their faces in her shoulders, both clung to her and to each other.

And they sobbed—the deep, resonant sobs of inexpressible joy replacing inexpressible grief. When Amon could finally find his voice, he couldn't find any words to speak. He leaned back, looked her in the face, then began to sob again.

As the sobs finally began to subside, her boys let her go and stood back, wiping the tears from their faces. Each continued to hold one of her hands. Finally, Amon whispered, "How?"

Tabitha gave a small shrug. "I heard Peter's voice say, 'Tabitha, get up!' So I did."

Amon looked at Peter, who also shrugged. "Our God is a mighty God, and the name of Jesus a powerful name."

Amon shook his head slowly. "But . . . she was . . ." He couldn't speak the word.

"Yes, Amon," Tabitha said softly. "I was dead. But now I am alive."

The widows in the room had been screaming for joy and passing the word down to the street. Now Amon heard a roar outside as if some great building had collapsed. He went to the window, pulled back the curtain, and saw twice as many people as had been there when he arrived.

All had their hands raised to heaven, shouting praises to God.

Amon gestured for his mother to come to the window. When she stepped into the light, the crowd cheered so loudly that Amon could feel the vibration of it in his bones. Tabitha waved, the widows wept, and Amon pledged to himself to never again doubt the power of God.

But then, marching in two columns, the Romans arrived.

✦ ✦ ✦

Peter presented Tabitha to the others after she had been raised from the dead. The word quickly spread throughout Joppa, and many people came to believe in the Lord because of it.

I wonder how much more God would accomplish on this earth if we, his children, were as willing as Peter to share the miracles, small and large, that God performs in our lives. I've been thinking a lot about this lately, because lately, God has answered many of my prayers in what can only be called miraculous ways. But I'm often terrified to talk to people I don't know well. So I've been hesitant in sharing those stories.

Here's a thought, and you'll have to decide if it's true or not: God doesn't work miracles in our lives just to make life easier or better for us; he does it to show others that he's still here, still in control, and still waiting for all people to turn to him. So let's you and I both get over our fears, tell others about the amazing things God does in our lives, and see how he uses us to draw them to himself.

Chapter Seventeen

Simon

Peter stood in the upper window, overlooking the crowd in the courtyard below. Tabitha stood next to him. In what was probably his most powerful voice he called, "Hear, oh Joppa! The Lord our God has this day shown you his power. I, Peter, an apostle of Jesus Christ, testify to his great mercy, through which he has given us new birth into a living hope through the resurrection of Jesus Christ from the dead, and into an inheritance that can never perish, spoil or fade. This inheritance is kept in heaven for you, who through faith are shielded by God's power until the coming of the salvation that is ready to be revealed in the last time."

Through the space between Peter and Tabitha, Amon watched as Roman soldiers pushed into the square from every street. *They must have thought the shouting was a riot*, Amon thought. As Peter continued preaching, Amon calculated that the Romans were about to act, so decided he should act first. "Stay with mother," he whispered to Jadon, then ran down the stairs and out into the crowd.

Amon had identified the commander of the squad by the fact that he was on a horse and wore the headdress of a centurion and now pushed through the mass of people as if trying to wade upstream in a raging river. When he got close, he could hear the centurion issuing orders to break up the crowd and arrest any who resisted. "Centurio!" Amon called. "Centurio! This is not as it seems!"

He pushed through the last of the crowd and burst out next to the centurion, still on his horse. Instantly two soldiers grabbed him by the arms and two others threatened his chest with the points of their spears. "Careful, Jew boy," the centurion said, almost bored. "I could have you executed just for talking to me."

Amon bowed his head. "Forgive me, Centurio, but I have some information I thought you might find important."

The centurion snorted. "What 'information' could a Jew boy have?"

"Merely the cause of this assembly." Amon nodded his head toward the crowd, then plunged ahead without being asked. "This is not a riot or protest. This is a celebration."

The centurion had been looking over the crowd, but now his head snapped toward Amon. "A celebration of *what*?"

Amon swallowed hard, then pushed his courage into his throat. "The woman in the window is my mother. She died of the fevers this morning. But the man next to her prayed for her in the name of Jesus the Christ, and she was brought back to life."

The Roman scowled. "Apparently she was not as dead as everyone thought."

"No, sir, she was," Amon replied. The centurion's face flared in anger—he wasn't used to having people argue with him. Amon pushed ahead. "I was there. I closed her eyes myself. They were dead and lifeless eyes. But now she is alive, and that is why everyone is celebrating and listening to how she was raised."

Another centurion rode up behind the first. "Marcellus! What are you waiting for? Let us stop this riot before they tear down the city."

Marcellus looked at the crowd, thought, looked at Amon, thought. "No need," he yelled to the second centurion. "It is only a celebration."

The other Roman seemed disappointed. "Are you sure?"

Marcellus looked at Amon again, then back to the other leader. "I am sure. Take your men back to the gate. I'll watch here." He looked down at Amon and stared for a moment. "Out of my sight, boy."

"Yes, sir," Amon said, and pushed his way back to the house.

When Peter was done preaching, many in the crowd yelled that they wanted to be baptized. "Many" turned into "most," and Amon and Peter spent several hours baptizing believers in a pool just outside the gates, under the ever-present gaze of Marcellus and his men.

Tabitha insisted on making dinner for her sons, Peter, and the rest of the house. Everyone wanted her to rest and relax, but she said, "Nonsense. I've haven't felt this good in many months!"

When dinner was finished and the day was getting ready to be done, Peter announced that he'd made lodging arrangements for Amon and himself. Amon was reluctant to leave, but he gave his mother one last hug, said he'd see her in the morning, then followed Peter out the city gate to the cliff overlooking the sea. "Where are we going," Amon asked, "and what is that *smell*?"

"To the house of Simon, a friend I baptized this afternoon. He said he has plenty of room for us and would be honored to host us while we're here."

"And the smell?"

"Oh, that. He's a tanner. Which may be why he lives alone, and so far from the city."

Amon rolled his eyes. "A *tanner*?" He thought about his own small experience tanning a hide to make a parchment for writing his ketubah and how bad that smelled. He knew that commercial tanners used an even greater number of stinky and poisonous mixtures to cure big hides for clothing and other uses. But he also knew the tanners were shunned by other Jews because they were almost always ceremonially unclean from handling dead animals. "Wait a minute," Amon said as he considered this. "Did you choose to stay with a tanner just to make a point?"

Peter gave Amon a coy smile but said nothing.

The smell seemed to get ten times worse every step Amon took. When they finally reached Simon's compound, he was sure he'd throw up. "Sorry about the smell," was Simon's greeting. He wore a thick leather apron, stained black, over his clothes. "You get used to it," he said. "But the house is upwind, so it's usually not too bad." Amon saw that his bare arms were also stained and burned, but he otherwise seemed to be a very pleasant and gentle man.

Simon's compound consisted of two wooden sheds and a larger stone house, all surrounded by a short wall with a gate. After storing his things in a corner inside the house, Amon went outside for some fresh air. The wind was coming off the sea and moving inland, so he stood at the edge of the cliff. He could see the white foam of the waves breaking in the moonlight on the shore below. He sucked in a deep breath and was relieved to smell only the salt of the air, not the stink of the tannery.

The next days quickly filled up with baptizing, teaching, and encouraging new members of the Way. Tabitha kept up her schedule of finding food, shelter, and clothing for the poor, widows, and orphans. Amon was amazed at her energy. As Sabbath came to a close the next Saturday evening, she announced to the leaders of the Joppa church that it was time for her and the rest of the Jerusalem church to return home. "You have enough resources now to thrive," she explained, "and my husband is anxious to see for himself that I'm alive, so all we're doing by staying here is eating up your food."

After a long talk with her and Peter, Amon decided he would stay with the apostle and finish the work in Joppa. The next morning, many tears flowed between the family as Tabitha and Jadon prepared to depart. "Please talk to Tamar for me," Amon said to his mother, "and tell her I'm sorry to be gone so long. But Peter seems to think I need to stay, even though I think I need to be preparing for our wedding and—and working at . . . other things God has called me to."

Tabitha hugged him, whispering, "The rest of your life will be so long that this one short delay will only seem like a moment."

As the group left through the city gate and headed up the road, Amon yelled one last request. "Jadon, ask Tamar and Benjamin to keep working on our other project, so we can carry out our plan as soon as I return."

Jadon waved acknowledgment, and then they were gone.

"Now what?" Amon asked Peter.

Peter looked at the city behind them. "Now we get back to work. There are still many people in Joppa who have not heard of Jesus."

For several weeks, Amon and Peter preached and baptized up and down Joppa. The streets on the city's seaside were so steep that Peter could usually only walk one street a day. Often Amon would canvass the steepest and most remote streets himself. Most people had heard about Tabitha being raised from the dead, but many didn't believe it—until Amon explained that he was her eldest son, and he himself had closed her eyes.

"It's always the closing of the eyes thing that gets them," he said to Peter and Simon over dinner one evening. "As soon as I say that, it's like proof to them that my mother really was dead, and they believe."

Peter reached for some salt to put on his fish. "As long as in the end they know that it's God and his Holy Spirit who did the work."

"Of course," Amon said with a smile. "Not even *I* want to make my mother into a god by giving her the credit for raising herself!"

In the evenings, Amon almost always brought out his parchments and quills and tried designing an addition to his father's house. He tried many strange variations, none of which he liked.

And always, in the back of his mind and sometimes on parchment, Amon was thinking about more ways to get Herod removed from office. So far, that hadn't done much good either. Just about every day he'd come up with a new idea and become more excited about it as the day progressed. One such idea was to wait for Herod to leave Jerusalem, which he often did, traveling to one of his other palaces for a time. Amon thought that perhaps he and the others could block Herod's path with a fake mudslide and divert him onto a side road they'd create. The side road would lead directly to a "tunnel." Once Herod's party was inside the tunnel, Amon would close an iron gate and lock it. Only then would Herod realize his party was in a cave and not a tunnel. Amon would simply refuse to let Herod out until he agreed to leave Judea and go back to Rome.

Usually it was about dinnertime that Amon would realize just how dumb his idea of the day was.

Late one morning, on a day they had decided to rest, Peter came to the table where Amon was drawing house designs. He pointed to a sketch. "I like that one."

Amon shrugged. "It's not bad, but I'm really looking for something . . . different."

Peter laughed. "Never let it be said that Amon of Jotham does anything the normal way."

Amon frowned and looked up at his elder. "That's exactly what Benjamin keeps saying."

"Your friend Benjamin is wise. Do you miss him terribly?"

Amon nodded. "And Uri. And my father. And most of all, Tamar."

"Ah, well, it won't be long now. I'm feeling like we shall soon leave this place."

"Truly? How soon?"

Peter patted him on the shoulder. "As soon as Jehovah commands. In the meantime, I'm going up to the roof to pray."

Three drawings later, Amon was still thinking about home. Especially after the episode with his mother, he ached to be back with his family. And while there was no doubt in his mind that God had raised his mother from the dead and was watching over her now, the whole incident had scared him and scarred him, and no amount of faith would take that away completely. *I am just human, after all*, he thought.

But Peter had said they would return home soon. So Amon thought about what he needed to do to prepare. He had only his one backpack with clothes and his writings and drawings, which would take only moments to pack. He needed to gather skins and fill them with water, and he should probably take a loaf of bread and some cheese. Simon would help with that, he was sure. "So I can be ready to leave on a moment's notice," he said aloud to himself. Home seemed a little closer now.

Amon went back to his drawings. About an hour later, he heard Peter calling from the roof. He stood and went over to look up the stairs. "Yes?"

Peter's face appeared above. "I'm getting terribly hungry. Could you please prepare a lunch for me and bring it up?"

This was not an unusual request, and Amon said, "Certainly." He had just finished frying some vegetables in olive oil when he heard the bell at the gate clanging. Simon the tanner was in the city delivering some leather, so Amon went to see who was there and what they needed. As he left the house, he saw three men—one of them a Roman soldier. He glanced up to the roof to see if Peter was watching, and he got nervous when he couldn't see the apostle. He took a deep breath to calm his nerves, then went to the gate.

"Greetings, young man," the Roman said, and Amon thought he sounded safe enough. "We are looking for Simon, who is known as Peter. Is this where he is staying?"

Instantly Amon's defenses sprang up. *A Roman looking for Peter? Surely it can be for no good. The only reason a soldier would be here is to haul Peter off to his death!*

Before Amon could answer, he heard Peter's voice behind him. "I am the one you're looking for. Why have you come?" Peter came to the gate, and Amon stood beside him, trying to look bigger than he was.

The Roman shifted his weight to one foot and studied Peter up and down. "You are Simon known as Peter, not Simon the tanner, correct?"

"That is true," Peter said.

The Roman smiled. "We have come from Cornelius the centurion. He is a righteous and God-fearing man, respected by the Jewish people. A holy angel told him to ask you to come to his house in Caesarea so that he could hear what you have to say."

In his head, Amon was screaming, *Nooo! Say no, Peter!*

But then Peter opened his mouth and spoke the words that would take Amon down a path he did not want to follow. "We'd love to," Peter said.

✦ ✦ ✦

Why did Peter choose to stay at the house of a tanner? Not only were tanners considered very low class because of their handling of unclean animals, they lived and worked around rotting animals and a stench that would knock your socks off. It was so bad, in fact, that tanners were usually pushed outside the city, to remote places where their stink wouldn't bother anyone.

Wouldn't some believer in Joppa (modern-day Tel Aviv) have had a nice house Peter and Amon could stay at? We can't know for sure, of course, but maybe Amon's suspicions are correct: Peter stayed at the house of a tanner to make a point.

What point?

The point that Jesus doesn't judge other people the way we do. We often judge people by how they look, how clean they are, where they live, or other things we think are important. Jesus couldn't care less about any of that. He sees—and values—the person inside.

I've always found it strange that we think we need to "dress up" to go see Jesus. In reality, he welcomes each and every one of us no matter how we're dressed—and no matter how badly our sins and prejudices and mistakes make us smell.

Chapter Eighteen

Sheets in the Wind

It was a day-and-a-half walk from Joppa to Caesarea, or one very long day. Peter suggested they rest for the evening and leave in the morning.

That gave Amon the whole night to figure a way out of this.

He couldn't. So in the morning, he and Peter gathered their few belongings and stuffed them into their bags. Simon the tanner put together food and water for them. The men Cornelius had sent to fetch them were down on the beach, cooling their feet in the surf and clearing their lungs in the salt air.

It wasn't that Amon was afraid of the journey. On his first trip away from home with Saul three years before, the unknown dangers of traveling a long distance on an unknown road scared him—thieves, leopards, lions, snakes, and basically any people he didn't already know. But that trip had taught him how to handle those fears. His second fear—the fear of what Saul's persecution of believers in Jesus might bring—had also been instantly cured when Jesus himself appeared to Saul on the road.

So it was neither of those that caused spiders to crawl through Amon's tunic now. There was a new fear, a very real one: the fear that they would be leaving the familiar surroundings of Jewish cities and towns and heading into a decidedly Roman city.

Amon had never been to a Roman city, and the thought of it was terrifying. From the descriptions he'd heard, everything there would be different, and everything there could be deadly if you didn't know how to act.

Amon did not know how to act.

As he was lost in his thoughts of these things, five other believers came from the town and offered to accompany the group. "For safety," one of them said. "And because we're curious," another added. Peter welcomed them. The group gathered, then Simon handed over the food and water and said blessings for their journey. On the way back through Joppa, Peter and Amon said goodbye to their new friends, then headed up the road on the other side—the road that ran along the coast, overlooking the Great Sea.

Even when he'd gone to Damascus, the city had been "normal" to Amon. Though not completely Jewish, at least it looked, smelled, and behaved much like Jerusalem. The towns he'd visited more recently—including Joppa—were likewise Jewish. Even Sebaste, though it had a Roman flair, was Jewish in its heart and soul.

Walking into Caesarea would be like walking into Rome. And about all Amon knew of Rome was that when a Jew enters that city, he dies. Or so Amon had heard.

Peter, being Peter, kept up a running conversation with their fellow travelers, talking politics, history, current events, and the possibility of a coming war. While Amon enjoyed the spectacular scenery along the coast, his heart and mind were locked in battle—

Enough!

Amon took a deep breath then blew it out, and with that made a decision to stop thinking and worrying about what lay ahead and concentrate on planning for more important matters.

He had a home to build.

He had a king to humiliate.

Those were the only matters worthy of his attention right now. For the rest of the day, and the next, his mind jumped between the two problems, looking for solutions to both. Could he simply add two walls to the upper room to create a separate space instead of building a whole new addition? Could he uncover some embarrassing fact about Herod's relatives, something bad enough to cause the emperor to disown him?

The road they walked was fairly flat, with only gentle ups and downs. To their left was the Great Sea. Along it sat many stretches of beach, some covered in small, rounded rocks, others in sand. The water was a deep greenish-blue, a color Amon had never before seen in his life.

It was a busy road they traveled, and at first they would stop every time they met someone coming the other direction. Amon knew it was customary and good manners to exchange information with those you met on the road: "Where have you come from?" "Where are you going?" "Are there any dangers ahead?"

"But such good manners can turn a two-day trip into a six-day trip," Peter said. "We will be polite, and exchange what greetings we can as we walk, but will not stop to talk. When Jesus sent seventy-two of us out to prepare the way for him, he told us not to greet anyone on the road. I'm beginning to understand why."

They continued to walk and at one point climbed a hill that rose a short distance above the coastline. Amon saw a single house near the beach below, two stories high with a corral of goats and mules. He wondered who would be brave enough to build a home out here, so far from the protection of a city.

"This is my departure point," one of the messengers said. "I will run ahead and alert Cornelius that you will arrive tomorrow afternoon." The man took off at a run, looking fit enough to run completely around the Great Sea without stopping.

Someone came out on the roof of the house below, and it reminded Amon of what he'd been wanting to ask Peter. He pulled his elder away from the others and spoke in a quiet voice. "Yesterday, these men we follow arrived as you were praying on the roof. It almost seemed to me that you were expecting them."

Peter nodded. "I was not expecting them, but I was not surprised. Right after I asked you to fix me something to eat, I went back to praying and fell into a trance."

Amon looked at him with skeptical eyes and a crooked mouth. "You mean, you fell asleep."

"No no no," Peter insisted. "I was not asleep, but I was not awake either. Before me I saw heaven open up and something like a large sheet being let down to earth by its four corners. It contained all kinds of four-footed animals, as well as reptiles and birds. Then a voice called out to me, 'Get up, Peter. Kill and eat.'"

Amon stopped in his tracks and turned to stare at his mentor. "A voice told you to eat unclean animals?"

Peter nodded. "Exactly. And I reacted exactly as you just did. I said, 'Surely not, Lord! I have never eaten anything impure or unclean!' But then the voice spoke a second time, saying, 'Do not call anything impure that God has made clean.'"

Amon's mouth hung open and his eyes blinked rapidly. "God has— How can *unclean* become *clean*?"

"I had that same concern, so twice more I asked. And twice more I heard the same answer."

"And then what happened?"

"Immediately the sheet was taken back to heaven. Then I woke up from my trance, and I heard you talking to these men at the front gate."

They started walking again. Amon stared at the ground, his mind far, far away as he thought about the enormous shock this would be to the believers. Like him, they had lived their whole lives following the laws that forbade them to even touch unclean animals. The thoughts spun around in his head until finally he whispered, "Dancin' camels!"

~

Late in the afternoon of the second day, shortly after a light rain had passed over the region, Amon realized they'd made a horrible mistake. They came to the top of a short hill, and he saw their error before them. "Peter," he said, as if he'd just seen a donkey riding a whale. "You must have made a wrong turn. That is not Caesarea in front of us. It is Rome itself."

Peter laughed. "Yes, I made a wrong turn on a straight road, and at the same time transported us half the world across the sea."

Amon was joking too, but only because the city in front of them was a sight his eyes had never before seen: a giant, modern city, sparkling in the sun after the rain shower, seemingly built of nothing but polished marble. Marble columns with palm trees planted in between lined the marble streets, and huge baskets of greenery hung from marble beams. There were marble buildings as tall as mountains. At the near end, a huge Roman amphitheater faced west, and a royal palace jutted out into the sea. A hippodrome with its long track dominated the center of the city, and beyond it was a harbor, built by human hands, large enough that many of the biggest ships could dock there at the same time. Around it all was a defensive wall that looked to Amon to be about twelve foot-lengths thick and fifteen high. At the far end of the city stood an aqueduct, like a giant bridge for water, as tall as two houses stacked atop each other and held up in the air by arched piers made of stone. The aqueduct came from the mountains, from springs, Amon knew, and brought water down to the center of the great city.

And the city was alive. People, horses, chariots, wagons. Flags waved, white linen canopies flapped, ships and boats sailed in and out of the harbor. Amon had never in his life imagined such a sight, and he returned to his original conclusion. "We took a wrong turn, and you brought us to Rome," he repeated.

Peter grasped him by the shoulder. "As bad a king as Herod 'the great' was, the man certainly did know how to get things built."

Amon nodded, almost sad. "His palace at Masada, his palace at Jericho, his palace at Herodium, his palace here. Too bad he only knew how to build things to his own glory."

"Ah, yes, that is true. Perhaps that is why he died a horrible and painful death."

Amon looked up at Peter. "Is it wrong of me to wish such a fate for his grandson?"

Peter sighed. "I will have to think about whether or not that is wrong, but it certainly is human. After what he did to James, I have those same thoughts."

They gawked for several more minutes, then headed down into the city. As they approached the main gate, they could see that guards stopped and searched everyone. The soldier with them talked to the guard in charge, and as soon as the man heard the name Cornelius, he passed the party through without further inspection.

Just like Sebaste, Caesarea was laid out in straight streets running either north and south or east and west. The buildings they passed were no less spectacular up close than they had been from a distance. Perfectly squared blocks of marble fit together so well that no mortar was needed. Not even an ant could find a hole to crawl through.

They walked down several streets, then came to a large house with a pillared entrance and gardens on every side. Standing near the front door, waiting, was Cornelius, Roman centurion. When he saw Peter, Cornelius fell to his knees and bowed his head.

Peter took the centurion by the shoulder. "Stand up. I am only a man myself, and a fisherman at that."

Cornelius stood, his head still bowed. "I am honored, and my house is blessed by your presence. Thank you for coming." Finally he looked up and saw the other travelers. "Amon? Is that you?"

Amon grinned. "Yes, Cornelius. And may I say what a pleasure it is to see you again. It has been too long."

"I should say so. I would wager that you are twice as tall as when I saw you last, and your eyes shine with twice the wisdom."

Amon bowed his head at the compliment, then looked back up. "I am betrothed."

Cornelius looked at him, smiling but a bit confused. "Oh, uh, congratulations."

"Thank you, but I am not telling you this to impress you—I'm telling you this because my father-in-law is a disciple of Jesus named Bartholomew."

"Oh. Um, that's a good name. I have known many men named Bartholomew."

"Yes, you have, including this one. When my father-in-law was a boy of ten, he ran afoul of a Roman citizen named Festavian here in Caesarea. The Roman was going to have terrible things done to the boy, but a centurion name Cornelius helped him escape. Through an aqueduct."

The centurion's eyes opened as wide as an owl's. He stared at Amon, mouth open. Amon could see the centurion's mind racing and figured he must be remembering the escape of Bartholomew the slave boy decades before. Finally Cornelius said, "Oh, *that* Bartholomew!" Then his face lit up. "And Nathan? What of Nathan? I've not seen him in so many years."

Amon shrugged. "I have only heard the name and know nothing of the man except that, I believe, he is still alive."

"Well, Amon, it is good to have you visit my home. We will have to talk more later. But for the moment, may I invite you all to come in?" He stepped inside the doorway and gestured for them to enter.

Peter had been waiting patiently as the two friends reunited, but at Cornelius's invitation his face turned white and he stared down at the door threshold they had to cross. Peter looked terrified, as if the threshold were made of spiders and the doorframe made of snakes.

✦ ✦ ✦

You've probably been taught all your life not to stick your fingers into an electrical outlet, and for good reason: it will hurt, and there's a good chance you'll die.

So what if one day your parents or boss or teacher told you to do just that—stick your fingers in an electrical outlet.

Hopefully you'd hesitate. Hopefully you'd refuse, until you absolutely knew you'd heard them correctly and could trust them completely.

But that's the dilemma now facing Peter and the other Jews. All their lives they've been told not to eat or even touch unclean animals, and never to step across the threshold of a Gentile house. "It will hurt," they were taught, "and you'll probably die." Not because of electrons or chemical reactions or blunt force trauma, but by the hand of God, because of their disobedience.

What would you do?

Peter is hesitant, of course.

But when Jesus was resurrected and ascended to heaven, and after the Holy Spirit had come to believers, a lot of the old rules went out the window because Jesus had fulfilled them.

That doesn't mean it isn't still difficult to do that which you've been trained all your life not to do.

It may take Peter and the other Jewish believers some time to fully adjust to this new world, just as it usually takes *all* of us some time to adjust when we come to know Jesus and discover that everything in our lives has changed. Sooner or later, though, we'll once again realize that we can trust the Father and follow him everywhere.

Chapter Nineteen

Gentiles

Amon stared at Peter, who was still frozen by his side. He looked at the doorframe, then back to Peter. Finally he looked up at Cornelius. "Forgive us, friend, but this is very difficult for us. We have been taught all our lives that it is against our law to step into a Gentile home." He turned to the apostle. "Peter? You must lead us. What are we to do?"

Peter nodded his head firmly once, twice, then a third time. He looked up, straight at the Roman, and said, "We enter!" Without further hesitation, Peter stepped across the threshold and into the house.

Two of those with them made a little gasping sound, as if Peter had just slapped a priest or set the Torah on fire. Amon was next, but he had a difficult time forcing his foot to step across. He looked up at Peter, now on the other side, and saw that he hadn't turned to ash or been struck dead. His heart pounding and his mind praying frantically, Amon pushed his big toe across the threshold as if testing the temperature of a pond. Nothing happened. He put his foot the rest of the way inside the Gentile's house. He still felt fine. In one quick and bold move, he stepped all the way in, with his whole being.

Amon's heart still pounded inside his chest, but otherwise he felt completely normal.

The others fought back their own fears and entered. Cornelius led them to a courtyard in the center of the house, a gathering place the Romans called an atrium. Amon was shocked to see it full of people of all ages—old, young, and all ages between. "My family and my closest friends," Cornelius announced. "I have gathered them today to hear your words of the God I have believed in since a monk named Nathan first told me of him in my youth."

Faces stared at the Jews from benches around the walls and from the balcony above, which circled the entire room. A pool with a fountain sat in the middle, but it was low and modest, so didn't make much sound. The floors were made of beautiful small, square stones in many colors, creating what they called a mosaic.

Peter looked over the crowd, then his face changed. *It's as if the Holy Spirit has entered him anew*, Amon thought.

"You are well aware that it is against our law for a Jew to associate with or visit a Gentile," Peter began in a loud voice, and Amon wondered where this was going. "But God has shown me that I should not call *anyone* impure or unclean. So when I was sent for, I came without raising any objection." He looked directly at Cornelius. "May I ask why you sent for me?"

Cornelius hesitated, and Amon figured he must be deciding if he really wanted to say what he was going to say in front of his family. "Three days ago I was in my house praying at this hour, at three in the afternoon. Suddenly a man in shining clothes stood before me and said, 'Cornelius, God has heard your prayer and remembered your gifts to the poor. Send to Joppa for Simon who is called Peter. He is a guest in the home of Simon the tanner, who lives by the sea.'" His eyes left his family and friends and turned to Peter. "So I sent for you immediately, and it was good of you to come. Now we are all here in the presence of God to listen to everything the Lord has commanded you to tell us."

Peter stood and gazed across the room at the Gentiles, people with whom he was never supposed to associate, and knew he was there to tell them about the Son of God. "I now realize how true it is that God does not show favoritism but accepts from every nation the one who fears him and does what is right. You know the message God sent to the people of Israel, announcing the good news of peace through Jesus Christ, who is Lord of all. You know what has happened throughout the province of Judea, beginning in Galilee after the baptism that John preached—how God anointed Jesus of Nazareth with the Holy Spirit and power, and how he went around doing good and healing all who were under the power of the devil, because God was with him."

He stepped to the side and held his arm out toward Amon and the other five who had come with them. "We are witnesses of everything he did in the country of the Jews and in Jerusalem. They killed him by hanging him on a cross, but God raised him from the dead on the third day and caused him to be seen. He was not seen by all the people, but by witnesses whom God had already chosen—by us who ate and drank with him after he rose from the dead. He commanded us to preach to the people and to testify that he is the one whom God appointed as judge of the living and the dead. All the prophets testify about him that everyone who believes in him receives forgiveness of sins through his name."

Even as Peter spoke, Amon noticed that many of those across the courtyard and up in the balcony began speaking in foreign languages. One of the travelers who had come with them from Joppa whispered, "I cannot believe this. The Holy Spirit has been poured on the Gentiles out of faith alone!"

Peter went silent and stepped slowly backward, staring at the scene, stunned. He bumped into Amon, then spoke in the voice of a man utterly shocked by what he was seeing. "Surely no one can stand in the way of their being baptized with water. They have received the Holy Spirit just as we have."

As if he hadn't even realized he'd bumped into Amon, he turned. "Amon! We must baptize these new believers in the name of Jesus Christ."

For the rest of the afternoon until the time for the evening meal, Amon and Peter baptized all those present. They used the pool in the center of the house of Cornelius—Roman centurion, Gentile, and now member of the Way.

Cornelius and many of his family begged Peter to stay and teach them for a time, to which he agreed. Amon understood the importance and significance of this but was still disappointed that his Jerusalem plans must wait yet again. "I must confess," Peter said to Amon as they later enjoyed a warm evening in the garden behind the house, "I was skeptical when you told me Philip had baptized a Gentile Ethiopian. I did not believe that the Holy Spirit would come to those who had never observed the law. But now"—he leaned back to look at the stars and sighed—"now I have seen it myself, and I understand."

After that, Amon and two young men from the house, Cornelius's nephews Linus and Darius, chose to sleep on the roof to get away from the crowded floors below. Darius was a year older than Amon, Linus a year younger. Amon had baptized both of them, and now they barely left his side. Darius was the more serious of the two and asked many questions about the proof that Jesus was the Messiah—not because he didn't believe, he explained, but because he wanted to be able to tell others. Linus was full of energy and wanted to know what Jesus was like, even though Amon had never really spent much time with him. Their older sister, Octavia, had also been baptized that afternoon, and seemed to Amon to be very kind and wise.

"I hope we don't miss anything that Peter says down there," Darius said as he laid out his sleeping mat. "But even if we were down there, we wouldn't be able to get close. The adults are all crowding in to make sure *they* don't miss anything. Everything Peter utters seems terribly important."

"Ah, yes, of this I can testify," Amon answered as he stooped to roll out his own mat. "The snores of Peter are most profound!"

Both boys laughed, then kept Amon awake late into the night with questions about their new faith. It was still dark outside when Amon felt himself being shaken, and heard Darius saying, "Amon! Awake! It is already the fourth hour."

Amon opened his eyes with great difficulty and squinted at the face of his new friend, which was lit up by an oil lamp in his hand. "How can it be the fourth hour? The sun is not yet up."

Darius looked confused. "The rooster has stopped crowing, and the clepsydra points to the fourth hour."

Amon had no idea what Darius was saying and wondered if this was all a dream. "Why are you up when it's still dark outside?"

"It is our uncle's way. He was a commander of soldiers for many years, so all of us have to be up before sunrise just like those soldiers did."

Amon rubbed his eyes and sat up. "So what's all this about roosters and clepa . . . clepto . . ."

Darius sighed loudly and stood. "Come, I'll show you."

Amon stood and followed Darius down to an alcove outside the atrium. On a shelf sat a machine such as he had never before seen. It had a bowl of water on top, some copper tubes, a wheel with six small chambers, and a little statue of a man with a pointer standing on a rod. Next to the statue was a gold-looking column etched with numbers. The pointer was pointing at the number four. "What is this?" Amon asked.

"I told you, a clepsydra. In your language you would say, uh . . ." he looked toward the ceiling and thought, then back at Amon. "A water clock."

Amon had never heard the word *clock* but a moment later understood. "Oh, I get it! The water drips out of the bowl at a constant rate, filling a chamber on the wheel. When the chamber is full, the weight of the water turns the wheel, and the water spills into the dish holding the rod. As the rod rises, the statue on top of it rises, and the statue points at the hour!"

Darius grinned. "Exactly!"

A moment later Amon was again confused. "But how is this the fourth hour if it is still dark outside?"

Darius answered as if this were a question so obvious even a child would know the answer. "Because the new day starts at midnight, and this is the fourth hour since midnight."

Finally Amon understood. "Ahhh, now I see! In Jerusalem, the day starts at sunrise, so the fourth hour is almost midday. Here, time is counted differently."

With that cleared up, the two young men got dressed, woke up Linus, and went down to breakfast and a day of converting and teaching new disciples.

Five days after their arrival in Caesarea, at eight in the morning, Cornelius invited Amon to go on a tour of the city with him. He was wearing his full uniform, with a vest of mail studded with victory medallions, bronze armor covering his shoulders, leather wrist guards, bronze leg shields, a helmet that looked as if it were made of gold, and a sword and dagger in his belt.

Amon looked at the armor curiously. "I thought you were retired?"

Cornelius nodded and led Amon out to the street. "I am. But we who are retired have been 'requested' by our superiors to wear our uniforms when out in public."

Amon cocked his head to one side, analyzing. "To make it feel like there are more soldiers in the city than there really are."

"Correct. As for our tour, I really just wanted a chance to talk with you alone. It's been quite a busy week."

Amon laughed softly. "It has. Linus and Darius should be apostles by now, for all the teaching I've given them."

Cornelius smiled. "Ah, my nephews. They're good boys. I guess in your world they would be considered men by now, but in our world, they still have much to learn. Which reminds me, do you still observe the Sabbath?"

Amon nodded. "Yes, we do. But, at least for my family and me, it's different now. It's no longer a ceremony looking forward to the coming Messiah but a time of praise for the Messiah who has already come. We still follow the rituals, but they have new meaning for us and are not laws as they were before."

They turned a corner and were now on the busiest market street, which had shops lining both sides. "I didn't get to see you again after your father was released from Antonia. Is he doing well?"

"Yes, very well. That was a crazy day."

The centurion laughed. "I'll never forget how you yelled at Pilate, and how everyone ran to get away from the lightning bolts they thought he'd throw."

Amon cringed. "That was not my finest moment."

"On the contrary. It was the best thing I'd seen in a Roman court in thirty years. And then to see Pilate back down like that. It was amazing. And I never will forget the look on your face when I explained that your father was still alive."

Amon felt tears come to his eyes and looked away. "Yes, that was a most amazing moment."

Cornelius came to a stop in front of a large, ornate house. "And here we are."

"What? Where?"

Cornelius looked pleased, as if he had just won a chariot race. "This is the house from which your father-in-law escaped when he was ten."

Amon's mouth dropped open. "The truth you tell! I can't believe it. It really exists?"

Cornelius laughed loudly. "Of course it exists. Did you think he made it up?"

Amon shrugged. "It is such a fantastic story that I sometimes wondered." His face flashed with fright. "Does Festavian still live here?"

"No, no. He died long ago. It is now owned by another family. But I thought you might like a tour of Bartholomew's escape route."

Amon grinned. "Yes indeed."

Cornelius led them up through the market along the waterfront, then halfway up the street that led to the Temple of Augustus. Everywhere they went, they saw beggars asking for food or alms. Amon asked, "Why are there so many poor here? There should be plenty of jobs in a city this size."

"Not always. Many employers only hire for a short time, and then their workers are on their own until the next job comes. There are also many old, injured, and sick people who cannot do hard labor. We followers of Jehovah do what we can for them, but we cannot buy food for all the poor in the city."

"My mother feels the same way, which is why she works so hard for the poor, especially the widows and orphans." He then told Cornelius about the miracle of his mother.

"You must share that story with the others tonight, after dinner."

They turned into a courtyard that had a platform against the far wall. "Bartholomew ran in here, chased by several soldiers," Cornelius explained. "At the time this was a slave market, and it's where ten-year-old Bartholomew was sold, up on that platform. Also at that time a pit of snakes laid right there in front of the platform. Threat of being thrown into it kept the slaves from trying to escape. All except for your father-in-law."

Amon stared at the courtyard, now a seating area for an inn. "That's amazing. How did he ever get out of here?"

Cornelius pointed to the wall at the back of the platform. "He climbed up there. But first, he was saved down here"—he pointed to the ground where they stood—"by a monk pretending to be a fool."

"Nathan!"

"Exactly. Nathan."

"Nathan saved my own father as well. Did you know him before that?"

Cornelius nodded. "Oh yes. I had already known him for some time. He had been telling me about the Jewish God, and I was starting to believe. Anyway, Nathan confused the soldiers, then grabbed Bartholomew, climbed that wall, and ran across rooftops with him. Later they escaped through that aqueduct." He pointed to the waterway running across the top of Caesarea. "I never saw him again."

Amon crossed his arms and smiled. "Actually, you did."

✦ ✦ ✦

Someone really messed up. Some angel or something didn't get the right message at the right time. The apostles had finally figured out this new Jesus system so it all made sense:

Step 1: Preach to person.

Step 2: Person confesses their sin and asks for forgiveness.

Step 3. Person is saved.

Step 4: Person is baptized.

Step 5: Person receives the Holy Spirit.

Simple.

But now this house full of Gentiles—not even "good" Jews—didn't make it past Step 1 before the Holy Spirit fell on them! What's going on here?

Here's a fact: we humans always, always, always want to put God in a box and make a relationship with him a simple matter of following the right steps in the right order.

Here's another fact: God always, always, always refuses to be put into a box. He does what he does according to *his* will, not ours.

And one of the biggest things he wills is having a saving relationship with *you*.

It's natural for us humans to want to organize and simplify things. The ancient Romans did it with roads and rules. We try to do it with task lists, calendar apps, reminders, and schedules.

But God will do what he will do according to his own desires and purpose, not ours (though always for our own good).

Peter is a bit befuddled because things aren't going the way they're "supposed to."

When we're befuddled, perhaps it's because we've already decided what God is going to do and then are surprised when he doesn't do it. Let's be open to recognizing new ways in which God is moving, even if it goes against how we've always thought things should work.

Chapter Twenty

Summoned

Cornelius didn't understand what Amon meant about meeting Bartholomew, so Amon explained. "The day Jesus was crucified, you brought another centurion, Titus, to our house to hide. Bartholomew was upstairs. But he was all grown-up and was by then a disciple of Jesus. He looked down the stairs to see what was happening, and you looked up at him."

Cornelius laughed. "Well, I don't remember that, but I wish I had known who he was. I have often wondered what happened to that boy."

"What happened to *you* after Bartholomew escaped?"

"I continued to serve the Roman legion but also continued to serve your Jehovah." A sudden sadness fell across the centurion's face. "I married, but she died after three years. We never had any children. But my sister did, until both she and her husband were taken by the consumption. That is why I now care for my niece and nephews."

Amon nodded, not knowing what to say.

They continued their tour of the city, walking past the Temple of Augustus to the waterfront. "It's an entirely man-made harbor," Cornelius said. Amon studied the two long rock walls, called breakwaters, that jutted out into the sea for what seemed like two hundred steps. The left wall turned toward the right one, but the right one didn't meet the left, leaving an opening about fifty steps wide where ships could enter. Along the inside of the walls were wide docks for loading and unloading cargo. Amon estimated there was enough room for at least fifty ships to use the harbor at the same time.

They walked along the wooden docks between the two breakwaters. Just past the harbor was the hippodrome, an oblong stadium for chariot races. It ran parallel to the beach. *If the docks are two hundred steps long*, Amon thought, *the hippodrome must be a thousand!* Two dozen rows of seats lined all sides of the stadium, except for the closest end, where stone barns held the horses, chariots, and drivers before a race. "It seats almost twenty thousand people," Cornelius said as Amon gawked. "Have you ever been to a chariot race?"

Amon shook his head. "No. I've been inside the hippodrome in Jerusalem, but never during a race. It was forbidden by the priests."

"Well, if you're here long enough, I will take you to a race. They're quite exciting, and not shameful like the gladiator games."

At the end of their tour now, Amon looked back over the city. *It's magnificent*, he thought. *But with a temple to a human emperor, it's almost like the pagan opposite to Jerusalem*. While he was thinking this, Linus and Darius ran up. Darius was yelling something. Cornelius held up his hands. "Slow down, boys. What is the message?"

Darius caught his breath. "Travelers have arrived. From Jerusalem. There has been trouble. Peter and Amon must go back immediately!"

~

Amon didn't wait for Cornelius. He took off at a run, followed by the nephews. He found Peter at the house, packing his bag, and was shocked to see Benjamin and Gaius with him. Amon hugged Benjamin. "It feels like a year since I've seen you!"

Benjamin patted his best friend on the back. "Tamar is well and sends her greetings." Amon stood back to look him in the eye. "Yes," Benjamin answered before Amon could ask. "She misses you, and told me to give you a kiss for her."

Amon's mouth dropped open. "Uh, let's just pretend you did that."

"My thoughts exactly."

Amon turned to Gaius. "It is good to see you as well, but what are you doing here?"

Gaius shrugged. "The apostle John came with Benjamin as far as Sebaste but was tired. So I said I would accompany Benjamin on the walk down here. It is only two short days."

"So what is the trouble in Jerusalem?"

Benjamin scoffed. "I'll give you one guess."

"Herod."

"Exactly. He's gone even madder than he was before, threatening to arrest the followers of the Way and have them executed."

"Did the Romans ever come looking for two runaway squirrels?"

Benjamin shook his head. "Nope. They finished the foundation of the wall, then stopped."

"They stopped? Why would they do that?"

Gaius answered. "John suspects that Herod finally figured out what the rest of us already knew. If his good friend Emperor Claudius found out Herod was building a new defensive wall, he'd see it as a slap in the face and a challenge to his authority. John thinks that rather than losing his throne—and his head—Herod probably decided it was prudent not to continue building the wall."

Instantly a plan formed in Amon's head: he and his friends would finish building the wall, Claudius would blame it on Herod then recall him to Rome. But it took only seconds for Amon to decide this plan was ridiculous.

"So you see, Amon," Peter said from where he was still packing, "Jerusalem is no more dangerous than it was. We must go at once. We can make Sebaste by lunch tomorrow if we go now, and Jerusalem the day after that."

Amon started packing. "Has Herod found any of our meeting places yet? Or Uri's Place?"

Benjamin shook his head. "No. Our secrets are safe so far."

Amon said goodbye to everyone in the house. Livia, the cook, loaded them up with bread, cheese, and water, Cornelius said a prayer for the travelers, and then Peter, Amon, Benjamin, and Gaius left Caesarea.

The road was crowded with travelers headed toward Jerusalem for the annual Feast of Unleavened Bread and Passover. They even met a few people they knew from previous Passovers. At Sebaste the next day, they traded Gaius for John and continued on after a short break for lunch.

They reached the hill overlooking Jerusalem late the next afternoon.

From that point, it should have been a quick trip to Amon's house, but with the people camping in the fields outside the walls, streaming through the gates, and pushing their way through the narrow streets, it took almost an hour. When they finally arrived, John and Peter went to the house they had been staying at and Benjamin went to his home, so it was only Amon who walked in the door to his own house. His family jumped up to greet him, and hugs were given. Soon dinner was set out as well.

Amon thought his mother looked amazingly well for someone who had been dead.

As his father caught him up on more of the news, Amon ate his dinner in the time it took for a thirsty dog to lap up a bowl of water. Then, with his father still midstory, he jumped up. "That was a wonderful dinner, Mother. Thank you for the news, Father. I'll be back soon."

His parents didn't even bother to object.

Amon ran back up the street, grabbed Benjamin out from the middle of his own dinner, and dragged him to Mary's house. Benjamin pounded on the door and an irritated Rhoda opened. A minute later, Amon felt like he could breathe for the first time in many weeks as he sat at the table in the back yard across from Tamar. He gave her the highlights of the events during the many weeks he was gone—and his version of his mother's miracle. Tamar told him all she had been doing—which was basically sitting around the house waiting for her wedding day—then they turned the conversation to business.

"Perhaps this is God's hand turning all things to his will," Amon started, "and I think it is good that Peter was summoned home for this week, and me with him. There are five times more people in Jerusalem now than at any other time of year, and five times more Roman soldiers and officials. If we can humiliate Herod in front of all Jerusalem, the word will be back to Rome within days, and Herod will be gone."

From behind her veil, Tamar asked, "How do we do that?"

Amon shrugged. "I'm leaving that up to Benjamin."

Benjamin snapped up straight. "Me? I don't know how to do that!"

Amon laughed. "It was just a joke. We need to work together to think up an idea."

But when Rhoda cleared her throat an hour later, the only plan they'd come up with was still one none of them really liked. "Okay, to summarize," Amon said quickly as he stood, "when Herod makes his appearance at the end of Passover, we'll start yelling, 'Hail Herod, our emperor and king!'"

Tamar nodded, but unenthusiastically. "If we can get the whole crowd chanting that, the news of it will surely get back to Emperor Claudius."

"It will make Claudius jealous"—Benjamin picked up the story—"and mad enough at Herod that he'll fire him."

Rhoda stood and Amon knew he was in trouble, so he and Benjamin quickly left through the gate.

After so many days of walking, all Amon felt like doing was falling into bed and sleeping through the festival. But after he laid down that night, between his two brothers on the roof of the house, Amon's mind refused to stop spinning. *What else could humiliate Herod bad enough that it would also humiliate Claudius and make him want to fire Herod? A scandal about money? A scandal about love? A scandal about power?*

When finally Amon felt sleep slipping into his mind, he thought about the house design and quickly shooed sleep away again. Many hours later, sleep snuck back in and took over Amon's mind before he could argue. When he awoke, sunlight was just hitting the tops of the mountains around Jerusalem. He shook what was left of sleep from his head, then jumped up and ran downstairs. His father found him an hour later, studying the sheep pens at the right side of the house.

"Are you looking for our paschal lamb?"

Amon was startled but quickly recovered. "Huh? Oh, no. I was just studying the house."

"Ahhh, another important tradition."

Amon stared at his father for a long moment. "Is it? I mean, are any of our traditions important anymore? I'm not sure that either the lamb of peace sacrificed at Passover or the traditions that lead to marriage really mean anything now."

Jotham walked over and leaned on the fence next to his son. "These are questions with which we all struggle these days. I will tell you, that the longer we spend living in the new world of the Messiah, the less I am inclined to practice the old ways of the law."

Amon nodded agreement, then suddenly stood up straight. "The law! Herod will use this week to do his evil. Any Jew not keeping the law will be executed!"

Jotham's eyes opened wide, as if he were staring at some terrible beast. "Yes, you are correct. I'm sure that is his plan. You must speak to the apostles."

Amon's eyes locked onto his father's for several moments, then he turned and ran. First he went to the home where James the brother of Jesus stayed.

"Ah! Amon. I was meaning to come and find you after the feast. We need to finish my letter and make copies."

"Yes, yes," Amon answered, "and I'm sorry there have been so many delays. But right now we must talk of more urgent things." Amon explained his theory. James agreed with Amon's assessment, then left to put the communication chain in motion.

Next Amon took the message to Peter at the house where he and his wife stayed. Peter brushed him off. "I just spent two hours with the council having this same argument."

Even though he wasn't an official member of the council, Amon was surprised there had been a meeting he didn't know about. "What do you mean?"

"I mean, as soon as we returned to Jerusalem, I was cornered by several people and the council, upset that we had stepped into a Gentile house and eaten with them."

"What did you tell them?"

"I told them exactly what happened, of course."

"And?"

"And they understood and accepted it, and all is well."

"Okay, but now we're not talking about the Jewish believers of the Way. We're talking about Herod. We must not give him an excuse to do us more harm."

"Nonsense," Peter shouted. "The old law is dead, or at least fulfilled, and we live by the new law of love through the living Spirit."

"Yes, yes, I know," Amon pleaded. "But right now, it would seem prudent to *act* according to the old law while we *celebrate* the risen Lord."

It took over an hour, but finally Peter relented and agreed—mostly for the sake of the others in his house—to keep the Passover traditions.

Jadon had spent most of the afternoon waiting in line at the temple to make the proper sacrifice, and as the sun set that evening, Amon, Benjamin, and both their families joined together as they always did for the Passover Seder—a dinner of many rules, rituals, and regulations. It was in the middle of that meal, as Amon was asking the traditional question, "Father, why is tonight different than all other nights?" that there was a loud pounding on the door.

The adults looked at each other, and Benjamin's mother looked terrified. Amon's father went to the door and opened it.

Standing on the other side were two temple guards and a sour-looking priest Amon did not recognize.

✦ ✦ ✦

Law versus grace.

That's the story the Bible tells us, and the story we see lived out every day.

The Old Testament laid out a long list of laws and told God's people they not only had to live by them but had to make sure every other Jewish person did as well.

When God's people failed miserably, as God knew they would, he gave an alternative.

"Believe in the Lord Jesus, and you will be saved," the New Testament tells us. It's just that simple.

Some, like Herod, are trying to enforce the law of God, while the new believers are trying to live under grace. The two ideas have been in conflict ever since, even until today.

Law or grace.

As we seek God, interact with others, and move through our world, let's make sure we're living under grace.

Chapter Twenty-One

Peter

The temple guards at Amon's door looked as if they were fully expecting to arrest everyone in the house. As they glared, the priest said, "We are here to verify conformity of this house to Jewish law. Stand aside."

Jotham squared his shoulders. "On what authority do you—"

The men pushed their way past Jotham as the priest said, "On the authority of King Herod Agrippa, keeper of the law."

The priest looked over the food on the table, saw the paschal lamb, the unleavened bread, the bitter herbs. He went to the cooking area and searched for any leavening—yeast, or anything made with yeast. He could find none.

Jotham stood by the table and crossed his arms. "You are interrupting our Seder dinner. My eldest son had just asked the traditional question, and you have interrupted. Is *that* part of Passover?"

The priest glared, scanned the table once more—*hoping to find something wrong*, Amon thought—then stormed out of the house without a word.

It was quiet for a long moment, until Amon said seriously, "I hope Peter is following the law tonight." The others nodded.

They went back to their meal, with Jotham telling the story of how God saved their ancestors from slavery in Egypt and brought them across the Red Sea on dry land.

In the morning, Amon went first to see Peter, who was still alive and free, and then Tamar. Though they would still eat unleavened bread during the week of the festival—to remind themselves of what their ancestors went through after leaving Egypt—Amon treated the week as any other: he had important work to get done. On the third day, he found his father tending the animals, giving salt to the sheep. "Father, I have something to tell you."

Jotham continued working as he looked up. "Yes?"

Amon cleared his throat. "My mind has found the design I would like to build as an addition to your house."

Jotham stopped working and grinned. "Let's see it!"

They went into the house, Jotham washed, then Amon laid out his design on the table. His father loved it and told Amon to get to work immediately.

A few days later, while his parents and brothers were visiting friends in the north end of the city, Amon was in the upper room, working on the list of actual construction materials he'd need for the new addition. He heard the front door slam open.

"Where are you?" Benjamin screamed, and Amon instantly knew something was wrong.

"Up here!"

Benjamin took the steps three at a time and stopped when his head was just above the second floor. "They arrested Peter!" he yelled, out of breath. "Your parents sent me to get you."

Amon leaped from the table and followed his friend out the front door.

"Do you know the charges?" Amon asked as they pushed through the streets.

"No, there have been none posted."

"Who knows about this so far?"

Benjamin had to push between a husband and his wife to catch up. "Everyone. Bartholomew was the first to find out, and he immediately put it on the news chain."

They neared the temple and finally got off the main streets and into the back alleys. They made several turns, then entered what looked like an abandoned storage building, where the apostles met.

In the chamber below, seated around the table, sat several of the apostles, along with James the brother of Jesus, John Mark, as well as a few other leaders of the church, including Amon's father and mother.

James looked up. "Amon! Benjamin! What news have you?"

Amon shook his head. "No news. I just found out and we came straight here." He searched the faces of the people in the room. Their looks told him the situation was desperate. "What was he arrested for?"

Andrew answered without looking up, disgust dripping from his voice. "For believing in the one and only true Messiah."

"And what do we do?"

James sighed. "We wait," he said with great sorrow. "Until we see where this leads and where God would lead us, we hide. We've already sent the word across the city—finish the celebrations of Passover this week, pray for Peter, but be very, very careful what you say, and who you say it to."

Amon searched the faces in the room again. "That doesn't seem like the bold and confident things Jesus did and said when he was here."

James shook his head slowly, his eyes still looking at the table. "No, it does not." He finally looked up at Amon. "We will be bold and confident when we know what the Spirit would have us do. Until then, we need to be cautious."

Amon nodded his agreement, then John Mark spoke up. "I think we need to keep meeting, in small groups, and be in constant prayer for Peter." There were murmurs of agreement, then he continued. "I know my mother, Mary, would be happy to host such a meeting. And I believe I know a few people here who would like to attend." He looked straight at Amon, who smiled.

"A meeting would be most welcome," Amon said, then glanced at his parents who also nodded agreement.

Over the following days, as Peter sat in prison, Passover ended and the city went back to normal. Given the circumstances, Amon abandoned his plan to humiliate Herod. Instead, small groups of believers gathered and prayed at all times of the day and night. Amon, Benjamin, and their families often went to such gatherings, hosted by Mary. Tamar and Bartholomew also attended. Rhoda saw to it that Tamar always wore a veil, and that Benjamin, if not a half dozen others, was always between Amon and Tamar. *But at least I get to be in the same room with her, and get to pray the same prayers*, he thought.

At first, Amon saw that the church was in chaos. Believers were leaving Jerusalem and moving to other towns. Herod's temper tantrums led to daily searches of homes and businesses by both the temple guards and the Roman soldiers. What they'd been calling a church was now just little packs of scared and timid mice hiding in dark corners and underground holes, too terrified to come out into the light. *Not at all like Jesus*, he thought. *More like scared children*.

But then one day he realized he was wrong. *No, not like scared children. Like obedient children, waiting for instructions from their Father.*

From that moment on, he approached the prayer meetings with confidence that this was exactly what they *should* be doing, not something they were doing only because they didn't know what else to do.

One afternoon, four days after Passover had ended, the word spread across Jerusalem: the trial of Peter would be held the next morning in front of Herod himself in the praetorium.

"The praetorium?" Amon yelled when he heard the news. He and Benjamin were once again in the hidden chamber with the leaders of the church. "Who does Herod think he is?"

"I think," James said slowly, "he thinks he is the Jewish-Roman king of Judea, trying to be everything to both sides. He needs the old Jews to love him for being Jewish, and the Romans to accept him because he acts as a Roman does."

Amon sat on the bench next to Matthew. "So what do we do now?"

James shook his head slowly. "Exactly what we've been doing. We pray. Every moment, without stopping, until—whatever happens, happens. Or until God reveals some other course of action."

They all agreed, prayed together, and then went out to lead the rest of the church in prayer.

All that afternoon, Amon and his family and friends remained in the house of Mary, praying. Rhoda set out some food, but no one except the children ate. The prayers were constant and moved naturally from one person to another. All the prayers asked for God's will to be done, but those present were hoping his will would be the release of Peter.

They prayed late into the night, prayed for Peter to prevail at his trial the next day, though they knew that the trial was already decided, and the sentence was already passed. The actual gathering of the officials and the speaking of the words was simply a formality.

At one point Amon took Benjamin aside. "We need to go into the tunnels under the temple," he whispered. "There were many more than we explored three years ago. Perhaps we can find a tunnel that leads to the praetorium."

Benjamin looked at Amon with a crooked smile. "Amon, you said it yourself. We are much bigger now than we were then. We couldn't get a hundred steps inside those tunnels."

Amon looked away in frustration. "Well, maybe we could send Jadon and his friends."

Benjamin sighed. "I love your brother, and he has grown into a fine boy. But he *is* still a boy, and not yet a man. He does not have your wisdom or intuition. Not only could he not stop Herod, he would get lost down there and we'd never see him again."

Amon nodded, giving up on the scheme. They returned to the prayer group. A short time later, well past midnight, there was a light knocking on the door of the house.

All praying stopped. Everyone stared in the direction of the door at the other end of the entry hallway. They watched as Rhoda went to answer the door, listening to hear who would be foolish enough to be out and about on such a night. They were shocked a moment later when Rhoda returned, giggling like a young girl and as excited as Amon had felt the day he saw Jesus rise into the air. "Peter is at the door!" she shouted in a whisper.

A shock wave stunned every person in the room, leaving them staring and speechless.

The knocking on the door continued.

Finally one man said, "You're out of your mind."

"No, no, it is so. I recognized his voice!"

The knocking continued.

The others stared toward the door. Benjamin's mother said, "It must be his angel," which Amon knew was an old belief about people who have died.

The knocking continued.

"Well, we can't just leave him out there," Amon's mother said. Then everyone jumped up and crowded into the entryway. Rhoda approached the door slowly as if now afraid that what she'd heard was a ghost instead of a man.

Another knock. She jumped back at the sound, then finally reached out and opened the door.

There stood Peter in the flesh, perfectly healthy, though a bit dirty.

No one said anything; no one moved.

"May I enter?" Peter said quietly.

Finally Mary, John Mark's mother and owner of the house, squeaked out, "Yes! Come in!"

As soon as Peter's foot crossed the threshold, it was as if the others suddenly woke up. "Peter!" they yelled, each in their own way. "What happ— Who let you— How did—" The questions tumbled from every mouth. Peter held up his hands and shushed them as he closed the door behind him. "Quiet now. Quiet! I will answer all, but please, move back into the house."

The talk continued in whispers as they moved back to the center of the house and sat. Rhoda brought Peter a large jug of water and a chair with a soft cushion. Peter sat, gulped much of the water, then wiped his mouth and looked up at the people. "Now then, let me tell you my story, though I still can hardly believe it myself."

✦ ✦ ✦

Why are we so amazed when God answers prayer?

I often feel amazed when God acts. But wait a minute—if I *often* feel that way, doesn't it seem like, at some point, I'd no longer be surprised?

If we truly believe God will do what God says he'll do, and then he does, our attitude should be closer to, "Yeah, of course he did. What's the big deal?"

I guess the answer is that God's miracle working never ceases to be amazing—it's always a big deal. It's kind of like when you watch the Olympics and some snowboarder does a double-triple squatting leaping loop-de-loop with a triple axel spiral and sticks a one-point landing. It's something we're not able to do, so it just never gets old.

And maybe that's why we're always amazed when God completes yet another miracle.

Peter was apparently just released from prison, against all odds. His friends, who have already seen plenty of miracles—not the least of which was the resurrection and ascension of Jesus—simply can't believe what they're seeing. They're amazed that God actually, once again, stuck the landing.

We really shouldn't be surprised.

Even so, it just never gets old.

Chapter Twenty-Two

Angels vs. Chains

Peter leaned back in the chair and closed his eyes. Amon could see that he was remembering the events of an hour before. *Probably trying to get them straight in his head*, he thought. When Peter finally spoke, it was almost as if he was in a trance, so miraculous were the events he was describing.

"I was sleeping between two soldiers," Peter said, and Amon leaned forward to better hear. "I was bound to them with chains. Four squads of four soldiers each had been assigned to watch me all night." He opened his eyes and looked across the faces of all those in the room. "I'm sure Herod had heard stories of the angel that released us from prison when Caiaphas was high priest, and he wasn't going to allow that to happen again."

Amon thought back to that amazing day, when the disciples of Jesus had simply walked out of the jail.

"Suddenly," Peter continued, "I felt a sharp jab in my side. I woke up. The cell was filled with bright light, and an angel stood in front of me." A gasp swept across the room. Peter shook his head slowly, and it seemed to Amon that the apostle still couldn't believe that what he was saying was true. "The angel had jabbed me in the side with his staff to wake me. He said, 'Quick, get up!' The chains simply fell off my wrists as if a key had unlocked them. Then the angel said to me, 'Put on your clothes and sandals.' And so I did. 'Wrap your cloak around you and follow me,' the angel said. So I followed him out of the prison. But the entire time I had no idea that any of this was really happening; I thought I was just seeing a vision. We passed the first and second guards, but they didn't see us. We came to the iron gate to the city. It opened for us all by itself, without anyone unlocking it. We went through it, and when we had walked the length of one street, suddenly the angel was gone!"

Amon's analytical mind had been listening to this, calculating the odds, searching for logical explanations. Now he stopped, sat back, and let the miracle of the story wash over him. *God really does exist*, he thought, as if he hadn't already accepted this, and hadn't just seen his mother raised from the dead.

Peter continued. "Then I realized I was awake and that this really happened. I said to myself, 'Now I know without a doubt that the Lord has sent his angel and rescued me from Herod's clutches, and from everything the traditional Jews were hoping would happen.' So I came here to tell you." He looked into the eyes of those gathered and finished with his own instructions. "Now go and tell James and the other brothers and sisters about this. I will go to the secret chamber and pray. Send them to me later, Amon, and we will see what God calls us to do."

Without another word, Peter stood and slipped out into the night.

Those gathered at Mary's house sat and stared at one another for a long moment. *They're probably thinking what Peter thought, and what I'm thinking*, Amon thought. *Did any of this really just happen?*

Then everyone broke into laughter, holding their hands over their mouths to keep any sound from escaping. They clapped their hands without making any sound, raised their hands and shouted, "Praise be to God!" without any words actually coming from their lips, and a few even got up and danced quietly on their tiptoes, waving their arms in the air.

After a time, they finally sat again, still grinning, and whispered.

"We must take care not to be seen out and about before it is normal," Jotham said. "It is almost first light. As soon as we can safely do so, we must spread out and pass the news to the entire church. Amon." He looked at his son. "Give Peter some time to pray and rest, but by midmorning you should gather the apostles."

Amon nodded, then the household broke into silent praise once again.

The sun was a quarter of the way through its journey across the sky when Amon and Benjamin set out to pass along Peter's request to meet with the apostles. After sneaking home at dawn, they had spent the morning baking bread. Most of it wasn't even burned. They knew the meeting of the apostles might go long and that they'd need bread to fuel their thinking. Amon took four of the seven houses where apostles were staying, Benjamin the other three. A short time later, most of the apostles had gathered in the underground chamber, where much quiet rejoicing and backslapping was enjoyed. Previous tests had shown that they could make as much noise as they'd like and no one above ground would hear them, but their sense of caution was now well ingrained, so the celebration continued in hushed voices.

The apostle Jude was the last to arrive. "I had to take great care," he reported. "Roman soldiers and temple guards are going door-to-door again, searching for Peter and for any followers of Jesus." He sat at the table. "Oh good, bread. I'm starving." He reached for a piece.

Philip the apostle was just finishing a piece. "Amon and Benjamin made it."

Jude stopped his hand just before he touched the bread and looked at the two younger men. Benjamin shrugged. "We brought a lot of oil. If you soak the bread thoroughly, it's not too bad."

The group laughed, and Amon thought, *That's exactly what this group needed right now.*

Peter turned to the two younger men. "Amon, Benjamin, this is likely to be a long meeting. We thank you for the bread, but you don't need to stay. I believe, Amon, you have an important task to attend to, one that has been interrupted several times for the cause of Christ?"

Amon nodded and smiled. "Yes indeed. And what could look more natural to prying temple guard eyes than a young Jewish man building a house for his new bride?"

The others thanked Amon and Benjamin as the two left and headed home.

It didn't surprise Amon that the streets were quiet as they walked. *All the followers of Jesus are in hiding*, he realized, *and everyone else is just scared*. They checked in at Mary's house to make sure Tamar was still safe, and Benjamin stopped at his house to see his family.

At home, Amon found the house empty. *Perfect*, he thought. *Now I can finally finish my plans.*

He went outside and started climbing all over the house. He'd lived there most of his life, but hadn't paid attention to details. Now he looked at how the house had originally been built. Like most houses in Jerusalem, Amon's was built on three layers of solid stone laid in a trench to create a solid foundation. *Exactly like the city wall we worked on*, he thought. The stone provided a foundation that could hold up against rainwater running down the street.

On top of the foundation, the walls were built with mud-and-straw bricks. Amon knew that the straw dissolved and mixed with the clay, making the bricks strong. Both the outside and inside of the walls were then covered in plaster to keep rain away from the bricks and to keep insects and other creatures out of the house.

Large log beams of cypress or sycamore were laid across the tops of the walls to create the floor of a second story. Across these were laid bundles of reeds to hold up the next layer of mud plaster. This was followed by a dry mixture of chalk, earth, and ash, which provided insulation, and finally a mixture of mud rich in lime, to keep out water.

On the next level up, a roof was formed using the same "waddle and daub" process. The builder would then roll the roof with a round stone to make it flat and smooth. Once the house was finished, the rolling stone would be left on the roof for use after heavy rainstorms.

Amon was very familiar with the law set out in the book of Deuteronomy that required a safety wall around the outside of the roof "so that you may not bring the guilt of bloodshed on your house if someone falls." But he remembered several times that Uri had almost fallen over the usual height of two foot-lengths, so decided to make his two and a half.

Now that he knew exactly how the house had been built, he sat at the family table next to the cooking area and finished the specific construction designs for the new addition. At the same time, he added to his running list of materials he would need and began to worry. *This will cost much more than I thought. I'd have to put window glass and water systems in every house in Jerusalem to earn this much money.*

When his family walked in the door a few hours later, the table was spread with drawings and lists, drawing tools, and worn-out quills. Amon looked up at his father. "I think I have finished my designs."

Jotham raised an eyebrow. "That was fast. The proverbs tell us that the plans of the diligent lead to profit as surely as haste leads to poverty. Are you being diligent or hasty?"

Amon sighed and rolled his eyes. "Father, I've been thinking about this for *months*. It was all in my head. I just had to put it down on papyrus."

Jotham smiled. "Show me."

As his mother and Jadon watched from the other side of the table, Amon pointed out the details of the plan to his father. "Instead of adding on at the ground level, as most people would, or adding on a two-story high structure, I'd like to come straight out over the sheep pens and make the addition at the same level as the current second floor. The addition will be held up by nine posts and will provide a roof over half of the sheep pen, so you no longer have to work in the rain or hot sun."

Amon's father smiled and nodded, his mother clapped softly, and Jadon said, "Finally I won't get soaking wet when I feed the sheep." His mother went to work grinding wheat for the next day, and Jadon went to play with Uri. Amon and his father continued at the table, going over every joint and seam of the plan, until a knock at the door interrupted them. Jotham reached back and opened the door.

"Peter!" Amon said, half-happy and half-scared to see the apostle.

Jotham invited him to come in and sit at the table.

Peter sat. "Ah, I see you finally have the plans ready for your house."

Amon pointed out the important details.

"So, as soon as you can build this, you can be married." Peter laughed.

Amon looked at him, suspicious. "Yes, that is the idea."

"Ah, well then, I will not keep you in suspense. My visit this evening comes on the heels of some news, and a decision made by the council today."

"What's the news?" Amon asked, even more suspicious.

"Herod and his entourage have left Jerusalem."

Amon was surprised. "Just this morning he was going to execute you. Now he's going on vacation?"

Peter shook his head. "Herod was humiliated this morning. His prize prisoner," Peter pointed at himself, "simply walked out of his prison. So he's going somewhere he can feel royal again."

Tabitha came over and set down a mug of water for their visitor. "How did they leave so quickly? They must have had no time at all to pack."

"That's Herod. He decides on a whim to pack up and move to one of his other palaces, so his servants are always prepared for that."

"And where are they going *to*?" Amon asked.

"Caesarea."

Amon nodded, glad that he was no longer in that city if Herod was going to be there.

"And what of this decision you mentioned?" Amon's father asked.

Peter seemed to become sad. "Ah, yes. Well, the council of apostles has decided, against my one vote, that I should leave Jerusalem immediately and go to Sebaste. Both the Roman legion and the temple soldiers still search, and the others feel it is too dangerous for me to remain. So I am actually on my way out of town this very moment."

Amon looked at the apostle sideways. "And you stopped here because?"

Peter took a deep breath, then let it out slowly. "Because, Amon, the apostles say I need to take a traveling companion. Someone who knows the route to Sebaste, and someone who can run ahead to Caesarea and warn the church that Herod is coming before he can get there."

Amon stared for a long moment, then finally understood what Peter was saying.

The sheep outside in the pens started bleating madly as a loud cry of "NOOOOOOOO!" shook the house.

✦ ✦ ✦

Who would I have been like?

I often wonder that when reading through the stories in the Bible. Would I have been like Peter, who was bold and fearless?

Or would I have been timid and just a bid afraid, like Timothy (a companion of Saul)?

I'm afraid the real answer is that I wouldn't have been like any of them. Even Timothy faced far more trials than I ever want to. I'm not sure I have the courage, strength, or faith to do the things they did.

Yet.

It's possible that those challenges still lie ahead. It's possible that in my lifetime, and in my homeland, we will once again see persecutions of the church and its people, just as there already are in some parts of the world today.

Let's choose to be bold and fearless when sharing Jesus, and let our timidity be covered by God's grace.

Chapter Twenty-Three

Preparing a Place

Amon wasn't angry. He was sullen, he was quiet, he refused to look Peter in the eye, but he kept telling himself he wasn't angry. *Only a child would get angry over such a thing. I'm just . . . disappointed that . . . that my other plans must wait. Again.*

It wasn't until his father had helped him pack his clothes, his mother had helped him pack some food, Jadon had collected his writing tools and tablets, and he had waved goodbye to his family, that Amon fully realized what was happening: he was leaving his home again, possibly for months again, and leaving his bride and his best friend behind. Again.

They stopped at Benjamin's house to say goodbye, and Amon asked him to watch over Tamar. "Like she needs any watching," Benjamin had said. Then they all went to Mary's house so Amon could say goodbye to Tamar.

That one was more difficult. Her shoulders fell, her head drooped, and she gave a long sigh before she said, "Very well."

Amon looked back and forth between her and Benjamin. "I wish you both were coming with me. Herod will be there, and this may be the best opportunity to humiliate him."

Tamar nodded, looked away with tears in her eyes, then went back inside Mary's house.

Now Amon and Peter were headed out the Damascus Gate, back toward Sebaste. Amon wondered why there were no guards at the gate watching for Peter, but he decided that if an angel could walk Peter out of prison right under their noses, then an angel could probably distract a couple of guards.

Once out of sight of Jerusalem, Amon relaxed a bit.

"I am so sorry about this, Amon," Peter said. "But the council felt that, because you know Cornelius, you know the church in Caesarea, and, I suppose, because you know *me*, that you are the only person for this assignment. Though I wish my wife could come along."

Amon swallowed the last of his anger. "It was a logical decision, and I am happy to be going with you." *Besides*, he thought, *I don't have enough money to build the house anyway. I might as well go on a trip.* Aloud he added, "Perhaps your wife will soon be able to accompany you on your journeys."

Peter nodded in hopeful agreement.

After three hours of walking, they stopped for the night in Rammalah, staying at the home of some new converts from Peter's previous journey. On the road the next morning, with the sun bright and warm, Amon felt much more like talking. He asked the apostle, "Why do we still keep so many of the old traditions, when we live in the new ways of the Messiah now?"

Peter eyed him suspiciously. "Would you be meaning traditions such as those that say you must build your bride a home before you can marry?"

Amon was sure his face was turning bright red, so he pretended to look at something on the opposite side of the road. "I really meant many things, but, yes, the marriage traditions would be some of them."

"I often think it is sad," Peter answered, "that you were not able to spend more time with Jesus when he was here with us. You would have learned so much."

"About marriage traditions?" Amon asked, not believing that Jesus had much to say on that subject since he was never married.

"Exactly. He used the marriage traditions to explain much about the Father and about our relationship to him."

Amon let out an "Ow!" then stopped to pull a thorn from his sandal. "Such as?"

"Such as the fact that God uses the term 'bride' to describe the church of Jesus. Just as in the older days when a father chose a bride for his son, God chose *us* to be the bride for his son Jesus. Metaphorically speaking."

Amon looked at the older man as if Peter were telling a joke. "You're saying that you and I are brides?"

Peter laughed. "No. I'm saying that, together with all other believers, we, the church, are the bride of Christ."

Amon still had trouble believing this, but said, "What else?"

"When you decided you wanted to marry Tamar, you wrote out a legal contract that included the amount you promised to pay her should your marriage dissolve for any reason. Jesus paid a price for us, individually and as a church, when he took on our sins and paid our debt with his blood."

This got Amon thinking more deeply, and he turned serious. "What else?"

"Before you can marry, you must build a home for your bride, adding on to your father's house.

One day, Jesus said to us something like, 'I go to my Father's house to build a room for you.' In other words, he returned 'home' to heaven to prepare for the arrival of his 'bride'—the church."

Amon became glum. "I hope it doesn't take as long for him to build a house for his bride as it is taking me to build one for mine."

"Well, on that matter," Peter continued, "you must also wait until your father says it is time for you to bring your bride home before you can marry. Jesus told us that none of us know when God the Father will decide it is time for Jesus to bring his bride, the church, home to heaven. Not even Jesus knows when that will happen. Only the Father."

Amon looked at Peter. "I'm beginning to think that maybe our marriage traditions are more important than I realized."

"Trust me, we had realizations like that every single day we were with Jesus."

"Anything else?" Amon asked.

Someone had built a long bench next to a small spring so that weary travelers could rest. Peter sat and removed his sandals. "Only this. Once your father says it is time for you to marry, there will be a huge celebration—and I'd better be invited, by the way. There will be seven days of feasting, dancing, telling stories, and renewing friendships. That is exactly how Jesus described the celebration when we, his church, are reunited with him in heaven. He told us that he and his bride will come together at last, dressed in robes of his righteousness." Peter stopped rubbing his foot, tilted his head back, and closed his eyes. "Oh, what a glorious day that will be."

~

They reached Sebaste late that evening. Gaius was happy to see them and happy to have Peter stay with him for a while. He also agreed to accompany Amon down the hill to Caesarea. They arrived two days later, weary but once again amazed by the sight of "Little Rome." They went straight to the house of Cornelius, where they were welcomed. Linus and Darius were thrilled to have their friend back, and Octavia seemed especially happy to meet Gaius.

Privately, Amon explained his mission to Cornelius. "Peter said Herod will probably stop at Lydda and Joppa for a day each, just to prop up his reputation in those places. So he should arrive here two days from now."

The centurion frowned. "That should give us time to prepare the church, but I wish Herod would just go home."

Amon laughed. "That's exactly what the believers in Jerusalem say when Herod is *there*."

Gaius had planned to return to Sebaste the next day, but after meeting Octavia he decided to stay in Caesarea for a few days. Cornelius and Amon carefully spread the news about Herod's impending arrival and his persecution of believers. After that, Amon decided, he needed to take some time to rest and enjoy the beautiful city and its beach.

Herod arrived two days later in a parade that was as long as the city itself. Most of the city turned out to wave and shout as riders with trumpets blew fanfares and Herod rode by in his golden chariot pulled by six white horses. The next day, banners went up along the main street announcing games and theater shows to be held for a month in honor of Emperor Claudius, Herod's boss and friend.

"Ahhh, fortune shines on you," Cornelius said to Amon as they walked again along the city waterfront. "I will be taking our entire household to the chariot races tomorrow. You are welcome to join us."

Amon nodded, taking him up on the offer, then looked out over the harbor. Dozens of ships would come and go, loading and off-loading, throughout the day. Most of the ships were similar in design. Most would curve up sharply at both ends, and most would have one large square sail in the middle and a smaller one at the bow. On deck, near the stern, there would usually be some kind of small, wooden building. Amon guessed it would take eight or ten men to sail such a ship.

The cargo came in all shapes and sizes, from barrels to boxes to bundles hauling grain, wine, olive oil, textiles, smoked fish, and a thousand other products. There was even a baby giraffe being led off one ship, and Amon wondered where it was headed.

The men working the cargo also came in all shapes and sizes, but with one common trait: looking rough and tough, as if they were about to break into a fight at any moment.

Amon and Cornelius left the docks and passed the hippodrome. Beyond the hippodrome was another rock jetty jutting out into the sea. This one held the palace. "Let me guess," Amon said. "That's where Herod is staying."

Cornelius nodded, a look of disgust on his face. "As you can see, it's big, excessive, and ridiculously lavish. And there's the man himself—also big, excessive, and ridiculous."

Amon looked to where Cornelius pointed. He recognized Herod immediately. He walked along a stone-paved patio around the outside of the palace. His hands were clasped behind his back, and he looked like he didn't care that he had murdered one of the apostles and was ready to murder more. "He's a devil."

Cornelius tipped his head toward Amon. "Actually, both the Romans and the Jews who are not followers of Jesus love him. He's almost kind to them, and very generous. It's only us people of the Way he hates. Mostly because he sees us as troublemakers."

Amon gave a "humph" but said nothing else.

The afternoon ended with a walk past the amphitheater, which held five thousand people, on semicircular steps facing toward the water. "This festival Herod is holding is all for free," Cornelius said. "He says it's his way of giving back to the people."

"The *Roman* people," Amon muttered. "Not the Jews in Jerusalem and Jericho and Hebron and Joppa who pay for it. I often think Herod has forgotten he is a Jew, not a Roman."

Suddenly, Amon stopped walking. He sucked in his breath, his eyes opened wide, and he stared at the horizon.

"What is it?" Cornelius asked. "Did you get stung by something? Are you hurt?"

Amon didn't answer his friend. He was too busy thinking to himself, *That's how I'll humiliate Herod!*

✦ ✦ ✦

In marriage, two lives become one. Two people join together emotionally, physically, spiritually, financially, and in every other way. The two become one.

It shouldn't be surprising, then, that Jesus used so much marriage language in describing our current and future connection to God. He was getting us ready for the day—yet to come—when we Christ followers (the bride) are joined together with Christ (the bridegroom) in the home he is even now preparing for us. In Jewish wedding tradition, the father of the bridegroom must inspect the bridegroom's preparations and decide when they are complete so the wedding may go forward. As Christians, this is what we wait for, resting in the knowledge that Jesus is preparing the place and that when the time is right, the Father will call us home.

Amon is frustrated that it's taking so long to get to his wedding day. I remember that feeling waiting for my own earthly marriage, and I feel it in my spiritual life every time I hear news of what's happening in the world. I am so ready for God to say it's time!

But we wait, patiently or impatiently, for the house to be ready, and for the time of our new life together with Jesus to begin.

Chapter Twenty-Four

Bake-Off

Linus and Darius sat on Amon's left, Cornelius on his right. Sweat poured down Amon's face and under his tunic, and it was still well before lunchtime.

They were sitting in the hippodrome, on the side facing the Great Sea, waiting for the first chariot race to begin. The entire household was there and seated together, as it was the only place where men and women were allowed to sit with each other. In all other places of entertainment, such as the theater, men and women sat separately. Octavia, who was two years older than Amon and sister to Linus and Darius, sat one row down and next to Gaius.

"The chariots will come out of those gates to the left, where those barred doors are," Cornelius explained, teaching Amon the sport. "The bars open at the same moment, giving all racers a fair chance."

Amon counted twelve gates. "How many horses on each team?" he asked, but his mind wasn't really paying attention.

"For the first races, with the less experienced drivers, only two. But as the day goes on, the teams will get bigger. I've seen as many as eight horses per chariot, but I've heard of as many as ten."

"Ten horses to pull one chariot? That must be spectacular," he said, but he was still thinking about Herod. "How does the driver control so many at once?"

"Much experience. But often they do *not* control them, and the track becomes chaos. I've heard charioteers brag about their skills and all their tricks for driving, but in the end, I've also seen many charioteers thrown off their chariots and killed, yet still they win the race. The horses just know what to do."

"Why the wall down the middle of the track?" Amon was looking at a brick wall taller than two men standing on top of each other and as wide as his house. It ran the entire length of the track except for a hundred paces or so at each end. Stairways led up to balconies along the top. At each end stood three tall, round pillars.

"That is the *plina*. It separates the racers. The Greeks don't use a plina, so sometimes a chariot going one direction will run head-on into a chariot going the *other* direction. As you can see, they run in an oblong circuit, traveling up the one side of the plina and down the other, turning around those three pillars at each end. Do you see the seven brass dolphins on top?" Amon nodded. "Those count the laps. There are seven laps in a race. Each time the lead chariot passes the lap counter, he flips one of the dolphins so its tail points up."

Amon gazed across the stadium, taking it all in. People in their finest robes entered along walkways above and below the seats, then took one of thirty stairways up or down to their row. Most carried skins of water with them. The sun was at the back of Amon's head and lit up the faces of those on the far side of the plina. Already the rock seat he sat on was getting uncomfortable, and he noticed that many people brought blankets or other padding to sit on.

Trumpets blared a short fanfare and the crowd cheered as a processional left the gates and paraded down the track. In the lead was the host of the day's races—King Herod Agrippa. Many of the horses, drivers, and chariots that would be racing followed Herod in a grand parade.

Amon leaned toward Cornelius to make himself heard. "The people seem to love their charioteers."

"Only in connection with the races," the centurion answered. "Unless they are champions, they are considered one of the lowest classes of people. Almost as low as actors and entertainers."

A few minutes after the processional, a man in Roman robes came to stand inside a box atop the seats to Amon's right. "Herod!" Amon whispered. *He looks like he's more interested in being a Roman than a Jew*, he thought again. *Now all I have to do is figure out how to make him look Jewish in front of the Romans, and Roman in front of the Jews.* Herod held a white cloth high in the air. The trumpets blared another fanfare, and he dropped the cloth.

"Let the games begin," Cornelius muttered. He turned his attention to the gates, and Amon's eyes followed. A few moments later the gates slammed open. Eight chariots flew out into the sunlight, each pulled by two horses. Everyone in the stadium stood to their feet to cheer on their favorite.

Some part of each of the chariots was painted either red, blue, green, or white. The horses also wore feathers or other decorations of the same color, as did the charioteers. Cornelius leaned over and yelled to Amon over the cheering of the crowd. "Those are the faction colors. There are four factions that race chariots. Red and green are the most popular."

Amon looked at the enormous animals pulling the chariots. *Those aren't horses*, he thought, *those are demons!*

He next looked at the drivers and gasped. "They're just boys," he yelled to Cornelius. "They're no older than my brother Jadon."

"Those are the *auriga*, the beginners. That's why they only drive two horses. The later races will be driven by experienced *agitators*." Each driver wore a thick leather helmet and a leather vest around his chest. The reins to control the horses were wrapped around the waists of the boys, and in one hand each held a whip.

The chariots reached the end of the plina and made the turn around the three pillars. From ten rows up on the shaded side, Amon could just see the heads of the drivers bouncing up and down on the sunny side of the center wall.

On the third lap, one of the chariots flipped up high in the air in front of Amon. The horses kept running but the driver was thrown against the plina, still attached to the reins. He bounced off and was dragged away by the horses, but he pulled out a knife and cut himself free. Spectators on the plina quickly hauled him in before the horses came around for the next lap. Amon never saw the empty chariot or its horses again.

Between races, entertainers came out onto the track to do horse tricks and demonstrations, clown acts, and even short comedy plays. One act had a chariot pulled by tigers, and another by ostriches.

All morning and into the afternoon Amon watched—but he wasn't really watching the races. He watched the people, watched how every worker went about their job, watched every driver to see what techniques they used. Between races, he studied every door, gate, tool, and mechanism to see how it all functioned together.

Near the end of the races—now running six horses for each chariot—he heard Darius say to Octavia that he was hungry, and he saw her pull a piece of bread from a sack. *I'm hungry too*, Amon thought inside his head, but Octavia didn't hear him. He remembered seeing a small stand outside the stadium where people could buy skewers of smoked fish, and now wished he had known to purchase one. *Too bad they don't* . . . he started to think, but then he had an idea that made him gasp and consumed his mind for the rest of the day.

The day ended with the Green faction winning the most races. The trumpets sounded, and one of the drivers ascended stairs to a platform below Herod. The entire stadium shouted the name, "Aloysius! Aloysius!" over and over. Herod handed the young man—no more than twenty years old—a sack of coins and something else. The young man then ran a victory lap on the track, waving at the cheering fans.

"How much do you suppose he won?" Amon asked Cornelius as they walked home.

Cornelius shrugged. "Probably twenty-thousand sestertii."

Amon's eyes flashed wide, and he stared at the centurion as they walked. "That's enough to give every poor person in Caesarea a loaf of bread every day for the rest of their lives! How can a boy—a young man not much older than myself—have that much wealth?"

"Keep in mind," Cornelius said, "that today's winnings might be everything Aloysius ever earns. His next race may well kill him. Few drivers make it past their twenties, and a large number don't live past their first race."

"When is the next one? Race, I mean."

"Next Sunday. It's part of Herod's monthlong jubilee."

They entered the house and most everyone said it was time for a nap after so long in the hot sun. Instead, Amon went straight to the kitchen. "Livia," he said to the old cook, "could you help me with a little experiment?" Livia agreed, and Amon asked her to make him a piece of flat bread. He watched as she mixed together some flour and other ingredients, then kneaded it into a dough, and finally a flat circle. She fried it and gave the thin flatbread to Amon, who took a bite. "Mmm, very good. Now, how many of those could you make in an hour?"

Livia did some figuring in her head. "Maybe fifty, if I was fast."

Amon frowned and thought. "May we try something else, please?"

Livia nodded and stepped back. Amon held up his hands and shook his head quickly. "Oh no, I'm not going to cook! Bad things happen when I cook. You cook, please. I'll give you ideas."

Livia laughed. "Very well, what is it you want done?"

"Um, we need to be able to make the bread more quickly. Could you add more water to the bowl when you mix it?"

The cook looked surprised, but nodded and started a new batch.

"Even more," Amon said as she mixed in the water.

When it was well mixed, Livia stared at the bowl. "This is as thin as soup. How am I supposed to knead it?"

Amon smiled. "You don't. You pour it into the pan."

Livia shook her head and mumbled but fried the strange mixture. When it was cooked, she lifted it out of the pan. Amon waited a few minutes so it could cool, then picked it up. It crumbled in his hands.

For the next hour, with Livia offering many suggestions and doing the actual cooking, they tried various combinations of flour, sugar, water, and yeast. They got the mixture to hold together better but still didn't like the taste. And it still took the yeast a long time to activate.

Amon thought, then said, "I'll be right back." He ran out to the street and down to the market. He returned and added a white powder and some sour milk to the mixture. The next batch created thick, soft discs of golden-brown bread, without yeast and without waiting for the mixture to rise. But once again they fell apart when Amon tried to pick them up. He looked around the kitchen. "What will hold the particles of wheat together but still taste good?"

Livia's mouth twisted into odd shapes as she thought. "Well, I've heard that in Pompeii they put eggs with flour to make something they call a *cake*." They added an egg to their mixture, and the next test produced discs that were golden brown, fluffy, full of air bubbles, and held together when Amon picked one up.

Livia tasted it. "By Jupiter and all the other gods I no longer believe in. How did you do that?"

Amon showed her the white powder he'd bought. "Instead of yeast, I added this trona and some sour milk to the mixture. Trona is a powder used in medicine. Our physician gave it to my father for his upset stomach, so I knew it was safe to eat. It mixes with the sour in the milk and makes bubbles, and takes the sour taste out of the milk at the same time. I thought the bubbles in it might make the bread thicker and airy, and it did! When we added the egg, it all held together."

"A magical powder and an egg. In bread. Who would have ever thought?"

Amon shrugged. "We *didn't* think. Together we experimented and came up with something new." He flashed her a smile. "What should we call it?"

Livia was still surprised, but looked to the ceiling and searched her brain. "Well, it's like those cakes they make in Pompeii, but it's flat and made in a pan. How about 'pan-made cake'?"

"Excellent. Now for the next part. We need a thick, sweet sauce."

At Livia's direction, they stewed some chopped figs with honey and water and a bit of lemon, boiling the concoction until it was thick. They then spread the mixture down the middle of the pan-made cakes and rolled them up. They both tasted the cakes and decided that heaven had arrived on earth.

After dinner that evening but before the table was cleared, Amon asked the servants to join the family. "Livia and I made something special for you today. I think it's something we can use to help the poor and unemployed in Caesarea, but first you have to tell us if it's a good idea."

Livia brought out a platter filled with rolled-up pan-made cakes and passed them out. As people took their first bites, every face smiled in delight.

Cornelius seemed particularly fond of the cakes and asked for seconds.

As everyone finished their cakes, Amon said, "Now, let me ask you this. How many of you would pay one quadrans for one of these while watching the chariot races?" Every hand shot up. "How many would pay a semi?" All but two hands shot up.

Amon smiled and nodded, and spent the rest of the evening explaining his plan to Cornelius. The older man was surprised and thought the plan might work.

But a few days later Amon was staring up, red-faced, at a Roman centurion, having an argument over things about which neither Jewish men nor Roman centurions normally argue.

✦ ✦ ✦

Amon is cooking up some scheme to help the widows, orphans, poor, and unemployed in Caesarea. Where did he ever get the idea that the followers of Christ should help the needy?

Maybe it was from the example of his mother, Tabitha, who was "always doing good and helping the poor." Maybe from helping James write his letter, where he wrote, "Religion that God our Father accepts as pure and faultless is this: to look after orphans and widows in their distress" (James 1:27).

Or maybe he heard the apostles talking about the time Jesus said, "Go, sell everything you have and give to the poor, and you will have treasure in heaven. Then come, follow me" (Mark 10:21).

Or maybe it's simply from the softening of his own selfishness, which seems to be a natural process when one follows Jesus.

Wherever it grew from, Amon has a hunger to help others as real as the hunger he had while watching the races. To not act on a hunger means starvation, and eventually death.

Or to put it more positively, for Christians to have a yearning to help those less fortunate is to be like Christ.

Chapter Twenty-Five

Hawkers

Amon and Cornelius were arguing in the atrium, with Gaius as referee. "Amon, I cannot afford to both feed *and* clothe half of Caesarea!"

Gaius nodded. "He's right, you know. It is much to ask of one man, and Cornelius has been more than generous already."

Amon tried to tame his impatience. "Yes, this I know. But we cannot send our workers out to represent us looking . . . like they do."

Gaius nodded. "He is correct, you know. The public will not want to do business with you if your workers have a bad look and smell about them."

They debated for another sixth of a turn on the clepsydra, then Amon hit on an idea. "Wait a moment." He stood and paced. "What if we required them to bathe just before they work for us? The public baths are free to everyone, are they not?"

Cornelius nodded. "Yes, and that would take care of half the problem. But many of them would still be wearing rags, as you say."

Amon thought some more. "What if I designed a simple, loose fitting tunic that they would slip over their regular clothes while working for us? They would give it back at the end of their shifts so someone else can wear it. After washing. That way, we only need to buy material for thirty or forty tunics, and only once."

Cornelius's eyebrows raised, and he nodded. "Yes. Yes, that might work."

Gaius nodded. "I was sure we could find a solution if only we worked together."

"And," Amon added with a grin, "we could make them from four different colors of cloth."

Five days later, before the sun even gave thought to rising, Amon's new plan was put in motion. For this first attempt, the members of the Cornelius household helped. Linus and Darius brought in many stacks of firewood and started a fire in a large, square box made of stone. At the same time, Livia supervised the mixing of huge quantities of batter in an enormous copper pot. Meanwhile, Octavia set up a grid of twenty-five small copper cups inside an iron frame on rollers. Soon, some of the beggars and invalids from around the city began arriving, all freshly washed in the public baths. Those who were old or disabled helped in the kitchen. The rest prepared to follow Amon to the hippodrome.

When the fire was hot and the batter mixed, Octavia's crew quickly filled the twenty-five copper cups with batter. A solid sheet of metal, pounded smooth, was set across the square fire box, then the grid of cups rolled over it on tracks. Livia pulled a lever and the cups flipped over and dropped their batter onto the now-hot metal plate. At the same time, a small cone of sand was turned upright, and sand started flowing out the narrow end into another cone.

The grid was quickly rolled back and refilled as the batter on the metal spread out to form circles. In less than a minute, the sand in the cone ran out. Two women with flat sticks quickly flipped the twenty-five circles. At the same time, the cones were flipped back. When the sand ran out a second time, the circles were loaded onto waiting plates and taken to the next station. Meanwhile, the copper cups and been refilled and were wheeled out over the metal plate. Octavia dumped them and the process started again.

At the next station, workers each took a pan-baked cake, spooned a line of fig-and-honey spread down the middle, then rolled it up and placed it in a waiting cloth-lined basket.

Once a basket was full of the rolled cakes, it was covered and set in a cart. When the cart was full, it would be dispatched to the staging area under the stadium.

While all this was happening, Amon, Cornelius, and a large group of able workers arrived at the hippodrome. Cornelius had made a deal with the manager earlier in the week: he and Amon would sell the pan-made cake rolls to the spectators and give the hippodrome fifteen percent of the income. The manager had been skeptical, until he tried one. That required an additional line on the contract, allowing the manager to eat all the cakes he wanted for free.

While they waited for the first cart of treats to arrive, the first of the day's chariot races started. Amon asked a dozen questions while watching with Cornelius. "How does one become a charioteer?"

"Almost all are slaves hoping to buy their freedom. At the other end of the spectrum are the truly rich and powerful, such as Emperor Caligula, who would drive for the fun of it."

"What's the strategy?" Amon asked.

"There are many strategies, such as start out in front and stay there, or come up on the leader on the inside and force him to your right, but that one is extremely dangerous." Cornelius continued to teach Amon most of what he knew about the sport.

During the second and third races, Amon supervised the staging area for the workers. It was under the stadium, in the stables, right next to the gates where the races started. When not supervising, he was able to watch as boys younger than himself were strapped into the chariots, a few of them crying in fear, each wearing a tunic the color of the faction for which they drove. A bell gonged, the gates slammed open, and the chariots took off like arrows shot from a bow.

He couldn't see what the charioteers looked like after the race since they left the track through a different gate.

The first cart of cakes arrived. Thirty former beggars each grabbed a basket. They all wore the loose tunics with four colored stripes representing the Reds, Greens, Blues, and Whites—the four competing factions in the race. Just as the third race ended, the thirty salesmen each climbed a stairway in the stadium and started selling. "Get your warm and sweet pan-made cakes here!" they each yelled as they climbed the steps. "Fresh off the stove! Pan-made cakes filled with fig and honey! Get them while they're hot!"

No one had ever seen such a thing, so Cornelius had asked a friend sitting in each section to buy one, "Just to grease the goose." Those first buyers made such a fuss over the taste that others quickly wanted one.

The first batch was gone before the fourth race began.

Shocked but pleased, Amon made sure the salesmen restocked for the next break between races. From underneath the stands during that break, he could hear them screeching all over the stadium and decided they sounded like a bunch of hawks.

Halfway through the day, Amon heard one of the hawkers in the stadium overhead yelling, "Get your warm and sweet pancakes here!" When the man returned for more, Amon asked him about the name. "'Pan-made cake' is just awkward to say," the man explained, "so I shortened it to 'pancake.'"

Since that man had sold more than any other, Amon quickly told everyone they were now selling a new thing called "pancakes."

Toward the end of the day, Cornelius took Amon aside. "I can't believe how well this is working. Even after the hippodrome's cut and us holding out enough to buy supplies for next time, our workers will have enough money to feed themselves and their families for at least a month. Do you realize what you've done here today, Amon?"

Amon looked at his huge friend and shook his head.

"Instead of using my money to buy food for the poor for a week, you invested it in this new idea that will allow them to feed themselves for the rest of their lives. I have never seen such a thing. If I weren't retired, I'd hire you to be on my general staff."

Amon was still dazed by the compliment when Cornelius returned to the stadium to supervise. Two hours later, the last race—the championship race with eight horses per chariot—was about to be run, and Cornelius went outside to see if people would buy the pancakes as they exited the hippodrome.

In the stalls next to Amon, a commotion broke out. He looked up in time to see the eight horses in lane one bucking and kicking at the gate. As they did so, the chariot they were connected to flipped up and sent its driver flying back toward the wall of the stable. The driver smashed into the stones.

The yelling started.

First the Red faction manager started yelling that he needed another driver. Then the race official started yelling that he needed to start the race. The driver—no older than eighteen—was just yelling in pain from a dozen breaks and bruises. And all the other drivers were yelling to start the race, no doubt because the injured driver was the *best* driver and the others wanted to take advantage of his elimination.

The eyes of the Red manager shot around the stable and finally landed on Amon. He pointed. "You!" he screamed. "Come here! You're my new driver."

Instantly, three rough-looking men surrounded Amon and grabbed him by the arms. He struggled and screamed, "I know nothing of driving a chariot!" They threw a red tunic over his head. Amon looked back to see if Cornelius had returned, but the centurion was still gone. All the sellers were still out selling in the stadium above.

Even as Amon fought them, the men and the Red manager slid a thick leather helmet over his head and a thick leather vest, with thicker leather ribs running sideways, around his chest. They set him up on the chariot and Amon thought it felt as weak and flimsy as a child's toy. He was still fighting as they wrapped the reins around his waist and tucked in the ends.

All the while, the manager was yelling instructions in his ear. "If you get thrown off, use the knife to cut yourself free. Use your hands for the whip. Try to get out in front and stay there, but if you can't, use the inside lane to cut in front of your competitor."

Amon had no idea what the man was saying—he was still screaming, "I'm not a charioteer!"

A moment later, before he knew what was happening, a bell was struck, the gates slammed open, and Amon was flying through the air on a thin piece of wood with wheels, pulled by eight monster stallions.

✦ ✦ ✦

If he weren't a fictional character, Amon would be one of my heroes. He just came up with an idea that would take the entire world by storm: selling treats to people, in their seats, at sporting events. Flat cakes you make in a pan, no less.

Brilliant! He'll be a billionaire before he's eighteen!

Wait a minute—no he won't. He just . . . what?! He just *gave away* the whole idea, simply to help some poor people eat? What a fool! He could have been filthy rich.

But then, that's why he'd be my hero, if he were real. Just like the widow who gave her last two coins to help the poor (Mark 12:42). Jesus said she was the most generous, even though her offering was tiny compared to those who gave from their riches.

The defining characteristic of Jesus is his selflessness. When he came, he could have had glory and power and money and palaces. But he gave up all of that to help you and me.

Here's a thought: let's be just as selfless and generous as Jesus and change our world!

Chapter Twenty-Six

The Race

Amon had often heard it said that, at the moment of death, your entire life flashes before your eyes. It wasn't a saying from the Scriptures, he knew, or from the doctors, or even from the rabbis. It was just a saying, and no one really knew if it was true.

But flying down the length of the hippodrome a moment after the gates opened, hanging on to the railing of the chariot with all his strength, hearing nothing but the thundering beasts all around him, and feeling the bouncing of the thin piece of wood that was all that separated him from the metal wheels, metal frames, and pounding hooves of sixty-four angry monsters, Amon had the thought cross his mind that death was passing before his eyes in his last moments of life.

Had Amon been asked in advance to drive a chariot, he would have analyzed the situation carefully, weighed the positive benefits of such a venture against the negative consequences, and taken an entire day to educate himself before he came to a decision. He had no such luxury now, thrown into the race as he was, against his will, with no training or preparation, and not even a moment to pray. He had absolutely no idea how to drive a chariot or make a horse do what he wanted it to do, let alone eight horses. So he had only an instant to decide on a course of action to save himself. In that instant the words of Cornelius echoed through his mind: *I've also seen many charioteers thrown off their chariots and killed, yet still they win the race. The horses just know what to do.*

"Hyaw!" Amon yelled. He had never in his life held a whip in his hand, but he quickly figured it out and now cracked it over the heads of his horses. "Hyaw, you beasts! Run for your lives! And mine." Since he was already in the lead, being in the lane nearest the plina, Amon decided the only way he could live through this was to just encourage the horses and let them do what they already knew how to do. *They've been in many more races than I have*, he reasoned.

The eight chariots and sixty-four horses thundered toward the first turn. Amon knew he could be dead in the next few seconds, but if he could keep the lead at this turn, he had a chance of surviving. He cracked the whip again and yelled, "Run, you lazy mules!"

He knew the theory behind turning a horse, pulling the reins in the direction you want to turn, but for some reason, the Red coach had wrapped the reins around Amon's waist, so he had no idea what to do.

They reached the three pillars. As if following a giant carrot, the eight horses all leaned as one to the left. The pillars sped past Amon in a blur and suddenly he was traveling down the other side of the track, back toward the gates. *I made it!* Amon gasped to himself.

An instant later he saw a team of horses from the Blue faction edging up on his right. He turned to look, then realized that every time he turned, he was pulling on the reins and turning the horses. His head snapped to the left, to look over his shoulder. Sure enough, another Blue team was waiting to cut in between him and the plina. He tugged the reins back to the left, moved in against the wall again, and cracked his whip. *Nice trick*, he thought. *Distract me with a fake attack on my right so his friend can sneak up on my left.*

They approached the second turn, and Amon was tempted to pull on the reins and drive the horses around. *No, you don't know what you're doing. Let the horses run.*

As they rounded the corner, Amon noticed that the lead horse, on the left, pulled ahead of the others and seemed to be setting the pace. He also noticed that only the horses in the middle were actually attached to the chariot. *The outside horses must be the fastest and make the middle ones run faster.*

A few turns later, Amon felt exhausted. After coming out of a turn he glanced up and saw that only three dolphins had been tipped on their noses—still four laps to go.

The Blue chariot on his right made another push for the lead. Amon cracked his whip, and his team gave an extra surge. They pulled away from the challenger.

Amon had figured out that there would be thirteen turns. He entered the eighth turn the same way as all the others—rotating his body slightly to ease up on the reins. Each time, the left horse kept the others leaning into a tight curve.

Just as they came out of the turn, Amon felt the board beneath his feet move and heard a loud *CRACK* even over the thundering hooves. He looked down and saw that the floor had cracked in two and was now sitting directly on top of the axle. In moments, he realized, the spinning pipe would burn through the thin wood. Still holding on with his left hand, he jumped in the air just as the board split completely in two and flew out behind him. As he came down, he spread his legs so that both of his feet landed on the axle mounting brackets.

Now he watched the sand of the track fly by in a blur just below his feet. *If one foot slips, I'm dead.*

He glanced behind him again: the noses of the Blue horse team following him were so close he could easily reach out and scratch them.

Six laps—twelve turns—gone. Amon knew he only had to hold on for one final turn. *But my feet are both slipping. How can I make it?*

He decided he needed to get more room between him and the teams following. He cracked his whip over the head of the lead horse, then again twice more. They turned into the corner so fast that Amon felt the right wheel of the chariot come up off the ground. He threw himself to the right to put more weight on that side.

The wheel dropped down to the track again, but when he had leaned over, his horses got the wrong message and started turning to the right.

The white chalk finish line was directly ahead, but now he sensed the two Blue teams behind him edging up, one on either side. *I don't care who wins*, Amon thought, *as long as I'm alive at the end*. He reached down and pulled the reins off from around his waist.

Free of any control, the horses took over the race themselves and bolted for the finish.

In his first chariot race ever, Amon sped across the finish line three full chariot lengths ahead of the second-place team.

Amon looked back and saw that the other teams were slowing down. Anxious to get out of the damaged chariot before his feet slipped, he pulled back on the reins.

The horses slowed to a stop.

Amon stepped out the back, off the chariot, and fell to his knees. *A few minutes ago I was filling baskets with pancakes*, he thought. *Now I'm a charioteer!*

He heard a loud roar and thought maybe he should get out of the way of whatever race or act or show was coming up behind him. But when he looked up, he saw he was alone in the middle of the sandy track. Even his team and chariot were gone.

And all the people in the stadium stood, cheering *him*!

The Red coach ran up, huffing and sweating. He grabbed Amon by the arm and pulled him to his feet. "That was a magnificent performance!" he roared. "I— I've never seen— I'm Maximus, coach of the Reds. What's your name?"

Amon was panting hard, his mind still reeling from the events his body had just put him through. "Amon—Amon, son of Jotham."

The cheering of the crowd still shook the stadium. Maximus lifted Amon's arm and waved to the crowd, which sent them into a frenzy. "That will never do," he yelled over the noise. "Your name is now . . . Titus Magnus."

Amon had no idea what was going on. His mind was still somewhere in the middle of the race, trying not to fall off the chariot and under the hooves that chased him.

Maximus held up Amon's arm and yelled, "Titus Magnus!"

First those in the seats closest began to chant, but the sound quickly spread around the entire stadium like a wave. "Ti-tus! Ti-tus! Ti-tus!"

Maximus pulled Amon by the arm toward the seats. "Follow me!" he yelled, the chant of the crowd still bouncing around the stadium. They climbed a wide stairway up through the middle of the seats. At the top, below the *pulvinar*—the imperial box from which the emperor or the sponsor of the race watched—was a platform. Amon was terrified to see King Herod Agrippa waiting there. He stared at the king, who was grinning.

Suddenly his grin turned to a scowl. He cocked his head as if trying to locate a memory. He stared for several seconds. "Where have I seen you before?"

The aches and pains of driving the chariot were nothing compared to the terror Amon now felt. *You've seen me in Jerusalem*, he thought. *On the Garden Gate, watching them build your useless wall*. Aloud he said, "No doubt you have seen me watching *you* at your public appearances."

Herod thought a moment, then nodded, and his grin returned. "A magnificent performance, young Titus. Such horsemanship! Such bravery! How many races have you run?"

Amon looked to Maximus, who gave him no clue as to how to answer. He looked back at Herod. "This was my first."

Herod's face melted into a look of shock. "Your first, you say?" He shook his head in wonder, then raised Amon's right arm and yelled, "Ti-tus! Ti-tus! Ti-tus!" along with the crowd. Then he handed Amon a gold palm leaf, placed a wreath of laurel leaves on his head, and gave him a bag of coins.

Herod faced the crowd and shouted, "Our champion!" which brought another round of cheers.

Amon and Maximus went back down to the racetrack. Amon knew that the champion at the end of the day was expected to take a lap around the track, so he started off. Maximus immediately grabbed him by the tunic and turned him around. "Wrong way," he said, then pushed him in the direction the horses had run.

As he circled the stadium, Amon heard his new name shouted over and over: "Ti-tus! Ti-tus! Ti-tus!" He finally made it back to the starting gates, panting, and was led inside by Maximus. "I'll take that," he said, grabbing the bag. He opened it, and Amon saw a sackful of gold coins. "Ten for you," he placed the coins in Amon's hand, "fifty for me," he counted out fifty coins for himself, "and the rest to our owner." He pulled the purse string tight. "Next week it will be twenty coins if you win."

Amon opened his mouth to say he had no intention of racing again, but Maximus turned and walked away. Amon turned around to go to their staging area and ran into a wall—a wall covered in armor. The wall pushed him back and looked at him with eyes as big as apples. "Amon!" Cornelius gasped, looking him up and down, then in the eye. "What happened? What were you doing in a chariot?"

Amon explained quickly, wanting to get out of there.

"But you were so brave!" Cornelius said. "I have rarely seen a soldier in battle as brave. You were driving your horses without fear and with great skill."

Amon sighed. "I was not brave, Cornelius, I was terrified. I was just trying to keep in front of the other horses so they wouldn't trample me. In fact, I wasn't even driving the horses. I just let them run wild."

"Well, terrified or not, you—"

"There he is!" The shout from a young man came from the other end of the stables, which was off-limits to spectators. But this spectator and his friends wore the fine silks and jewelry of the rich, so Amon figured that *they* figured they could go wherever they wanted.

The group ran toward Amon, who was half-hidden behind Cornelius. He looked around for a better place to hide, then realized he was standing next to their cart of supplies. He quickly slipped one of the multicolored tunics over his head. The group slid to a stop in front of him. "We've been looking all over for you," the same young man said.

"I am not Titus Magnus. I just look like him."

The young man scrunched up his face. "You don't look *anything* like him, and he's not who we were looking for. We were looking for *you*!" He leaned in closer and lowered his voice. "Do you have any more of those pan-made cakes?"

Amon was flustered but checked the cart. "Uh, no, we're sold out."

The entire group was disappointed. One young woman said, "Will you be at the theater next week? Could we get some then?"

Amon's head snapped up as a plan instantly formed in his head. "Yes," he whispered, looking over at Cornelius. "Yes, we will be there."

✦ ✦ ✦

Checklist for today:

1. Kick winning goal in FIFA World Cup
2. Design system to eliminate world hunger
3. Depose ruthless dictator

Not a bad day's work, if that's your to-do list for today. Could you do it?

Today Amon worked at all three jobs: champion racer, inventor, secret agent. He's a great example. Now go and do likewise.

Oh, wait.

Amon is a fictional character. In a fictional story. Of *course* he can do three amazing things in one day. You and I probably can't.

But maybe there are some amazing things we *can* do today, or at least work on. Maybe we could, for instance, be kind to our siblings and the neighbor kids? Obey our parents? Help someone who's struggling with something?

As we get older, maybe we could do things like finding a way to help actual widows and orphans. Help the elderly. Help our children learn to truly love Jesus and not just go through the motions.

What Amon accomplished this day was truly amazing. But that's how God feels about us—amazed—when we get over ourselves and do something for others (Hebrews 13:16).

Chapter Twenty-Seven

The Challenge

Nobody knew who he was.

And that's a good thing, Amon thought over and over. The lure of fame and fortune was tempting, but such a future was not what he, or Tamar, really wanted. Still, he had earned a handsome reward at the races, which would build him a house and carry his new family through many difficult years. *If I ever get home to get married!* he thought, and his whole body ached to hold his bride in his arms.

~

After leaving the hippodrome, Cornelius had taken Amon directly to the public baths. While Amon bathed in pools that were warmed by hot air flowing beneath the floors, the centurion went to the market and bought Amon a new hooded tunic, since Amon's old one was now tattered and filthy. Then they had gone home as if nothing strange had happened. No one in the household had been there to see the last race. They had all been busy carting most of the day's supplies and equipment back to the house and cleaning the kitchen. So not a single other person knew that Amon was the hero Titus Magnus the whole city was talking about.

At dinner that night, the talk was about the day at the races—which none of them had attended—and the success of Amon's idea. Though the poor and the widows had been given two coins each, the entire Cornelius household had donated their time and services and now spoke of how good it felt to help others. Livia had been cooking since before dawn, so dinner was breads, cheeses, olives, and a few leftover pan-made cakes. "Oh, one of the sellers suggested we shorten the name to 'pancakes,'" Amon said. "I thought it was a pretty good idea." Most agreed, and it was decided. Overall, the group was completely impressed by how well the day had gone, even though they received no money for their work. "It will be one way we can help those in need," Cornelius said, "any time there is a race, or theater, or other public gathering."

Eventually the talk turned to the remarkable performance of Titus Magnus in the last race. Linus shook a half-eaten pancake at the group, saying, "I heard he was a giant that barely fit on the chariot."

"No he wasn't," Darius said, pulling three olives from a dish. "He was a skinny little guy that no one thought would survive the race. That's what makes him so great."

"I heard," Octavia said, "that he was handsome, and now he's rich, so I think Uncle Cornelius should find him and offer me as his bride."

Gaius gave her a look of panic. "You don't even know him. He could be a liar and a cheat!"

"Or he could be a warm and kind man who would love me with all his heart."

Amon felt his cheeks turning red.

"And what of you, Amon," Cornelius said with a grin. "What have you heard about our latest hero?"

"Uh, I heard nothing but the shouting of the crowds. I was busy at that time."

"Is that a new tunic you wear?" Octavia asked. Everyone looked.

"Oh, uh, yes. My old one got stained today, so Cornelius was kind enough to buy me a new one."

~

Amon slept little that night. The plan in his head was growing, and all night long he filled in the details.

The next afternoon, while Gaius talked with Cornelius, Amon, Linus, Darius, and Octavia volunteered to go shopping for Livia, to replace the supplies they'd used up making the pancakes. It would be terribly improper for Amon, being betrothed, to go with Octavia alone, but even Livia thought it would be all right for her to go since her brothers were going as well.

Amon was shocked at what he saw in the marketplace.

At the first stall, a seller of imported dried fruits also displayed fifty or sixty handmade flags on sticks. The flags were red in color, had a picture drawn on them of a young man that looked remarkably like Amon, and the name "Titus Amicus Populi Magnus" stitched across the bottom.

Linus put his face right up to the flag. "Hey! That looks like you, Amon!"

Octavia crossed her arms and frowned. "I thought his name was just Titus Magnus?"

Amon nodded. "It is. Someone must have added 'Friend of the People' in the middle."

At every stall, it seemed, besides whatever the merchants normally sold, there was also something with the name Titus Amicus Populi Magnus drawn, sewn, or stenciled on. Besides flags, the vendors had oil lamps, mugs, tunics for babies and children, and anything else on which the name Titus would fit. "Merchants must have stayed up all night making these things," Octavia said.

Several times someone in the crowd of shoppers would do a double take when they saw Amon.

Finally he pulled his hood up and tried to cover his face. He steered his friends through the streets, to the front of the house from which Bartholomew had escaped a horrible punishment more than thirty years before. He sat them on the curb of the street, in the shade of the very tree Bartholomew had used to break his fall from the second floor. "I have a secret to tell you," Amon started. He looked each of them in the eye, trying to make a final judgment about their ability to keep a secret. "But I must know you will keep this secret always and tell no one. Except maybe your future spouse. In twenty or thirty years. Or maybe a hundred."

Each of them looked curiously at him. "Of course," Octavia said. "We have had to keep many military secrets for our uncle Cornelius. If we didn't keep the secrets secret, someone would die."

"And that's exactly what would happen this time. But I need help. I can't do what I must do alone." They nodded, as if this were obvious. "All right then, here's the first part of my secret. I am indeed Titus Magnus."

Linus laughed. Darius frowned. Octavia's mouth dropped open and she whispered, "The truth you tell!"

"And only the truth," Amon said.

Linus stopped laughing. "Wait a minute. Are you being serious?"

Amon nodded, then explained all that had happened at the last race the day before. "But that is only the first part of my secret. The second part is much more frightening. King Herod is persecuting the believers in Jerusalem. He even murdered one of the apostles, James the son of Zebedee."

Darius nodded. "Yes, we know of this. It is no secret."

"But this part is," Amon said. And then he told them his plan.

~

Amon knew that, in any Roman city, just as in Jerusalem, it was common for people to write messages and draw cartoons on the walls of the buildings. Sometimes the message was to one god or another, sometimes it was a political statement, but often it was to make fun of some government official—often the king or emperor.

So when Amon asked Linus and Darius to write on the walls for him that night, he knew he wasn't doing anything wrong—it was an accepted form of public speaking.

When the people of Caesarea started going about their business the next morning, they were surprised to see huge messages on the stone walls of many buildings that read "Titus Amicus Populi Magnus challenges King Herod Agrippa to a chariot race in the hippodrome!"

As the four young people wandered through the market later in the morning, they heard many people discussing the challenge, and almost all thought Herod should accept.

"After all," a woman selling fish said as she wrapped, "Caligula was a brave man, if a bad emperor, and he *loved* to race the chariots himself!"

"And you know, don't you," her customer responded, "that Herod grew up in Rome with Claudius *and* Caligula. He should be well trained in the art of the race."

All over the city people talked of the challenge. Amon grinned to himself: he knew there was no way Herod would accept, and by refusing to race he would earn the label of coward, no matter his reasons. Once Emperor Claudius heard about it—which Amon would make sure of—he'd recall Herod to Rome and replace him. Herod might live out his life in luxury, Amon knew. *But who cares, as long as Herod is gone from here.*

The next afternoon, the four young people again strolled through the market. Some of the merchants and customers were still talking about the challenge, but most had moved on to other gossip. Amon noticed that some of the graffiti had been washed off.

On the third day, there was no talk at all of Herod racing a chariot, and the messages had all been washed away.

Amon was disappointed but not defeated. "At least we planted the seed," he told the others as he gathered them together on the roof that night. "It seems Caesarea has lost interest in my challenge. So it's time to add fuel to the fire."

Linus looked around the roof. "What fire?"

Amon grinned. "The fire we're setting under Herod's throne."

Linus leaned over to Darius and whispered, "How will we build a fire under Herod's throne?"

"It's a figure of speech," Darius whispered back. "He means we're going to put a lot of public pressure on Herod."

Amon took back his meeting, wishing Tamar, Benjamin, and Jadon were there. "Now, I remembered today that Herod's next public appearance will be at the theater on Sunday. They're putting on a big show he's designed, something about greatness and power. It will be first thing in the morning, so the sun will be at the backs of the audience and shining directly onto the stage. I have designed," he rolled out a sheet of papyrus, "a tool that will allow someone to speak from one place, but their voice to come out in another."

The drawing on the papyrus showed a long, cone-shaped tube made of dried and hardened leather stretched over a frame. It was curved and had a small hole at one end and very large hole at the other. "We'll put this on the roof of the theater," Amon continued, "with the small end hanging down on the back side. After Herod comes out on the stage but before he speaks, Darius will yell into the small hole, which will be down near the ground. His voice will come out the big hole, up on the roof, and fill the stadium. The guards will go to the roof looking for whoever yelled, but Darius will already be down the street."

Darius grinned at the thought of such intrigue. "And what is it I will yell?"

"You will yell, 'Herod! Accept the challenge! Race against Titus Magnus!'"

All of them grinned now as they pictured the scene in their minds. "Do I yell it just once, or more than once?"

"After you say the first line, you'll start chanting, 'Race Titus! Race Titus! Race Titus!' As soon as the crowd picks up the chant—which we'll help along—you run."

They thought this a brilliant idea, but Linus frowned. "What do *I* get to do?"

"Ahhh," Amon said, holding up his index finger. "You and I and Octavia have another important job."

For the remainder of the day, the four friends worked at gathering as much soft leather as they could find. They stitched it together until they had two pieces, each the size of a large door. On each, Amon wrote just two words: "RACE TITUS" in three languages. They rolled up the banners, tied them closed with a bow, and hid them in a shed.

"Friday night," Amon explained, "you three will write more graffiti on the walls of the city. Saturday night, Linus and Octavia will sneak into the theater and hang these under the eaves of the stage while Darius and I mount the speaking tube. Sunday, after Darius yells his challenge, Linus and Octavia will each pull a string to release their scroll. The banners will drop down between the columns behind Herod. I'll be in the audience to make sure the chant gets started." In the streaks of light and shadow inside the barn, Amon crossed his arms and grinned at his friends. "Herod will make some excuse about why he can't race, then we'll start our campaign to label him a coward. As soon as Emperor Claudius hears about it, Herod will be recalled to Rome and out of our lives."

The others grinned at the thought.

They spent the next two days building the speaking tube. Saturday night, as soon as it was dark, they carried the tube through back streets and alleys to the amphitheater. The guards only patrolled the various gates of the city, so none were at the theater itself. It wasn't difficult to see a path to the roof—the moonlight hitting the marble made the theater glow in the dark. Amon climbed up, then Darius pushed the long tube up a corner where two walls met. Amon leaned down and pulled up the device.

As he waited for Darius to join him, Amon looked out over the Great Sea in the moonlight. He had never seen such a sight, and this new view of God's creation made his heart race.

Darius arrived on the roof, and together they positioned the large end of the horn between two support walls, near the front of the roof, but in a place where it could not be seen from the audience's point of view. The other, smaller end of the tube hung down the back of the theater on the street side, hidden by a palm tree.

Meanwhile, Octavia and Linus also climbed to the roof and hung the two rolled-up banners just behind a row of pillars.

With everything ready, the plotters dragged themselves home to bed for a few hours of sleep. As Amon's mind drifted among a thousand thoughts, he suddenly remembered the most important thing of all. He sat up straight on his bedroll and whispered into the night, "Oh no."

✦ ✦ ✦

Many of us, young and old, dream of being rich and famous. We picture ourselves on late-night talk shows, plan internet content we're sure will go viral, or learn a sport or talent that will bring us fame.

We might even dream of doing those things . . . in the name of Jesus.

All for him, of course.

To build the church. Yeah, that's it.

There are a lot of reasons people feel the need to be famous. I'm no expert, but I think a lot of those come down to insecurity: we don't think we're special enough. We feel the need to do something to prove to others that we're just as good as—or maybe better than—them.

But as a pastor of mine once said from the pulpit, "*You* are special to God. Just like everyone else."

At first, that sounds like a joke—it seems to say nothing at all. "Special" means separate from others, individual, *un*like anyone else.

But when you look closely, it's true. The God of the universe knows you intimately and sees you, separate from all his other children, as an individual, unlike anyone else. He sees each and every person that way.

Kind of like a parent sees their kids.

What more could you want? What award, recognition, or amount of money could even come close to beating such a truth?

You are special—to God.

Let's use our "specialness" to reach others and build God's kingdom.

Chapter Twenty-Eight

Worms

Amon was awake all night, pacing and thinking. After much thought, he'd decided he needed to pray. When he ran out of prayers, he went back to thinking. But then he didn't like the thoughts, so he returned to prayer. From the very beginning of his pacing, praying, and thinking, he knew what he was supposed to do, but he really, *really* didn't want to do it.

Finally, when the little man on the clepsydra pointed at the number three on the column, Amon gave in. "Yes, Father," he whispered into the night. Then he returned to bed and was immediately asleep.

In the morning, as he heard the cooks preparing breakfast, Amon got up and went down to help light the dining room torches and set out the food. Even as he carried plates of delicacies to the table—including rolled pancakes the hired crew was making for the theater—and even as the household began to stir, he was again thinking of ways he might still get out of this.

Cornelius came into the banquet room first, probably to make sure everything was done correctly, Amon suspected. He was followed by Gaius, who was stretching and yawning. When Linus and Darius entered, they were almost giddy and kept looking at Amon, flashing him smiles and nods. The rest of the family finally arrived. They sat on pillows around the outside of the room. Cornelius prayed a blessing on the food, then everyone began to eat. After three quail eggs and two pieces of bread, Amon cleared his throat, then knocked on the floor. Everyone stopped talking and looked at him.

"I have something to tell you," he said, and curiosity filled every face. "For the last many months, ever since Herod murdered James, tried to murder Peter, and threatened to do the same to us all, I have been plotting a way to get rid of Herod." Shock crossed Livia's face, surprise crossed Cornelius's, and concern crossed the face of Gaius. "I wasn't planning to assassinate him or anything, but I thought if I could humiliate him badly enough, I'd humiliate his friend, Emperor Claudius, as well, and Herod would be recalled to Rome and retired."

Cornelius looked like he was about to faint and fall face-first into his dish of olives.

"So last week," Amon continued, "I had graffiti written on the walls of the city to plant the idea in the minds of the people that Herod should challenge Titus Magnus to a chariot race. I knew Herod would never agree to such a thing, so then I could label him a coward and humiliate the emperor. Then this morning," Amon sighed and took a moment to fuel his confession, "this morning, at Herod's celebration, I was going to release two banners that again challenged Herod to race against Titus, and at the same time start the crowd chanting for such a match."

Complete silence crossed over the table. Amon saw that the servants and household staff had crowded around the outside of the banquet room as well.

"But last night," Amon continued, "*all* of last night, I thought and prayed, and came to the conclusion that this—all of this—is wrong, and I cannot go forward with my plan." Disappointment filled the faces of Linus and Darius. "You see, at one time my father was convicted of a crime he did not commit and was sentenced to death. I worked and plotted and schemed to get him released. But nothing I did mattered. I failed. In the end, it was the hand of God, working partly through Cornelius, that saved my father. I learned then that my ways are not God's ways, and that his thoughts are much, much higher than my thoughts. I also learned that, sometimes, what I *believe* is God's voice whispering in my ear is really just my own desires pointing me in the wrong direction. I vowed to never make that mistake again."

Amon lifted his cup and took a drink, then set the cup down and continued. "But not even a year later, Saul went on a rampage, planning to kill all those who believe in Jesus. He even enlisted me to help him, not knowing that, by then, I was a believer myself. So I made it my mission to convert Saul, to make him see the truth of Jesus. And once again, my plans and plotting and schemes failed. In the end, it was the hand of God, working through Jesus himself, that made Saul see the light—literally."

Cornelius smiled and gave Amon a friendly nod to encourage him.

"Once more, after Saul's conversion, I pledged to never again take God's work into my own hands. But, once again, I failed. Almost. Last night, as I thought through these things, and as the Holy Spirit convicted me, I realized I was doing exactly the same thing again by trying to dethrone Herod in my own power. So before this goes any further, I'm going to say 'No. Enough. I will wait for God and accept his will.' Fortunately—for all of us—the Holy Spirit is difficult to ignore. And I hereby pledge, I will never make this mistake again."

A couple of people almost started to clap, but before they could, the quiet voice of Cornelius said, "Yes, you will."

Now everyone looked at *Cornelius* in surprise. "Amon, you are smart, you are clever, you are inquisitive, and you are truly a man of God. But you are also human. And all of us, all of us here and all of us across the world who believe in Jesus, are imperfect because we're human. We all have made and will again make mistakes, and we will mistake our own desires for those of God. The good news is," he leaned back and sighed, "God understands that, and has great patience with us as we learn." Cornelius lifted his cup. "To our God," he said, "who knows us completely, but loves us regardless."

They held up their cups to honor God, then left the breakfast dishes where they were and headed out to the show.

~

Since they were at the amphitheater and not the stadium, the men and women had to sit separately. Octavia went with Livia and the other women to one side of the seating, Amon and the other men and boys to the other. They sat about two-thirds of the way up, with Amon between Cornelius and Gaius, and Linus and Darius on the row in front of them. The theater was still dark, lit only by torches on the curved wall behind them.

The morning breeze off the sea was cool and salty. The hired crew was selling pancakes to the people entering the stadium. Even though he had invented them, Amon bought several to share, and decided they made an excellent food to break a fast.

The sun was just about to rise over the hills of Samaria behind them, so the entire city was blanketed in the dim, purplish light of predawn. The stadium was full to capacity even as people continued to stream in.

At the very moment the first rays of sunlight hit the stage, eight men holding long trumpets blew a fanfare that drew everyone's attention to the center curtain. As the fanfare ended, the curtains parted, and Herod stepped out onto the stage.

Amon could not believe that what he was seeing was real.

Herod was dressed in some kind of new robe that radiated light as if he were wearing the sun itself. It seemed to be made of small mirrors or jewels and reflected the first rays of dawn into the eyes of the audience. Herod walked slowly out onto the stage, arms held out to his sides, a faint but smug smile on his face.

The crowd jumped to its feet, terrified.

Amon heard shouts of, "Is this a god or a demon?" and "What terrible wrath have the gods brought upon us?" But as Herod reached the front of the stage, he turned around slowly, then walked to one end, his arms still outstretched, and then back to the other end. Gradually, everyone realized that it was not some demon but a trick of the light. After a moment, Amon could see that Herod's robe was made entirely of shiny rectangles—silver, he guessed. The early morning rays of the sun—in their strange red, yellow, orange, and gold mix—struck the silver and reflected back, appearing to come from the soul of Herod himself.

Now the people started applauding. A throne was brought out. Herod sat and gave a long speech of such grandeur and promise that the people of Caesarea began shouting again, this time praising Herod. "You are a god!" one woman shouted, and many other voices picked up the cry. "All praise to the god Herod Agrippa!" people yelled. Over it all, another woman wailed, "Be merciful to us! We thought you to be only a man, but now we see you are a god!"

Herod stood, stretched his arms to his sides once more, and bowed his head in acceptance of the honors.

In the next moment, Herod grabbed his stomach with both arms, doubled over, and made a sound like a man cut with a knife.

The crowd quieted.

Some said prayers to the Roman gods.

Herod fell to the floor of the stage, on his side, kicking and screaming in agony.

Some in the audience began to scream.

Herod's attendant, Aristo, was the first to reach his side, followed by many other servants and doctors. They gathered between Herod and the audience, hiding him from view. But nothing could hide the screams that screeched from Herod's lips even as they carried him away, out the back of the stage to the palace on the jetty.

Now a great weeping and mourning swept across the amphitheater. People stumbled and pushed toward the exits and across the stage and covered the amphitheater in grief. Amon and the others were pushed along as well. Amidst the shoving and kicking, Amon saw that someone had brushed against one of the strings they had hung the night before. A banner unfurled down the left side of the stage, a banner reading, "Race Titus!"

The crowd slowed as it reached the side of the theater, where there were only a few gates through which to exit. As he shuffled across the plaza, Amon heard from the top of the theater a booming voice saying, "Hello? Hello? Can you hear me?"

Amon looked up and saw that some workmen had discovered his voice-amplifying cone invention. "Can you hear me?" the voice continued to fill the theater.

At the house of Cornelius, everyone sat and prayed to Jehovah. They prayed for his will to be done with Herod and for salvation for Caesarea.

The prayers continued over the next five days. Except for the comings and goings at the docks, the city all but shut down, with only a few food shops open here and there. On the street in front of the palace, and even on the rocks of its jetty, people in sackcloth knelt and wailed, crying for the recovery of their god-king. All across the city, whole families cried and prayed for Herod.

During all that time, Amon could think of nothing but getting home to Tamar.

"Why do you think Herod got sick?" Linus asked Amon one afternoon.

"That's easy," Amon answered. "Because the people called him a god, and he didn't deny it."

"But he really was a great and powerful man, wasn't he? I mean, unless you happened to be one of us Jesus believers."

"Yes, he was the king of the Jewish nation. But he was not the *God* of the Jews. When the Romans called him that and he didn't argue the point, the one and only God struck him down."

On the fifth day, Herod died.

Amon heard rumors—which were later confirmed—that Herod had been eaten by worms from the inside out, and that he suffered a terrible and painful death.

Then an odd thing happened.

In the streets of Caesarea, the same people who had been mourning Herod now gathered in mobs to mock him and protest against him. Even the soldiers who had followed his orders joined the mobs. Soon they broke into the palace, stole whatever they wanted, smashed statues, and took furniture, dishes, and decorations. The city became an endless street party, celebrating the death of the puppet king.

It was in the middle of this that Cornelius brought home a guest one evening. "I found him wandering the streets, talking to people about Jesus."

Amon got up from where he had been teaching Linus and Darius. The man was standing in the shadows of the entry hall, the nearest torch behind him, so it took a moment before Amon could see his face. "Philip?" he said, when it finally clicked inside his head.

Philip the evangelist stepped further into the room. "Amon, my young friend. It is so good to find you alive and healthy."

"Wha—what are you doing in Caesarea?" Philip started to answer, but Amon interrupted. "No, let me guess—an angel told you to come here to preach."

Philip smiled. "It is so. For how long I cannot say, but it seems you and Cornelius have already done a great work here."

Cornelius invited Philip to stay for dinner, and for as long as the Spirit told him to remain in Caesarea. They were called to the dining room, where Livia served venison and lentils. When she first walked into the room, carrying a large clay pot and holding it with two pieces of cloth to protect her hands from the heat, Amon saw that Philip noticed her and, in fact, couldn't take his eyes off her. He stared at her with a crooked smile and wide-open eyes.

~

"I think it's time for me to go home," Amon announced, ten days after the theater show.

Cornelius thought, nodded. "Yes, I think that would be a good thing. You have more than done your duty here. Your duty now rests with your future family."

"I'm not sure what 'duty' I did here. I thought God sent me here to get rid of Herod. But he *really* sent me here to relearn that he has everything under control."

Cornelius patted Amon on the shoulder, then left the room.

The next morning, after long goodbyes and promises to meet again, and after Gaius said a very long goodbye to Octavia, the two friends left the house and stepped around the drunken partiers and revelers sleeping in the streets. As he took his first step out of the city and onto the long road back to Jerusalem, Amon wondered if he could survive three more days without Tamar, and what was to come after that.

✦ ✦ ✦

Herod the Great, who tried to have the baby Jesus killed, was an evil man.

His grandson, Herod Agrippa I, was also an evil man—completely self-centered.

So were almost all the kings of Israel and Judea, and the Roman emperors, and many, many of the world's leaders who came after them, in every country. There have been far too many leaders over the centuries who were more interested in helping themselves than helping their people.

Evil.

So it would seem right and natural that we should go out there and take them down. Get rid of them. Solve the world's problems by eliminating the evil leaders.

That was Amon's plan.

But then, God showed Amon (a fictional character, of course), as well as everyone else (for real, in the Bible) that *he* is in control, and *he* will deal with leaders who need to be dealt with.

It feels so good to try to do away with bad leaders—and, of course, we have every right, and a civic duty, to place our vote in the ballot box. But what God is *really* calling us to do is, well, what Jesus did: preach the good news of salvation, help those less fortunate than ourselves whenever and however we can, and change the world one soul at a time.

Chapter Twenty-Nine

Secondhand Traditions

Amon sat and stared at the piles of materials in the sheep pens. His father had moved their sheep to a friend's pen temporarily and had taken out the inner fences that isolated groups of sheep from each other. In their place sat piles of stones for a foundation, mounds of clay and straw for bricks, stacks of long, straight logs for beams, and bundles of reeds for filler. He had purchased all the material he needed for the addition to his father's house using the money he'd won at the chariot races. "There is no foul in using it to build your house," Gamaliel had assured him. "You earned that money honestly, even if not in a traditional Jewish way."

So he had everything he needed to build the house, except time. *I so wanted to be married before the seventeenth celebration of my birth*, he thought. *But now that's only a few weeks away, and there is no way I can build even the foundation in that time.*

Many young men were already married by their fifteenth year, but Amon had been so busy helping the apostles and the new church that there'd been no time to even think of such things in the past. Finally, at sixteen, he was betrothed to someone he loved, but even that had been more than ten months before. *I feel like I'll be an old man before I ever get married. Not as old as Gaius, but much older than I ever wanted.*

That made him think more about his new friend.

~

After he and Gaius had left Caesarea, they'd talked for almost the entire day-and-a-half journey to Sebaste. It cemented their friendship forever, and Amon was able to teach the new convert many things about the Torah and the history of their God. Gaius shared his deep feelings for Octavia, and the fact that he would soon ask Cornelius for her hand in marriage.

At Sebaste, Amon had said goodbye to Gaius and hello again to Peter. The news of Herod's death had already reached Sebaste, but Peter knew none of the details until Amon explained.

Back in Jerusalem, Amon and Peter had discovered a famine had fallen over the land, leaving food expensive and many people hungry. Amon found Benjamin and went to see Tamar before he even went to his house. Rhoda sputtered and Benjamin laughed as Tamar and Amon held each other so tightly that not even a Roman crane could have pulled them apart. When finally they sat at the well, she reported that the believers were taking care of the church as best they could, and that so far no one was starving. They then talked for an hour, until Rhoda cleared her throat.

When Amon walked in the door of his house, he had been instantly smothered in hugs. Even his brother Jadon was happy to see him. Then his family sat and listened in shock as Amon told of the things that had happened to him on his journey. Amon's mother just about fell off her bench when he described the chariot race, but they were even more shocked when he told them he had won. Amon pulled out flags, an oil lamp, and other trinkets etched and sewn with his face and new Roman name.

That night he made pancakes with fig-and-honey sauce for dinner. Benjamin took a whole basket full of them to Mary's house for Tamar and everyone there.

On his first full day back in the city, Amon had ordered the materials for his house. While he waited, James the brother of Jesus suggested they read his letter one last time and then start making copies. Down in the cistern of Jesse, Amon took the letter written in Greek and began to read to its author.

"James, a servant of God and of the Lord Jesus Christ," Amon began, "to the twelve tribes scattered among the nations: Greetings. Consider it pure joy, my brothers and sisters, whenever you face trials of many kinds, because you know that the testing of your faith produces perseverance . . ."

A few days later, Barnabas and Saul returned to Jerusalem, bringing with them gifts from the church in Antioch to help ease the famine. Saul found Amon and asked him to follow him. As they strutted past the mansions and palaces of the upper city, Saul explained. "I've decided we've waited long enough," he had said, sounding angry at himself. "We're going to tell Gamaliel about Jesus."

Amon sucked in his breath but kept walking. Tell the greatest rabbi in Jerusalem that everything he believed was out-of-date? Convince him to follow a crucified Messiah whom he never met? Go against the priests and scribes and the entire Sanhedrin? "This is a most difficult task you have set before us," he said as they stormed up the street.

"Difficult for us, yes. Difficult for God, no. I tell you, Amon, that God is working miracles all over the world. Everywhere I went in Asia, all we had to do was open our mouths and people started believing in Jesus and asking to be baptized."

Amon nodded. "I saw similar things in Samaria, and on the coastal plains."

"That is why I'm so sure we need to take many missionary journeys, much farther from Jerusalem than we have up till now. The message of Jesus is a message for all people, not just the Jews."

They arrived at the house of Gamaliel and found their teacher reading in the garden.

Two hours later, exhausted and drenched in sweat from arguing and pleading, Amon had no idea if their tag-team sermon to an audience of one had done any good or not. "Only Jehovah knows," Saul said as they strolled back across the upper city. "And only he *needs* to know."

With Herod gone, tempers in the city had cooled considerably, so the apostles felt it was safe to hold a large church meeting in caves of Uri's Place. Saul did most of the talking to the hundreds of people gathered, and all the people of the Way rejoiced at the news of their successful ministry. Just as the meeting was coming to a close, Barnabas got up and stood next to Saul. "By the way," he said, "our friend Agabus in Antioch suggested a new name by which we can call ourselves. Instead of 'People of the Way,' we are now putting Christ in our name and calling ourselves 'Christians.'"

The mood of the people instantly became subdued, almost shocked. They stared back at Barnabas, confused.

Barnabas held up his hands as if to stop a brewing riot. "I know, I know," he said. "The Greeks and Romans who came up with this name meant it as an insult. They thought they could shame us by calling us 'followers of Christ.' But we're turning their insult into a term of honor. From this moment on, we will be proud to call ourselves Christians!"

This had caused a great celebration that lasted another hour.

"Enough stalling," Amon chastised himself aloud from where he still sat and stared at the piles of building materials. "Get to work!" He stood, grabbed a pick, and, using techniques he'd seen the Romans employ, started cutting a trench along the right side of the house, the side that faced the sheep pens. The new addition would be directly above him, an extension of the upper room. But the existing wall wasn't strong enough to hold more weight, so he would build another wall against it, tying the two together to make it doubly strong.

He finished the trench—a miniature version of the one he'd helped build for Herod's wall—then laid the first stone below the level of the ground, up against the existing wall. He was reaching for the second stone when he heard a commotion down the street. He looked and saw a mob approaching, with people yelling and running for their lives.

A moment later, a large group of men and boys broke out of the crowd. They stomped directly toward Amon, feet pounding, and in the lead was his teacher Gamaliel. Looking past him, Amon saw his father, and his almost father-in-law, the apostles Peter, James the brother of Jesus, Saul, John, and several others. With them were Amon's best friend, Benjamin, his brothers Uri and Jadon, and then . . . Cornelius? And Gaius? And Linus, Darius, and . . . Octavia!

Amon almost fell backward as the group approached, looking stern and terribly angry, as if they were an attacking Roman legion. They stopped, frowning, in front of Amon. Gamaliel held up his hand for silence, and the crowd hushed.

"Amon, son of Jotham," he said loudly enough for all to hear, and Amon had never heard his teacher speak in such a stern voice. "What do the words of Jehovah, as written down by our father Moses, say must be done to one who has cursed his father or mother?"

Amon's head was spinning. Did he inadvertently do something wrong? Why had the whole community gathered, and why were they so angry? "Uh, that person must be put to death by . . ." Amon looked nervously at the crowd. "By the members of his community."

"And what does he say must be done to one who strikes someone with a fatal blow?"

Again Amon's mind scrambled to figure out when he had done such a thing. Even as he thought, his mouth answered, "That person must be put to death."

"And what of one who kidnaps someone?"

Amon saw the pattern now, and knew that someone had convinced his friends, family, and fellow Jews that he had done some terrible deed. In answer to the third question, he said simply, "Death."

Gamaliel stepped forward, away from the crowd behind him, and leaned in close, resting on his walking stick. Still just as loudly he said, "And what, please tell me, does Jehovah say is the punishment for a young man if he allows his family and neighbors to help him build the house to which he will bring his new bride?"

Now Amon was *totally* confused. He searched the Scriptures in his head, searched through all he'd been taught since he was five, searched the knowledge imparted to him by Gamaliel himself. Finally, he opened his mouth, and a squeaking sound came out. "I . . . uh . . . he says nothing about such a situation."

Gamaliel stared with cold eyes, then nodded slowly. "Your friends and family are most terribly disappointed that in ten months since your betrothal, you have not yet managed to build a single wall of your house, let alone complete it. So we have decided we must take action to rectify this situation."

Though Gamaliel managed to keep a scowl on his face, Amon knew from the grins and smiles that now erupted on the faces of the others that no one was really mad, and that something wonderful was happening.

"Therefore," Gamaliel continued, "those of us you see before you, and anyone else we can coerce, are here to help you build your house, whether you like it or not."

Amon was even more confused now, and more than a little worried. "But, even if Jehovah says nothing about it, such help is against the rules of our tradition. I must build the entire house myself, having help only with tasks that require two people."

Gamaliel looked down as he stroked his beard. "Ah, yes, well, we had a meeting this morning, all of us, and discussed that very issue." He looked up. "That's when we realized that such a requirement is not in the scrolls of the Torah. It is not in the prophecies of the prophets. And it was not," he looked over his shoulder at Peter, "in the words of Jesus. It is, in fact, only a tradition. And while many of our traditions are important for our spiritual lives, this one is not. So we voted, unanimously, that it would break no rule of God nor any rule of common sense to enforce what someone has called," he looked over his other shoulder at Jadon, "'a silly rule.'" He looked back at Amon. "So, where would you like us to start?"

Amon grinned so big he thought his face might break. "Well, I could use some help digging more trenches . . ."

✦ ✦ ✦

Jews who do not believe Jesus is the Messiah live by a list of six hundred and thirteen laws that dictate every aspect of their lives. Following those laws is how they believe they can please God.

But Jews who believe Jesus is the Messiah—as well as all other Christians—live by a list of two, stated in various ways throughout the New Testament: believe in Jesus as the Christ, and repent of your sins.

Everything beyond those two falls into the category of "Other" and has no bearing on your salvation. What to wear, what style of music to sing, how often to worship, what day or time or place to worship, who can or can't administer this or that sacrament, when, where, and how often you pray—and on and on. These are just human ideas, usually offered with the best of intentions, and sometimes very practical or desirable, but still just human ideas. They are not God's rules—they are traditions.

Amon just spent almost a year worried about how he'd ever get married when the work of the church was keeping him so busy. He had a subconscious fear that if he didn't do things "just right," he would anger God. But as his wise elders, parents, and friends helped him see, traditions are not sacred—sometimes nice, sometimes necessary to keep up good family relations, but not sacred.

Believe in Jesus as the Christ, and repent of your sins.

Those are the only keys you need to enter the kingdom of God.

Chapter Thirty

The House

For the rest of the day, Gamaliel sat on a stool, pounding his staff on the ground like a dance instructor keeping a beat. "Keep it moving, oh you sheep, keep it moving, night to beat . . ."

Amon listed the tasks to complete, and the group of men and boys divided themselves into teams to accomplish those tasks. Cornelius and Bartholomew ended up on the same team and had a grand reunion, telling each other all that had happened in the thirty years since Bartholomew escaped from Caesarea.

Tabitha and Octavia kept the food and drinks coming, and they occasionally stopped to pound a nail or tie off a cord. By noon, the trench had been dug, three courses of flat stones laid, and the double wall finished up to the level of the upper room. After lunch, posts the diameter of a cantaloupe were stood up on top of the trench foundation about four foot-lengths apart. This created a rectangle with the long sides running across the sheep pens and the short sides about fifteen foot-lengths wide.

The posts were tied together with timbers across the top, then more poles were laid across the frame, from the double wall out to the side of the rectangle. This would be the foundation platform for a floor at the height of the upper room in the original house.

Two days later, a complete floor had been laid on the beams, brick walls lined the outside edges of the platform, more beams on top of those walls created a waddle-and-daub roof, and a door between the old house and the new had been cut in the original wall of the upper room. When it was whitewashed and the finish work completed, a celebration of thanks was held for the workers. Amon was thrilled with the work but sad that Tamar couldn't be there to celebrate with them. "That is one tradition I am *not* willing to give up," Bartholomew had said. Even Saul agreed with him.

"Tomorrow morning," Amon's father said, "I will inspect your work." Amon gulped and knew this would not be an automatic pass.

That night, while his family slept, Amon quietly dug out the dirt floor of the main house and replaced it with stones. He even used two different colors of stones to create a pattern. *Not exactly a mosaic like in Caesarea*, he realized, *but still sort of nice*.

When his mother came down in the morning, she actually screamed in delight. She danced around the whole lower floor, stomping her feet just to enjoy the feeling of an actual floor. He then showed his father that, if he lifted one particular stone, he would find a stone safe underneath. "To keep your valuables," he explained.

"A very nice gift, my son," Amon's father said. "But that doesn't mean I'll automatically give you a pass on the new addition."

Amon nodded and gulped.

The first time Jotham inspected the new upper room, he shook his head slowly. "Oh, no, my son. This is not yet right. You have holes at the top where the new wall meets the old building. Your wife would not appreciate this. She needs a place of privacy, where voices cannot be heard in the next room."

So Amon spent the better part of a day sealing all the holes between the old and new.

The second time Jotham inspected, he shook his head slowly. "Oh no, my son, this is not good. You have only mats on the floor for sleeping. Your wife deserves a proper bed on which to rest her weary body at the end of a long day."

"But we have *always* slept on mats on the floor! You and Mother grew up as shepherds, living in tents!"

"Yes, but never did your mother or I like that. Why do you think we moved into the city and raised you in a house?"

Amon stepped back and eyed his father, suspicious. "You moved into the city and built a house so that your son could have a proper education with the greatest mind in Judea."

Jotham smiled. "You truly are ready to be the head of this household." He took a deep breath. "But first, your wife deserves a proper bed."

So Amon spent the better part of two days building bed frames, stringing support ropes, and sewing thick mattresses, not only for himself and Tamar, but for his parents and brothers as well.

The third time Jotham inspected, he shook his head slowly. "Oh no, my son, this is most sad."

Amon looked shocked. "Now what? What is wrong?"

Jotham put his arm around his son's shoulders. "It is most sad that you have built a fine and proper house for your bride, because now you will be married and no longer belong to me."

Amon's face lit up when he realized what his father was saying, but just as quickly went dark and sad when he realized what his father was saying. "I will always be your son," he said, and pulled Jotham into an embrace. "And you will always be my father."

~

That evening, Benjamin trimmed Amon's hair, then he, Jadon, Uri, and Gaius all dressed Amon for his wedding. They bought, borrowed, and stitched fine and colorful silk clothes that made Amon look like a prince.

"Ow! You stabbed me with that needle," Amon complained at one point.

Benjamin checked the site of the wound for blood. There was none. "A minor irritation for one about the have the most joyous day of his life."

"If I survive long enough," Amon replied.

Benjamin looked up into Amon's eyes. "You know you can't retrieve your bride until I knock on her door, right?"

"Oh, uh, thank you for your fine sewing, Benjamin."

Benjamin turned back to his work. "That's better."

His friends finished the work of dressing him as a prince, complete with a crown made of papyrus and painted with something Amon couldn't identify.

"We tried to make it look gold using the edge of a bronze coin," Benjamin said. "Sorry, it didn't really work."

"I would never complain," Amon replied, "especially when someone has done their best."

A knock on the railing of the stairway caught their attention. "May I come up?" a man's voice called.

"Saul!" Amon yelled. He went over and hugged his older friend. "I was afraid you'd be off on some new journey."

"Not yet, and especially not before I saw you properly married."

"So why are you here? The celebration doesn't start for another hour."

"I came to give you this." Saul held up an actual gold crown. Amon and the others gasped. "Where . . . where did you get such a thing?"

"Did you forget? I am both a Jew and a citizen of Rome, and my parents enjoy many benefits of that citizenship. I borrowed this from them during my trip with Barnabas."

Benjamin knocked Amon's papyrus crown off, grabbed the new one from Saul, and centered it on Amon's head. He grinned. "Much better."

An hour later, as the sun stepped down onto the horizon, Benjamin, also dressed in fine clothes, led Amon and their friends and family down the street toward the house of Mary. Many of those walking with them carried torches, shouted, played instruments, and sang songs. When they reached the house, Benjamin knocked.

Tamar's father, Bartholomew, opened the door. "Yes, what is it you seek?"

Benjamin took a deep breath and threw his shoulders back. "I seek the bride of my best friend, Amon, son of Jotham. May she come and join him, that they may be as one."

"May they be so blessed, and so be a blessing to others," Bartholomew said. Then he stood aside. Tamar stepped to the door. She hugged her father for many moments, and many words passed between them which none could hear but them. Then she turned to face Benjamin. "Where is my bridegroom, that I may see him who would marry me?"

Benjamin finally stepped aside so Amon could see. Tamar stepped out onto the porch, and Amon thought his heart would fly right out of his chest. The words of the prophet Ezekiel came to his mind, and he understood them as he never had before: "You were adorned with gold and silver; your clothes were of fine linen and costly fabric and embroidered cloth . . . You became very beautiful and rose to be a queen."

Tamar stared at Amon for several moments, her face still covered with the veil. Finally she spoke the words to Benjamin that Amon had been waiting to hear. "I will accompany you, and you may take me to my home."

Jadon, Uri, and two of Amon's other friends ran forward with a litter—a fancy chair covered in royal blue cloth with gold braid and a gold canopy over the top. It was carried with two poles attached to the sides and had a gold cushion on the seat. Benjamin took Tamar's hand, led her over, and seated her. The four boys picked up the litter by the poles, and followed Amon as they walked back up the street.

Along the way, people who had watched the parade pass with an empty litter now saw a bride seated there for the return. A loud, strange, whooping-trilling sound erupted from the women. It jumped from window to window and door to door as the procession passed. People all along the way came out to the street to wish the new couple well. Some sang from the Song of Songs, saying, "Who is this coming up from the wilderness like a column of smoke, perfumed with myrrh and incense made from all the spices of the merchant?"

Finally, they arrived back at the house. Amon took Tamar's hand and led her to the door. He knocked. An excruciatingly long moment later, the door opened, and Amon's parents appeared, dressed in their wedding clothes.

“Mother, Father,” Amon said in a loud voice, “I have brought my bride home to live with me.”

Jotham answered, “Blessed is he who finds a wife to love and support him for all his years.”

Tabitha answered, “Blessed is she who finds a husband to love and support her for all her years.”

Together they answered, “Blessed are you both, and welcome in our home, where we pledge to love and support you, for all our years.”

Amon stepped across the threshold with his new wife.

And though the celebration and feasting would last another seven days, he breathed in a deep sigh of relief, for finally, after all the interruptions, and all the fear of persecution, and all the traveling and preaching and miracles, Amon had finally completed . . . his mission.

✦ ✦ ✦

Oh what a glorious day that will be, when Jesus returns for his bride, and takes us back to the home he has prepared for us, to live with him forever.

What a glorious day that will be.

Are you ready?

About the Author

Arnold Ytreeide is a former police officer, television producer and director, and university professor who now spends his days writing books. He is a gifted storyteller who cares deeply about spiritual growth in families. He loves travel, scuba diving, writing, filmmaking, and reading. He and his wife live near Boise, Idaho, and have two grown and married children and five grandchildren.

How do you pronounce his last name? It-tree-ide (*tide* without the *t*).

Learn more about Arnold at jothamsjourney.com.

Enjoy family stories by Arnold Ytreeide